NO STOPPING

NO STOPPING

NO STOPPING

No Justice Series: Book 5

NOLON KING
DAVID WRIGHT

Copyright © 2020 by Sterling & Stone

All rights reserved.

No part of this book may be reproduced in any form or by any electronic or mechanical means, including information storage and retrieval systems, without written permission from the author, except for the use of brief quotations in a book review.

The authors greatly appreciate you taking the time to read our work. Please consider leaving a review wherever you bought the book, or telling your friends about it, to help us spread the word.

Thank you for supporting our work.

To YOU, the reader.
Thank you for your support.
Thank you for the wonderful emails.
Thank you for the thoughtful reviews.
Thank you for reading and loving our stories.

Prologue - Victor Forbes

A soft ping on his phone woke Victor Forbes — a very specific alarm.

Someone's inside.

He reached under his pillow for his pistol, pointed it at his bedroom door. Waited.

Is this him?

Has he finally come for me?

Silence in his oceanfront penthouse apartment, except for the usual AC and humming electronics. But he knew the sounds of his place, same as his body's rhythms. Something was off.

He steadied his aim.

A soft knock made him flinch. If not for his extensive training, he would've pulled the trigger for sure. Instead, he focused his breathing, slow and steady even as his heart hammered hard in his chest.

"Don't shoot," said a man's familiar voice. "It's me."

The last voice he wanted to hear, other than the black man who'd done so much damage down in Mexico and threatened BlackBriar's operations.

Petr Sokolov, also known as The Raven — the notorious hit man employed by his boss.

It's worse than I thought if they're sending him.

He steadied his uncertain hand on the pistol. Could he really take out The Raven?

"If I wanted you dead, I wouldn't have knocked, nor allowed your alarm to trigger. The boss wants to speak to you."

His boss, Boris Molchalin, of MK LTD, the multinational company that owned BlackBriar.

"Come in," Victor said, still aiming at the door as it opened.

The Raven was in his late forties. Tall, intense dark eyes, broad shoulders, and graying hair. He was dressed in a heavy black trench coat, hands raised to prove he wasn't armed — not that he couldn't reach inside his coat in a blink.

Still, Victor felt foolish holding his pistol on the man, so he set it on his nightstand and stood, vulnerable in his silk boxers and nothing else.

The Raven reached into his coat.

Victor felt uneasy around the Russian but tried to mask his fear with a casual expression. He managed not to flinch.

The Raven pulled out a phone, dialed, then spoke in Russian.

Victor could understand a few words here and there, but not enough to know what the man was saying. He managed to take the cell with a steady hand. "Hello, Mr. Molchalin."

"Hello, Victor. What news have you about our little problem?"

Victor didn't have to be cautious with his words as the call was surely encrypted. Men like Molchalin never took chances. But Victor rarely felt comfortable enough to speak *too* openly on a phone.

He swallowed and got on with it. "We've not identified the man or located the item yet."

"What about the police, the woman he went there to save?"

"I've got eyes on her in case they make contact."

"Good. We don't have much time to retrieve the package or prevent the damage if you can't find and disable the website. You need to be more ... proactive."

"You suggesting I ... *pick her up?*"

"You know her, yes. Get her to tell you. If not, then yes, find this man by any means necessary."

"Yes, sir."

"And what about the feds? Are they done with their questions?"

"Yes. I answered everything, assured them Anderson was acting alone. But they've been snooping around, anyway."

"That is why you need to lay low. I'm placing you on administrative leave for the moment. Susan O'Connell will be acting CEO until your return."

"Susan?" Victor hated the idea of that bitch taking his place. "That'll only look more suspicious if BlackBriar's CEO suddenly steps aside."

"They'll understand. You're in mourning."

"Mourning?"

"Yes, your mother passed in her sleep tonight."

"What?" A chill ran through Victor as he met The Raven's eyes. "You fucker."

The Raven already had his pistol aimed at Victor. "Don't be stupid, not while you've still got a sister," he said with slow shake of his head.

"My sincerest apologies for your loss, Mr. Forbes," said Molchalin. "She went peacefully, if that's any consolation."

"How?" His voice cracked, struggling with the new reality that his mother was dead. He hadn't visited in months. She'd left messages on his machine last weekend asking when he was going to call, asking if he was okay. His poor, sweet mother who'd never hurt anyone. Ever. He'd ignored her calls, figuring he'd get back to her once this shit was behind him.

But now she was gone for good.

And while the man sitting across from Victor was directly responsible, and his boss on the other line was the one who surely issued the order, he knew the truth even as it settled like silt in his gut.

This was all his fault.

"You now understand how urgent this matter is?" Molchalin asked. "You *must* contain this."

"Yes, sir," Victor said through clenched teeth and the first hiccup of a coming sob.

How the hell could he keep Voluptatem from getting out? And once it did, how many politicians, celebrities, and wealthy men would fall?

The only thing Victor knew for sure was men like Boris Molchalin, even if he was somehow linked to the pedophile ring, would escape into anonymity. They had wealth and secret networks in place, designed to leave justice in the dark.

But he had no such escape hatch. For Victor, it was silence this scandal or die.

He hung up the phone.

The Russian said, "Grab some clothes. You'll be staying with us for a while."

"What? For how long?"

"Until this is over. Is there a problem? Should I call Mr. Molchalin back?"

"No," Victor said, throat full of bile. "No problem at all."

Chapter 1 - Jasper Parish

JASPER ADJUSTED his ski mask as he lurked in the woods surrounding the remote lake house. He watched in the dark and waited for the lights to finally go out.

His target was a man named Joseph Bremmer. A criminal, yes, but not the sort who normally wound up on Jasper's radar. Jasper hunted murderers and rapists. But Bremmer was a white-collar criminal — an accountant and money launderer working for Victor Forbes, using his cryptocurrency ATMs to clean cash for criminals.

So far as Jasper was aware, Victor hadn't yet fallen under suspicion for BlackBriar's role in either the kidnappings of Jessi Price and Mallory Black, nor for the company's role in breaking Paul Dodd out of prison or for anything to do with Madam Pandora's pedophile palace in Mexico. Outside of Anders Martin's involvement, the pedophile network was barely a blip on American news, believed to be a mostly Mexican and South American crime ring. If the FBI *had* tied BlackBriar to Jessi Price or Mallory's abduction, they had yet to act on it.

That didn't mean they weren't investigating behind the

scenes. And Victor was surely eliminating any and all evidence tying him or BlackBriar to the crimes.

Jasper was certain Victor Forbes was involved, but he couldn't go after him yet. He was likely being monitored by FBI agents. But he was also surrounded by his paramilitary guards, and Jasper wasn't in the condition to take them down.

The Feds could take him in. Jasper didn't need vengeance on the man, so long as he paid a fair price for his crimes. But until Spider decrypted the drive Paul Dodd said could expose the entire network — and found evidence they could either hand to the Feds, release to the media, or use for his personal hit list — Jasper was content to clip Victor's wings so the asshole couldn't easily escape.

That meant pursuing his money man.

Jasper's daughter appeared beside him in her pink ski mask and purple hoodie.

"We're not killing him, right?" Jordyn looked at her father's holstered gun.

Jasper sighed. "I already said not if I can help it."

"Don't sigh. I just want to make sure we're on the same page."

"I thought you were going to wait in the car? Didn't you say you wanted to catch up on your reading?"

"Someone needs to look after you."

"He's an accountant. I'm not worried."

"All the same, you're still recovering from your wounds."

"I'm good."

"Doesn't hurt to have back-up." Jasper could tell she was smiling wide under her mask. "Besides, you need my skills."

"I've been sitting on the house for hours. Nobody has come in or out. I think he's alone."

No Stopping

"Thinking isn't the same as knowing." Jordyn echoed something he used to say a few years ago when she started becoming a moody teenager who thought she knew everything.

Jasper rolled his eyes then moved toward the house, stopping at a side door leading to the garage. The best place to enter and least likely for him to encounter anyone.

He'd already cased the place to make sure there wasn't an alarm. Bremmer's house in Jacksonville was outfitted with the best in home security, but his lake house in the panhandle was not.

He turned to Jordyn, waiting for her psychic magic.

"Yes?" she teased.

"Is there anybody else in there?"

Jordyn closed her eyes, focusing. Then she touched the door. "Weird."

"What?"

"I'm not getting anything. At all."

Her gift didn't always come on demand.

"No worries." Jasper started picking the lock.

"I don't think you should go in there."

"Why?" Still picking.

"I ... just have a bad feeling."

Jasper looked at her and calmly said, "We'll be fine." He opened the door.

Jordyn followed him into the garage. They circled the Cadillac SUV, making their way to the door leading into the house.

On the other side, Jasper also felt something was wrong.

The house wasn't quiet. Music played over the sound system, classical music he vaguely recognized. Yet the house felt still, like death waiting to step on the scale.

He swept the bottom floor, gun drawn, finding nothing

3

but a plate on the coffee table in front of the couch with an uneaten sandwich and an empty wine glass beside it but no bottle. The TV was on, tuned to the classical music station.

Jasper turned to Jordyn, signaling her to stay back as he headed upstairs.

His daughter nodded.

He took the stairs softly, an uneasiness tightening his shoulders. The steps led to a hall with four closed doors.

His gloved hand turned the knob of the first door to his left. A bathroom.

Bremmer was in the bathtub, a washcloth over his eyes.

Jasper's heart skipped a beat, believing for a moment that the man in the bathtub was dead.

But then he moved, pulling the washcloth away from his face with widening eyes.

The man looked like he might scream, but stopped when he saw the pistol aimed at his forehead.

"Shh," Jasper said.

The man nodded, terror turning his pasty face even whiter.

"Is anyone else here?" Jasper asked.

"No." He shook his head and reached down to cover his crotch. "What do you want?"

"Victor Forbes's Pentz. I want you to transfer it to me," Jasper said, referring to his cryptocurrency stash. Once he had the untraceable money in his account, Victor could no longer access the funds or use them to escape justice.

"I don't know what you're talking about."

Jasper shook his head. "I'm only going to warn you once, Mr. Bremmer. You think I showed up here without doing my due diligence? I value time far too much to waste any of mine, let alone yours. Lying to me is always a mistake. Now, I'll ask you one more time, and please don't insult me with—"

"I swear, I don't—"

Jasper fired a suppressed warning shot into the tub, the bullet tearing through its fiberglass bottom.

Bremmer screamed, looked down to make sure he wasn't hurt, then immediately appeared to get the message. Something about his expression bothered Jasper, but then the man spoke.

"He'll kill me if I do that."

Jasper waved his weapon. "Better to worry about the man *not* here or the man who *is* here? The man with a gun aimed at your head?"

He stared at Jasper, wheels clearly turning in his head, seeking a way to stall or deny him.

Jasper took deliberate aim at his crotch. "Should I fire another shot?"

"No, I'll do it," he practically whimpered, pointing at the sink where his iPhone was sitting. "I need you to hand me my phone."

Jasper scooped it up, but stopped short of handing it over. "Try calling for help and you're dead."

He nodded. Jasper gave him the phone.

"He's going to kill me, then you," Bremmer said.

"Then take enough to get yourself out of town."

"Really?" He looked at Jasper, confused.

"I'm not here to get you killed. I just want to clip his wings. You know the shit he's into?"

"What do you mean?" Bremmer shook his head. "No, never mind. I don't want to know."

"Yeah, maybe not," Jasper said.

"There's just over a half-million Pentz in here. How much should I take for myself?"

Jasper shrugged. "How much will you need?"

"Maybe fifty?"

Another shrug. "It's all yours."

Bremmer seemed surprised by his nonchalance. "Okay, where am I sending this?"

Jasper gave him his info, then he checked the Pentz account on his phone to confirm that the money went through. "Now hand me your phone. I'll leave it in your mailbox on the way out."

Bremmer handed it over, then two things happened at once.

His eyes widened with the sound of a door opening.

Jasper spun around with his gun at the ready. Nearly fired, but stopped as his attention fell to the small boy, about ten-years-old or so.

Water sloshed behind him. Jasper turned to find Bremmer leaping at him, blade in hand.

Where it had come from, Jasper wasn't sure. He barely dodged it by falling back into the boy.

Bremmer screamed and lunged.

Jasper had nowhere to go. Nothing he could do beyond allowing his instincts to kick in.

He fired five shots until Bremmer stopped his attack.

"Daddy!" the boy screamed.

Jasper wheeled toward the child as he raced toward the stairs.

Fuck!

He ran in pursuit.

"What happened?" Jordyn shouted from downstairs.

"Get him!" Jasper yelled.

Too late, the boy had run out the front door and into the night.

"Fuck!" Jasper punched the banister and bloodied his knuckles.

"What happened?" Jordyn asked.

"His kid was here."

No Stopping

"I thought he'd be alone. He was divorced. His ex has custody. She lives in New York."

"Me, too." He sighed, imagining the child's horror and how terrified he must have been walking in on something like that. His life destroyed in seconds, and it was all Jasper's fault.

Tears welled in Jordyn's eyes.

He shook his head, trying to clear the mire of emotions threatening to pull him under. The kid would find a neighbor who would summon the cops.

"We need to get out of here."

Chapter 2 - Mallory Black

EDM MUSIC THRUMMED in the club's walls, in the ground, and through Mal's entire body as she adjusted her long red-haired wig in the bathroom mirror and gave herself a once over. Her black leather dress was tight, cleavage spilling out, and her makeup on the right shade of garish for this crowd. She looked a few years younger than her usual self, and Down To Fuck.

She took a moment not just to make sure she looked the part, but also to steel herself for what she was about to do. She patted the blade in a holster on her inner thigh, comforted to have it.

Two college-aged girls entered the restroom, laughing, practically tripping over themselves. One, a light-skinned black girl with a shaved head wearing a tank top and no bra, gave Mal a flirtatious look. She thought about complimenting the girl's bright pink eyeshadow but decided to smile and nod instead.

Best not to engage.

Best not to have anybody remembering her.

No Stopping

She left the bathroom. Stopped at the bar for a shot of whiskey, downed her liquid courage. Just enough to dull the edge, not her senses. She made her way to one of the many tables overlooking the dance floor below. It was packed with pretty people, mostly young, and nearly all of them looking to get drunk or high, maybe find someone to take home and fuck.

But Mal wasn't here for fun.

Had she missed her mark? His LiveLyfe post said he'd be here tonight. But Mal had been here for nearly an hour and had yet to see him. Maybe he'd already gone.

She considered leaving, maybe trying another night or another place, but then she saw him take a seat at the bar beside a blonde in her early twenties.

He looked different from his mugshot and social media photos. Douchier in person.

Eddie Marshal, age twenty-three. College dropout. Accused rapist. He got off two years ago thanks to a technicality, with a certain assist from his very rich parents. Eddie was six-foot two, muscular. Had enviable shoulders, a nice smile, and nicer hair. Might have been handsome if not for his weak jaw, beady eyes, and penchant for rape.

He'd left Volusia County and went north to Jacksonville six months ago, a place where the fucker was still unknown.

And in that time, there'd been five *reported* rapes from girls at clubs who had been drugged and couldn't remember who took them home.

Mal had a decent guess.

She watched as he chatted up the blonde. The music was too loud, so their words weren't even a mumble by the time they made it all the way to Mal, but judging from the blonde's smile and flirty body language, she was into him.

He ordered drinks for them both.

Mal watched as they drank and flirted. She kept touching him, but Eddie was playing it cool, not appearing overly interested. Before becoming a cop, she might've wondered why a good-looking guy with obvious charm would ever resort to drugging women. Seemed like a move from the desperate loser's playbook. But the job had taught her rape wasn't about sex for guys like this. It was an act of violence. Whether that violence was borne of pent-up frustration with women, anger issues, or some other trauma, Mal didn't care. The result was the same — dangerous men walking around hurting whomever they wanted, without giving a damn about the long-term damage they caused.

Men like Paul Dodd.

He'd raped and murdered her daughter. Hadn't even been close to done when he kidnapped Jessi Price and Mal.

Yes, he'd been a victim to a pedophile as a kid, but the man still had a choice.

No one forced him to continue the cycle of abuse. Or elevate it to murder.

She could have ended his life. Twice.

The first time she'd let him go, trusting in the justice system only to watch it fail. Dodd escaped, then kidnapped and tormented Jessi and Mal again, taking them to Mexico where he planned to destroy them both in whatever ghastly manner his twisted soul could conceive.

And, somehow, fate had saved her and Jessi again.

But this time, Mal didn't make the mistake of turning him over to the authorities. She made sure Dodd would never escape or destroy another life again.

She killed him.

Nightmares plagued her nearly every night in the three weeks since that moment. And while part of her wished she hadn't been pushed to murder, another part of her knew the truth — she should have done it sooner.

She used her three weeks to research some local men who'd gotten away with sex crimes. Followed a few of them for a while. Last week, she'd pursued a particularly nasty piece of work named Dre Hamilton to a club, uncertain what she would do. She wanted to get close, see if she could observe him without getting caught. Mal got close enough to easily hurt him, and she wanted to for all the atrocities he'd gotten away with — some of them to a fifteen-year-old girl. But she chickened out at the last minute after realizing she was heading into action without any plan.

This time she came prepared. A different target, but still a pile of shit.

She stared at Eddie, wondering how many more girls he'd rape, how many more lives he'd shatter if given the chance. What if he went further the next time, and murdered his victim?

The man was a disease, who knew what sickness he carried in is head?

Someone had to stop him.

And that someone was Mal.

But first, she had to be certain.

Mal had plenty of circumstantial evidence pointing to him for these crimes, but no actual proof. He'd either been careful or lucky. She blamed it on the officers who'd botched the case with their ineptitude when Eddie was actually arrested.

She kept watching.

A waitress shouted over the music, "Can I get you something?"

Mal wanted another whiskey, but she'd already downed

a few shots and didn't want to decay her reaction time any further. So, she ordered a Coke instead.

As the waitress left, Mal saw what she was waiting for.

The blonde turned to the girl behind her.

Eddie waved his palm over her drink with precision. It was so fast, he must've practiced the move many times. A pro at drugging women.

As the girl turned back to him, he slipped something into his pocket.

She kept flirting and laughing, completely unaware.

She was about to take a drink when the girl next to her said something, distracting her.

Eddie looked annoyed.

Mal could feel his anxiety as he waited for the girl to take a drink.

The waitress returned and handed her a Coke. Mal said *thanks* with a ten-dollar bill and told her to keep the change.

She grabbed the Coke and went into action, acting tipsy as she approached the bar.

Fortunately, Eddie hadn't made eye contact with her.

The blonde was about to take a drink, but Mal stumbled forward, spilling her Coke on the girl's dress and knocking the blonde's drink from her hands.

The girl yelped.

"What the fuck?" Eddie shouted from behind.

Mal turned to him, then back to the blonde, apologizing profusely in slurred speech.

"I am *sssssoooo sssssorry.*" She grabbed a handful of napkins from the bar and dabbed at the giant brown spot on the girl's dress, doing a shitty job on purpose, trying to annoy her into leaving.

It worked.

No Stopping

The woman next to the blonde nudged her toward the bathroom. "Let's get you cleaned up."

Mal turned to Eddie, apologizing as they left. "I am sooooo sorry."

She let the strap fall from her shoulder, to show him more of her cleavage.

He looked down.

Mal smiled at Eddie, biting her lip.

"Whoa, I think I might've ... had a bit too—" she stumbled toward him, feigning dizziness as she fell into him, holding her head against his chest for a moment, her hand sliding, *accidentally*, over his stiffening cock.

She looked up and met his eyes, then leaned forward and whispered into his ear. "*Damn*, you're hot."

Then she pulled away — he was the predator here.

"I ... I, uh, I sh-sh-should probably go," she said, struggling to stand. "Could you walk me to my car?"

Any normal man might have responded by asking Mal if she's insane to think she could possibly drive in her condition. But Eddie was a predator looking for an easy mark, and damn if Mal wasn't turning their encounter into the ABCs of sexual assault.

"Um," Eddie looked around, either to see who was watching or to see if the blonde was out of the bathroom yet. "Sure."

He held Mal by the waist as she stumbled around the dance floor and toward the exit with him.

Outside, Mal pretended to not know where her car was. Truth was, she hadn't taken her car here. Nor did she have her phone or anything else that would tie her to this location.

She started walking down the center aisle, looking around the lot in confusion, exaggerating her drunken movements and slurred voice. She laughed and said, "Oh, my God ... I can't remember where I parked."

It was dark and starting to rain. She shivered. "I'm so cold."

Mal moved closer to him, his hand still around her waist.

"Maybe I should drive you home."

"Awwww, that's so sweet." She put a finger on his lips, drunk and overly-flirtatious manner. "I don't wanna t-t-trouble you."

"It's no trouble. I'm right around the corner."

She let him lead her to the side of the building where the lighting was mostly a rumor. His van was parked away from the crowd in a patch of pure black.

"Oooh, you have a van," Mal teased, running her hand over his crotch. "I've never done it in a van."

He smiled, his pupils dilating. "No?"

"No." She shook her head, leaned into him, then kissed him on the mouth. Even repulsed, Mal was fully in the moment, so excited by what she was about to do, she could mask her disgust and turn it to a cousin of interest.

He opened the rear door then reached inside, flicking on fairy lights strung up around the ceiling and illuminating a sleaze-ball's idea of a bachelor pad. Plush red carpeting, a mini fridge in the wall console, a bed with silk sheets, a comforter, and a half-dozen throw pillows.

"Nice." Mal climbed inside, careful not to touch anything.

His smile went from friendly and casual at the bar to a shark's toothy grin as he climbed in. He closed the rear doors behind her.

She turned to him, giving him a chance to change his mind. "Um, I don't think I should—"

But Eddie was already on her, kissing her on the neck.

No Stopping

His hands trailed to her breasts as he tried to press her down onto the bed.

He was moving too fast, so she grabbed him by the back of the head and kissed him, biting his lip in a tease before pulling him down and shifting her body on top, hoping the blade against her inner thigh wouldn't press into him.

She started to unbuckle his belt.

He met her gaze with a predator's smile. Then he leaned back and closed his eyes while she slid his pants and underwear down.

She grabbed his cock and squeezed it, teasing him.

He tried to sit up and kiss her again, eager to fuck.

But Mal pushed him back down, acting like she was about to swallow his cock. She spotted the handcuffs laying in the corner and wondered how many women he'd used them on.

If he thought he was going to put them on her.

He noticed her gaze and looked suddenly nervous, like she might be getting close to scared off.

"Ooh, you're kinky." She grabbed the cuffs before he could. "I've always wanted to suck a guy off while he was restrained. Do you want to be that guy?"

She squeezed his dick, hard.

It quivered in her hand, his balls practically ready to burst.

He shook his head. "No, I don't do submissive."

"No?" She pouted. "Not even for me?"

Mal leaned down, putting her lips near his dick, flicking her tongue teasingly at the tip. "You sure?" She held his gaze, challenging him, not backing down.

"Okay," Eddie said with a nervous little gulp. "I guess I could."

She reached up and cuffed his right hand, forcefully,

surprising him with her strength and immediacy, slipping the other cuff around a metal ring welded into the side panel like it was a single fluid movement.

"Um," he stammered, "just cuff me, not—"

"Relax," she cooed, running her fingertips softly over his exposed abs, slowly trailing them lower.

She bent over, letting her hair fall down so he couldn't see what she was doing until the blade was in her hand and touching his cock.

His eyes went wide as he writhed, trying to buck her off of his body.

"Sit still or I will cut it off," Mal said, now sounding perfectly sober.

He went still, save for the rise and fall of his chest. "What are you doing?"

"How many women have you drugged and raped?"

"What?" His eyes were wild and scared.

"I asked you a question. Answer it. No lies."

"I don't know what you're talking about."

She pressed the blade against his shaft, drew a ribbon of blood.

"No!"

"Answer the question."

"I ... I don't know."

"Ballpark it."

"Um ... six?"

"Six, you *think*? Or *definitely* six? Come on, Eddie. Don't be all humble now."

"I ... I don't know what you want me to say." Now he was crying.

"Try the truth," Mal growled, sick of his pathetic whining.

"Six, maybe seven or eight."

"Ah, that's more like it. See, that wasn't so hard."

No Stopping

His dick was now anything but. She squeezed to stiffen it for an easier, cleaner cut.

"Here's what's going to happen, Eddie. I'm going to give you a choice. And I want you to think about it very carefully. Whatever you do, *don't beg, cry, or try and talk me out of this.* I will gut you like a pig and leave you here to die. Do you understand me?"

"*Please.*"

"I said no begging!" She pressed the blade harder.

"I'm sorry."

"I know you are. In a moment, I'm going to do something you're not going to like very much. And you're going to want to hurt me or maybe call the cops on me, but I suggest you don't, Eddie, because here's the thing — I know where you live. I know where your parents, Ed Senior and Darlene water their garden every morning. I will gut your whole damned family if you tell a single soul even one damned thing about what happened here tonight. Do you understand?"

He cried, not answering.

"I said, *do you understand?*"

He nodded.

"Good. Now here's the choice. Do you want to me to cut off your balls or your dick?"

"What?"

"I can't have you out there raping any more women. You've got to be neutered, Eddie. It would be irresponsible of me to let you continue. And unless you want to die, this is the only option you have to walk out of here."

"Please—"

"What did I tell you?" Another press of the blade, another dribble of blood. "What do you want to keep? Answer now or I decide for you."

Eddie started to sob.

"I'll let you live. You can drive yourself to the hospital, but something's gotta go. So what's it going to be?"

He couldn't stop crying.

She had no sympathy whatsoever, not for a rapist like him.

He couldn't make a choice, so Mal chose for him.

And opted for both.

Chapter 3 - Mallory Black

MAL WOKE up to the worst headache of her life. At least the worst that didn't come with a head wound, and that was saying a lot.

Her phone was ringing, but as she fumbled around her bed and nightstand in the pitch-black hotel room, she couldn't find it. All she managed to do was knock several pill and beer bottles to the ground.

"Fuck." She wanted to leave the mess, but some of the bottles still had beer in them and at least one of the pill bottles was open. The last thing she needed was to ruin her perfectly good pain pills by drowning them in beer.

Mal flicked on the light, scooped a handful of pills off the ground before they got soaked, grabbed the offending bottle, then set it upright on the nightstand. She popped a pill into her mouth, dry-swallowed, then grabbed some towels from the bathroom to clean her mess.

Her phone rang again, but this time — on all fours, hung over and in her underwear — she saw it lying under the bed.

She reached for it, found her boss's name on the screen.

Mal had been on leave since her abduction and everything that happened in Mexico and still wasn't sure how long she'd take until she felt like going back. Or how long Gloria would wait. She'd told Mal to take as much time as she needed, but she had also asked twice since her return how she was doing and when she thought she might be up for more work. Mal was even offered light desk duty, but it was bullshit and boring to be out of the field.

Her phone kept ringing.

Voicemail was full — mostly from reporters wanting to interview her about Jessi Price and Paul Dodd as well as from people pitching books and offering her obscene amounts of money. But the lottery had already made her rich, and the idea of telling Jessi's story or giving Dodd any more attention for cash disgusted her.

She considered ignoring Gloria's call, but her boss was the persistent breed of pain in the ass that would surely show up at her door. Mal didn't want Gloria seeing her like this — strung out on pills, yet again.

"Morning," she answered, though it was one in the afternoon.

"I'm downstairs in the restaurant. We need to talk."

Downstairs? Fuck.

"You couldn't call first?"

"I've been calling all morning."

"I need to shower. Give me fifteen minutes?"

"See you then."

MAL FOUND Gloria sitting alone in a corner booth of the hotel's restaurant. She was sipping on a soda but not

No Stopping

eating. Her shades were large and dark, probably to hide the circles under her eyes, and her hair was pulled back tight into a bun. She greeted Mal with a sarcastic, "Good morning."

Mal sat with all the enthusiasm of a student called to the principal's office for a proper scolding. She hated feeling like a two-legged disappointment.

The server, an older woman named Roberta, came over to take her order.

She smiled. "Hey, Mallory. What can I get you today?"

"You want some coffee?" Gloria asked.

She knows I'm high or hung over. Or both.

"No, I'll take a Coke." Mal wasn't hungry, but she was also afraid pills on an empty stomach might make her sick, so she ordered a piece of cinnamon cake, one of the restaurant's specialties, and something she could pick at without getting any more nauseated.

"So, how are you?" Gloria asked once the server had left.

"Okay. How are *you?*"

Gloria removed the shades, revealing her exhausted eyes and worried expression. Something was off. "Have you seen the news?"

Mal's first instinct was to worry someone had discovered what she'd done to the rapist. She didn't think he told the cops what happened, but …

Maybe he's dead?

She didn't want another death on her hands. Paul Dodd was one thing — that man was a murderer. But so far as she knew, Eddie hadn't killed anyone. Why hadn't she checked the news? She braced for the worse and tried for a nonchalant expression and tone. "No. What's up?"

Gloria slid her phone across the table.

The screen displayed Cameron Ford's blog, Creek County Confidential, and a post with the title, *Where Are Calum Kozack and Brianna Gilchrest? A Tale of Incompetence at Creek County Sheriff's Office*.

Mal skimmed the article — a hit piece based on Oliver Kozack's wanting to know where his missing son and the other girl were.

Gloria looked around. You could never be too careful in public. "Did your friend have anything to do with their disappearances?"

My 'friend,' Jasper.

Fuck.

Gloria knew he was alive, and that Jasper was the prime, though unnamed, suspect for Wes Richardson's murder. She'd never said anything yet about liking him for Calum and Brianna's disappearances, but Mal's boss had been an excellent deputy before becoming Sheriff. She would eventually stitch two and two together.

Following Jordyn Parish's death, her father had complained to the sheriff's office about how Calum Kozack was responsible for his daughter's suicide. He wanted an investigation, but the District Attorney's office never pressed charges. Jasper was obviously a suspect, but he wasn't on anyone else's radar because nobody knew he was alive. He'd faked his death long before Calum or Brianna disappeared.

"I don't know. It's not like he ever volunteered information to me."

"Where are you on locating him?" Gloria asked.

Shit. Shit.

She looked around to make sure nobody was close enough to be listening in, or worse, recording their conversation. "He was in Mexico."

No Stopping

"What? Did you tell the Feds?"

"No," Mal said.

"Why the hell not?"

"Because it doesn't matter."

"Why not?"

"Paul Dodd killed him."

"What?"

"He died saving me. I left him out of it because, well, it would've needlessly complicated things."

"God damn it. It wasn't your call to make, Mal."

"I'd say it's for the best. It would be clusterfuck if word got out about him. Right now, they're frustrated, but they don't have any suspects."

Gloria breathed a long sigh. "How sure are you he's dead?"

Mal wanted to say one hundred percent, but if Jasper showed up later, Gloria would know that she'd lied to her face.

"I don't remember much, Gloria. I was pretty out of it. One of the people there said he was among the dead, but I dunno. I don't think you need to worry about him popping up out of nowhere."

"For all our sakes, I hope you're right. Otherwise, our old boss will bury us all."

"They've got nothing."

"Yeah?"

"A druggie loser and his girl took off, so far as anyone knows. Happens all the time. He was into some super shady shit."

"Yeah, but—" Gloria looked around again. "What if someone finds them?"

Finds their bodies.

"I want you on the case," Gloria finished.

"What?"

"I want you to work it. Meet with the man." She was careful not to use Oliver Kozack's name out loud. "Meet him, work him, let him know he's being heard."

"And what happens when I can't solve the case? He'll still be pissed."

"It's optics. Right now, you're the golden child. They can come after me, but you just saved Jessi Price. Again. You survived the unimaginable. Twice. Coming after you will only make them look awful."

"Ford was releasing videos of me just a couple of weeks ago, talking about what a damned train wreck I was. Did you forget or think it's gonna stop?"

"What you've been through, it's bought you time."

Mal shook her head. "How do you do this?"

"What?"

"Swim in these political waters so easily? Playing the game, manipulating perceptions? Don't you ... don't you feel dirty?"

"The game is the game, Mal. I don't make the rules. But I have to believe the good I can do is worth playing by their rules, whether I like them or not. What's the alternative? Give up and let a corrupt piece of shit back in power? You remember what it was like under him. How he and his cronies treated you, treated *all* women. And people of color."

Mal nodded.

Things were hell under the former sheriff. Barry was corrupt, crime was rampant, and he was complicit in a lot of shit. Not to mention the abusive deputies operating under his watch. Creek County was one more innocent black man being beaten or shot away from a riot. Gloria *had* cleaned things up. The crime rate was down and scads of innocents weren't fearing for their lives. Things were

No Stopping

better for everyone, except for some of the corrupt players that had to shift their dirty deeds out of the area. Barry's reelection would make things bad for those who already had them worst.

Even still, the politics always made Mal feel sick to her stomach. "Why's this getting press when Victor Forbes is still walking free?"

"The feds talked to him and cleared him. So far as anyone knows, Anders was behind it all."

"His second in charge had me and Jessi Price kidnapped and was working with an organized pedophile and sex trafficking ring — you think Victor's clean?"

"It's not my case," Gloria said. "It's out of my hands. And I'm sure if there's something on him, justice will be served."

"Ha. Justice."

"Listen, Mal, I know this has been rough on you. And if you're not ready, fine. But I could use a favor here."

Mal shook her head. "I'm ... I'm not sure I'm ready to come back yet."

"Are you using again?" Gloria asked, pursing her lips.

Something about the weight of that question got tears welling up in Mal's eyes.

"They drugged me, Gloria. Heroin. I was clean. I'd kicked it, but ... between that and the nightmares and everything that happened, it's been hard."

Gloria was quiet for a long moment. Mal wasn't sure if her boss was sad for her, disappointed, or angry that Mal had relapsed.

"I'm sorry you went through all that," Gloria said. "And I understand."

"Have Mike handle it. People love him. And he's untouchable."

Her partner was a good man, the kind of guy born to

do this job. He'd started as a beat cop where all the old ladies loved him, then went on to school resource officer where all the moms, dads, and teachers sang his praises, then eventually detective where he had an excellent closure rate. Hell, Mike could run for sheriff if he wasn't even more averse to politicking than Mal.

Gloria gathered her bag and left cash on the table. "Well, thank you, Mal. Please, take care. We need you better." She slipped on her shades and left in a hurry. Maybe Gloria was close to breaking down with all this bullshit. Or maybe she was pissed Mal had made a mess of herself yet again.

Mal looked down at her barely touched cake and sighed, feeling even worse than when she'd woken up. Not only was she suffering from a migraine, she was a big disappointment who couldn't even help her boss.

Fucking addict.

She was ready to burst. She needed someone to talk to but didn't want to burden Mike. Didn't want to talk to the therapist the sheriff's office suggested, at least not right now. She didn't even have friends anymore. Could probably call Tim Brentwood, the narcotics officer and her one-night stand in Jacksonville. He'd been leaving messages for a while. He was kind and not like most of the other cops she knew. But the last thing she wanted was awkward conversation about why she'd not called back. Or worse, awkward sex.

Mal was all alone.

She needed to get to a Narcotics Anonymous meeting.

Sobriety was a lonely battle, and sometimes it felt good just to be in a room with other people struggling — even if those people were oftentimes more ruined than her. Something about being in a group would help her right now. It would help her feel less alone.

No Stopping

She wanted to go to her home group, where she'd known a few people, but it was in town, and now that Mal was back in the news, she didn't want to deal with the stares. Or risk someone recording her there.

So Mal would have to find a meeting out of town.

Chapter 4 - Victor Forbes

VICTOR'S ARMS were shaking as he raised the weights over his chest and let them clang safely back onto the rack.

Exhausted, he trudged from the bench in his home gym to the rowing machine then grabbed his phone off the seat to see if his sister had responded to his encrypted message yet.

But still no word from Veronica.

Had they already gotten to her? Taken her somewhere until this all blew over, to ensure he obeyed his masters?

Or was his sister already dead?

He shook the thought from his mind while walking from the gym to his bathroom. After disrobing, he stepped into the shower. Left the water ice cold, as usual, then began to soap up.

Veronica was all they had left to hold over him. There was always torture, of course, but his capacity for pain was legendary. At least when it came to the physical stuff.

He cursed himself for not being better prepared. Since childhood, he'd always been ready for the worst. At first, he'd trained his mind and body to deal with bullies until

No Stopping

they were scared of him. Then he prepped for military service — denying himself creature comforts while exposing himself to harsh conditions, pain, and starvation ... anything to make him stronger than the enemy.

Once he'd realized his days were numbered as an enlisted man, Victor set his mind to becoming the shrewdest of entrepreneurs. He got close to the right people, found a way in with BlackBriar, then rose up the ranks to CEO.

But Victor now realized he'd stagnated in his job, grown too comfortable. He'd stopped preparing for the worst. Yes, he had money, weapons, and a few safe houses, but he'd foolishly not thought ahead to secure his mother or sister.

The people he worked for had no qualms when it came to killing innocents. Victor had overseen enough missions to know that all enemies, and their families, were the fairest of game. And he knew enough about the most powerful men and women in this country, and others, that he'd become a threat to them and the power structure that held them aloft.

If he couldn't contain the threat, then Victor became The Enemy as well.

Enemies of BlackBriar, and the group behind it, were never allowed to exist for long. And no enemy was too powerful to put down. King or soldier, capo or warlord, there was nobody they couldn't get to.

Even if Victor could do what they wanted and secure the information before it got out, would they allow him to live?

He had to figure something out.

Victor got out of the shower. As he dressed, a call came through on his encrypted line.

"Check your Pentz accounts," said The Raven.

Panic swelled in his chest as Victor logged in. He wasn't sure what was happening, but knew it couldn't be good.

He logged in on his phone and stared at the zero balance, stifling a scream, trying to maintain his composure.

Was this their attempt to make sure he didn't leave?

Were they going to use the money to keep him in line? Another insurance policy in case he didn't give a fuck about his sister?

He drew the deepest of breaths. If Victor lost his shit in front of The Raven, the man would know just how close to the edge he actually was.

"Where's my money?"

"You might want to ask him," The Raven said.

"Who?"

His messenger buzzed.

Victor looked down at an incoming photo, a man in a ski mask, roughly the same size and build of the irritant who had dismantled the Mexico operation.

"What is this?"

"The man who just robbed your accountant. Before killing him."

"What?" Victor asked.

"I'm following him." The Raven hung up.

With the line dead, Victor finally screamed.

Chapter 5 - Jasper Parish

JASPER PULLED up to the two-story tenement in the Butler projects just after midnight.

No surprise, there were still people awake, loitering in the parking lot, smoking, drinking, and probably selling drugs. Loud bass shook the ground. He could feel it in his bones, coming from a lowrider with purple neon glowing underneath it.

I really wish she'd move from this damned place.

He got out of his car and felt all the angry stares. Mostly men, but also a few women casting their raging gazes on him. No visible weapons, but most of the crowd was probably packing.

A trio of men stopped him as he approaching the front doors of the apartment complex. Two were buff, in sleeveless tees with lots of ink. The third, walking between them, looked barely eighteen. He was a pipsqueak, around five-six, and wore thick black-framed glasses, a hoodie the color of a bruise, black cargos, and yellow Nikes with a bright purple stripe.

"You come 'round here a lot," said the little guy, "yet I

don't know who you are."

Jasper met the young man's eyes with a nod. "Just visiting a friend."

The man leaned forward and sniffed the air. "You smell like cop."

"Yeah, it's a new cologne I got, *le Bacon*," Jasper said, mimicking a French accent. "It helps me get out of speeding tickets."

The man didn't smile. Nor did his buddies.

"Who the hell are you?" asked one of the big dudes, lifting his shirt to show his holster and the weapon inside it.

Jasper considered his options. This could escalate fast. He could take a few of them out, but doing so would surely get him killed, or at the very least, he'd have so many cops descending on this place that Spider's activities would likely be discovered.

Best to keep things quiet, play respectful to this little corner kingpin.

Jasper held up his palms to show he meant no harm. "I'm a friend of Spider's. Just passing through."

"Yo, Logic, he's cool," said a young man emerging from the entrance — Tyrell, the same young man in the tight black tee and skull cap who'd greeted him on his earlier visits.

"Yo, Professor Xavier." Tyrell greeted Jasper with a smile. "Spider's expecting you."

Jasper turned to Logic. "We good?"

Logic looked him up and down. "Yeah, we good." He and his guys backed off, as Jasper and Jordyn followed Tyrell into the building.

"What's his deal?" Jasper asked.

"That's Logic. You do not want to fuck with him. He's a'ight if you cool, though. Just protective of this place like he should be."

No Stopping

They took the stairs, following Tyrell to Spider's apartment.

Three quick knocks followed by two spaced apart, then another three fast ones. The door buzzed, then Tyrell waved them through. As the door closed behind them, he stayed in the hall, either standing guard or simply waiting to escort Jasper to his car.

Kim, one of Spider's friends and part of her security team, was in the living room. She was small, a twenty-three-year-old mixed-race girl, part Thai and part black. Her hair looked like cotton candy, dyed in shades of bright pink and blue, and she wore a pink-and-white track suit. She was seated at a table rolling a joint, her pistol at the ready.

She nodded. "Hey, Professor, how's life treatin' you?"

"Good. And yourself?"

She licked the joint then lit it. "All good. She's in the back, waiting for you."

"Thanks." Jasper walked toward the computer-filled room. The door was ajar, and he could see Spider inside, seated in her wheelchair, typing at a laptop.

"Be with you in a sec," she said, click-clacking even faster than Jordyn texted on her phone.

Spider finished whatever she was doing, drank from her large flask, then smiled. "Hey, Professor. What's up?"

"You get the Pentz transfer?"

He'd transferred half of Victor's crypto to her and kept the other half in his account. Wars needed funding, after all.

"Yes, and thank you. That'll go a long way." Spider was using her half to upgrade computers, pay for protection and information, and otherwise cover the basic overhead of their highly illegal vigilante venture.

"Good." He looked down, unable to shake the memory

of the little boy seeing him kill his father. "One more thing, we need to set some aside for an unexpected situation."

"What's that?"

"His son was there. Saw everything."

"His son was there? Did he see your face?"

"No. I had a mask. But … I want you to monitor the situation, see what happens to the kid. Set up a trust fund for him, give him access when the time is right."

Spider shook her head. "Such a softie. Can't help but go around saving orphans, can you? Maybe he'll be working for you someday."

She was kidding, trying to lighten the mood, but Jasper couldn't find any humor in it now. "Difference is, I didn't kill your family. You were already an orphan. And no, I don't want his son ever working with us. Hell, I'm not even sure I've got much left in me."

Spider raised her eyebrows.

Jordyn, leaning against the wall to Jasper's left, mimicked Spider's reaction.

"For real?" Spider asked. "Like, quit it all?"

"I thought I was helping, but no matter what I do, I can't save everybody. Those kids and women in Mexico — how many actually escaped that life after the place was shut down? I saved a few, sure, but how many others went from one abuser to another?"

"What if it was only one?" Spider asked. "You still made a difference. Every life matters."

"But what about tonight? What about that boy's life? I ruined it, and for what, to try and keep Victor Forbes from escaping justice? Was *that* worth it? If the lives I save matter, then how about the ones I destroy?"

Spider was silent, all three of them were. Then she said, "Do you want me to continue decrypting the drive?"

"Yes. How long do you think it'll take?"

"Hard to say. I'm running my best brute force on it. Could be any day. Could be months."

"*Months?*"

"Maybe years. Or never, if the password is long and complicated enough. Though I hate to say never. Quantum computing is on the rise, and when it's here, things like this might get cracked in seconds. Minutes at the most. But the not-too-distant future is still a ways off."

Jasper hated leaving a job undone, but if there was nothing he could do now, then maybe it was best to rest up like Jordyn had been begging him to do. If and when Spider cracked the encryption password, he could decide whether to turn the list of people in the pedophile network over to the authorities or pursue them himself.

"No need to choose now," Jordyn said. "Take a break. Relax a bit. You deserve it. Then you can decide."

"Maybe," he agreed.

"Maybe what?" Spider asked.

"Maybe I'll take some time off."

Spider was still quiet, and he wondered if she was worrying about the money they took tonight. They'd taken it to stop Forbes from leaving and help fund Jasper's war with the network. If he stopped the battle, then the money wasn't as necessary.

"Regardless of what happens to me, keep your half. If — or when — I quit, make sure that kid gets enough, then do whatever you want with the rest. Maybe you can finally get the hell out of here, stop working for ... *the locals.*"

Spider rolled her eyes. "And here you go again."

"What?"

"These are my people. You see them as thugs and gangbangers, but they're not all like that. Not the ones I work with. They were here for me when nobody else was, before you came along like a white knight."

"White knight?"

"I appreciate all you've done for me, Professor, really I do. I'm sure I'd be on the streets without you. But these are my friends. People I've known my whole life. And I'm not giving up on them."

"Yeah? Hate to break it to you, but they gave up on themselves. We all have choices in life. And none of them is *forced* to sell drugs."

Spider shook her head. "You don't know what it's like, trying to survive."

Jasper wanted to argue he did know what it was like. He grew up in a place a lot like this in South Florida. But he managed to make a different choice. But Spider didn't know Jasper's name or his past, and he wanted to keep it that way. She only knew the fiction he'd given her. That plus the one truth he was willing to share — he was hunting some human scum. Given his methodology, that didn't exactly give him the moral high ground in an argument like this.

He looked over, but Jordyn was gone. Then he remembered what he forgot all too often. His daughter was dead. "I'm sorry. I just get protective. You remind me of someone I couldn't keep safe."

"I'm fine, Professor. If someone ever hurts me, it won't be one of these guys 'round here."

Jasper nodded. Spider was probably right. They did seem protective of her. Maybe she was better off here than some place in the suburbs.

"Thank you. I'm heading out. I'll be in touch soon."

Spider met his gaze. She looked like she wanted to say something else but nodded instead. "See ya 'round, Professor."

Jasper left, missing Jordyn and feeling lonelier and more lost than when he'd arrived.

Chapter 6 - Mallory Black

MAL'S NA meeting was at a Baptist church in St. Augustine, a place she'd never been before.

She released her ponytail and let her hair hang in her face, glancing in the rearview mirror to make sure her features were obscured. She was also in baggy sweats, T-shirt, and oversized denim jacket — her best attempt at a fast but not too obvious disguise. Just blend in with the others.

Mal crossed the barely lit parking lot with her head down. Once inside the church, she followed signs directing her to a small classroom with several folding tables forming a square in the center. A half-dozen of them, with four seats at each, plus two other tables along the wall.

As she'd arrived late to the meeting, which started at eight, there were few empty chairs left. She chose a seat at the far end of the square next to a mousey, brown-haired woman in her twenties who was dressed for work in a green Publix uniform.

The woman looked at Mal. "Hi."

Not one for small talk, she nodded then faced forward to hear the person seated at the other side of the room, a short Indian man in his sixties, talking about this week's biggest hardships.

Mal listened as he confessed to his near slip-up. The only thing that had stopped him from using again was his daughter showing up at his house and asking if he could watch his granddaughter. If she hadn't been called to a last-minute shift at the hospital, he wouldn't be sober.

"So, I sat there looking after my beautiful six-year-old granddaughter, the sweetest, most precious girl. She was drawing pictures for me and talking about school and chattering on and on. I remembered how much I missed these days with my own daughter, how I'd been too busy working to enjoy them. Here I was, getting a chance to experience a special moment with my granddaughter, no work to preoccupy me since I'm retired, but … I *still* couldn't enjoy it. All I could think about was waiting for her to sleep so I could start using again."

He paused and wiped his eyes.

A few other people in the room's eyes were watering, too.

"And then, finally, I got her to bed. Once she was asleep, I just stared at the pills I'd been so desperately waiting to use."

The silence stretched on, as if he were trying to figure out how to say the next part. In that pregnant moment, Mal feared what he might say.

"And … I couldn't do it. I hated the pills, hated myself even more for wanting them more than I wanted to spend time with my own granddaughter. So, I flushed them. Thank you all for listening. Glad to be in my home group."

Several of the people responded with, "Fucking A."

"Thank you, Aaron," said a Hispanic man in his fifties. "Anybody else?"

He looked at Mal. She hoped he wasn't going to request an introduction. Being late meant she'd missed the part where someone would ask if there were any newcomers or guests from out of the area.

"Well, I guess I need to get this out," said the woman next to Mal. "Hi, my name is Maggie. My D.O.C. is opiates, and I'm five weeks sober this Tuesday."

"Hi, Maggie," the others said.

"It's been hard. Tommy is getting *sooooo* difficult and thinks this whole twelve-step thing is a scam or a joke or something. He practically laughed when I showed him my thirty-day keychain. He's always saying shit like, 'You know this isn't gonna last. What, you think you're better than me?' Or he'll accuse me of cheating on him with my friend, Jake. I'm not being unfaithful, but damn it if he isn't *making me* want to leave his ass. But I just can't do that to our kid. So, for now, it looks like I'm stuck."

A few nods from women in the room.

Mal looked closer and saw the bruise under her eye. Concealed with makeup, but still ,she could see the faint remains.

Is this bruise from her Tommy?

"Anyway, Jake is trying to convince me to leave him, but ... I can't. Tommy would make divorce a living hell. He's always bitching about men's rights, saying women always get the kid and he can understand why men kill their exes because 'the bitches' leave them no choice. I don't want to raise my daughter with a man who thinks like that, but I don't know what he'd do if I took her."

The woman paused and wiped her tears.

"I can't go on like this. Now that I'm sober, I see how

much I've let him treat me like shit for so long. But ... I can't just leave. I'm so angry and sad all the time. Pills were my only escape and without using, I ... I don't know. It's a real struggle. But I have to stay sober. I do bad shit whenever I give in, and I can't lose my daughter. I'm just glad to be here. One day at a time, right? Thanks for letting me share."

The skinny white dude sitting across from Mal went next. He had long hair, denim shorts, and an ankle monitor. When he started talking, she looked over at Maggie, who was back to wiping tears from her eyes.

Mal wanted to say something, but wasn't sure what she *could* say, other than yet another empty platitude. Besides, she wasn't here to make friends.

She listened to others share but avoided speaking. The last thing she needed was for someone to recognize her. People usually respected the anonymity, but that didn't mean she didn't get looked at. Sometimes, Mal heard the whispers.

Isn't that the cop whose kid was murdered?
Hey, wasn't she kidnapped, too? Do you think he raped her?
Didn't she win the lottery?

Mal wanted to blend in and maybe feed off the strength of shared suffering and recovery. Hearing the struggles of others helped her to remember this wasn't a battle she fought alone.

And right now, a bit could be all the difference between a normal life and losing everything.

Once everyone was through sharing, the Hispanic man — whom she'd heard someone call Louis — asked if anyone else wanted to share. Nobody spoke or raised a hand.

Then he asked if it was anyone's first time, so they could get a keychain and the *Basic Text*.

No Stopping

Nobody spoke.

He handed out keychains for thirty and sixty days. And an anniversary chip, which invited hugs and applause. Mal felt good as she clapped for the other addicts' achievements.

She hugged Maggie at the end of the meeting, then, just to avoid awkward small talk or coffee and snacks, asked where the bathroom was.

After freshening up, Mal avoided the classroom and went straight to the parking lot. Maggie was standing on the sidewalk, smoking, looking like she was waiting for a ride.

The skinny guy with the tracker on his ankle was chatting her up. Based on Maggie's body language, it was clear she was trying to avoid the conversation.

Mal considered leaving, but as she passed she overheard the guy promising Maggie a good time — either propositioning her for sex or offering drugs. It wasn't uncommon for drug dealers or predators to hunt for prey in rooms like this.

Now Mal couldn't leave. She turned around and headed straight toward them.

The guy looked at Mal approaching and narrowed his eyes. He planted a fake stoner smile on his dumb face. "Hey, you new here?"

"Yeah," Mal said, waiting to see what he would say next.

He was looking her up and down, his sneer like a wolf. "What's your D.O.C.?"

"Sobriety," Mal said.

"Well, I ain't got that, but I can hook you up if you want some real fun. Can hook both you ladies up."

Mal took an assertive step toward him and gave a sharp rise to her voice as others shuffled out of the church. "Are you trying to sell drugs at a fucking NA meeting?"

He looked around sheepishly then glared at her, "You don't have to be such a bitch."

Mal smiled. "Oh, I'm not even getting started."

He stared at her for a long, idiotic moment, as if his dumb brain was trying to get the message.

"Leave," she said. "We don't want your shit."

He looked like he might argue but then thought better of it and sighed instead. Then, as he turned, he said, "Whatever … bitch."

Mal watched him slink off toward the street, probably too spooked to approach anyone else.

"He a regular?" Mal asked.

"Seen him a couple of times, but this is the first time he approached me," Maggie told her. "Thank you."

"No problem."

"You waiting on a ride?" Mal asked instead of saying goodbye.

"Yeah. I texted him fifteen minutes ago. He should be here by now."

A fat raindrop fell on her face, followed by more. Mal looked back at the awning over the church entrance, where others were chatting and smoking. "You want to wait in my car?"

Maggie looked at Mal for a long moment, as if trying to determine if she was another predator. Finally, she nodded, "Okay, thanks."

They sat in the car near where Maggie had been standing, waiting for Tommy.

"How long you been sober?" Maggie asked, starting on the small talk.

"In hours?" Mal smiled awkwardly. "Kinda slipped."

"Sorry. Been there. A few times."

"How long have you been an addict?"

"Oh, God. Um, on and off since I was eighteen. Stopped for a while when I got pregnant with Emma. And I stayed sober for the first two years. Then, last year, I hurt my back at work and … one thing led to another."

"Ah, I know the feeling." Mal considered sharing a less detailed version of her story but then thought better of it. She barely knew this woman. And besides, Maggie needed to vent more than she needed to hear Mal bitch.

Maggie stared out the window, growing quiet, maybe contemplating how much she should share.

"Did Tommy put that bruise on your face?"

Maggie played dumb, but her lie crumbled as she met Mal's gaze, and so did her resolve to keep the secret. She wasn't crying, but her lip trembled all the same. "He doesn't usually hit me."

Mal had heard that song before, plenty of times. But instead of pushing Maggie, she asked, "What happened?"

"It doesn't matter."

"The hell it doesn't. Nobody should ever hit you, least of all your husband."

She shook her head. "You're right, but I don't know what to do."

"Leave," Mal said.

"It's not that easy."

"Sure, it is. There are places you can go if you feel unsafe. You can—"

"No, I don't want the police involved."

"So, what then? You wait until he hits your kid?"

Maggie glared at Mal. She'd pushed too hard, too quickly.

"I think I'll wait outside."

"Wait, I'm sorry."

"It's okay, but … I'm just gonna wait over there."

Maggie got out of the car, walked to the front door, then waited under the awning where people were still smoking in a huddle.

Mal drove off, pissed at herself and her stupid mouth.

Chapter 7 - Jasper Parish

JASPER WOKE to his buzzing phone and a sliver of morning light burning through the crack in his block-out bedroom curtains.

The number was unlisted.

He picked it up and heard silence on the other end. "Hello?"

Nothing.

His gut churned, gnawing at him. He sensed something was wrong but didn't know what yet. "Hello?"

A static crackling pop came from the other end, the kind he got when an automated machine called his number to see if a live person was on before passing the call to a telemarketer or scammer.

Jasper hung up. He considered calling the few people who had his number, just to ease his mind of the sensation that something was horribly off, but there was a knock on his bedroom door before he could, loud enough to startle him.

His hand was under his pillow and on his gun before the door exploded open.

Jordyn.

He was glad to see her. He felt some measure of relief — until he saw her eyes, and the look inside them that said she had some terrible news to share.

"Did you see it?"

"What?" Jasper asked.

"The vision?"

"Of what?"

She looked down at her feet. "I … I feel like I have to tell you but I don't want you to do anything."

"What?" Jasper repeated.

"Someone you know is in danger, but you can't get involved this time."

"What? Who?"

"You'll want to get involved if I tell you, and I doubt you have a way to contact him, so you're going to ask me to find him. Then it'll all begin again."

"*What's* going to begin?"

Now on the verge of tears, she said, "Something bad."

"Stop being so cryptic, Jordyn. Just tell me. Who is in trouble, and what's going to happen?"

"I can tell you who is in trouble, but … I can't tell you what's going to happen."

"Can't or won't?"

"Can't, I don't know, other than this awful feeling that if you go to help this person, it's going to trigger a chain of events you won't be able to undo."

"That's just your anxiety."

"No, it's not, Dad! I can feel it."

"Then you or me will get a vision and stop it from happening. Now tell me, who is in trouble?"

"That man, Cadillac."

"Cadillac?" Jasper hadn't thought of the man since he'd gotten his info on BlackBriar and had given him

No Stopping

enough cash to get out of town with his girlfriend, Keisha, and the two kids. "What's wrong?"

"He's going to die. And so is his family. They're going to kill them all."

"Can we stop it?"

"I don't think it's happened yet, but—"

"Then we need to try."

"Damn it."

"Can you find him?"

"*Please*, Dad."

"We can't sit by and do nothing. Clearly you know this or you wouldn't have told me. You would've kept it to yourself."

She let out a long sigh and closed her eyes, focusing as she searched for his location. Last they'd seen him was after he helped them by telling Jasper about BlackBriar's involvement with kidnapping Jessi and Mallory. He'd given Cadillac money and told him to get the hell out of town.

"He didn't go far."

"What?"

"Yeah. He's on the west coast."

"Can you find him if we start driving?"

"Please, Dad, do we have to?"

"You know the answer."

"God, I hate this psychic bullshit."

"I'll call Spider, see if she's got a number or can find a way to contact him. In the meantime, we need to get going. Okay?"

Jordyn nodded, defeated, then went to grab her bag.

He called Spider before realizing it was probably too early. Her voicemail came on and he said, "Hey, it's the professor. I need help finding a number for that guy, Cadillac. Whenever you wake up."

He hung up, got dressed, grabbed his go bag, then darted out the door with his daughter.

Jordyn sat in the passenger seat, reading and listening to music on her phone as they drove.

"Whatchya' listening to?"

"Lo-fi," she said, her eyes on the phone.

He drove a few more miles before taking another stab at some small talk. "Whatchya' reading?"

"*The Gay Science*."

"Ah, Nietzsche."

She yanked out an earbud and looked over. "You read it?"

"A long time ago. Don't remember much. What do you like about it?"

"Do you believe in fate?" Jordyn asked, but didn't wait for a response. "What if we live the same lives over and over, always making the same choices and repeating our same mistakes? Then do we ever *really* have a choice?"

Jasper considered her question, wondering what she was getting at. Was Jordyn pondering philosophical thoughts or making a point? Maybe it had to do with her fear that bad things would happen if they helped Cadillac.

"Sometimes I feel like things line up too perfectly not to believe in something. But when bad shit happens to good people, to innocents, then I have to wonder what kind of fate would allow that or dictate that such horrors must happen at all, let alone again and again. As for choices, I have to think we always have a choice."

Jordyn turned off the screen and stared out the window.

"Why?" Jasper asked. "What do you think?"

"I think there has to be a point to all of this. Even suffering has purpose. Maybe it's the only way we can appreciate the good."

No Stopping

"What are you saying? We should let people suffer? Let fate do as it will?"

"*Can* we stop fate?" Jordyn asked. "I mean, you didn't stop that cop's kid from being killed even though you warned her. You chose to tell her, but it still didn't save the girl."

"No, but we *did* save Jessi, twice. And Mallory, plus those other girls in Mexico."

"But maybe they were meant to be saved. Maybe fate had already decided and it was just meant to be."

"How do you determine if fate pushed me to intervene or if it was my choice?"

"I don't know."

"Maybe fate works through us."

"But if fate is going to do whatever it wants, anyway, then why bother saving other people? Why not just let it happen? If they're meant to be saved, then fate will save them. If they're meant to die, they die. And if they're meant to jump off a bridge, so be it."

"What does that even mean?" Jasper asked, feeling like he should know.

"Never mind." Jordyn turned her attention back to the world racing by outside her car window.

They drove in silence the rest of the way, but Jasper's mind was far from quiet. He kept thinking about Mallory who had argued with him how it wasn't his job to decide who should live or die. She'd wanted to let the system handle Paul Dodd but had lived to regret that decision.

Mallory had lived to change her mind and pull the trigger herself.

He wondered how much it was eating her up. Did she regret crossing that line?

Jasper had crossed it so long ago, and so many times, he didn't even remember where it used to be.

Death had become his life's only constant. In his waking life and in his dreams, he saw only bodies — those he mourned and those he'd murdered himself.

He thought about his conversation with Jordyn and prayed if he was indeed doomed to live the same life with the same choices on repeat, he'd at least find a way to make his peace with it. Because right now it was eating him alive, his mind aching with so much loss.

At least Jasper still had his daughter.

He looked over to see Jordyn sleeping, her head on the window, reminding him of when she was little and she'd fall asleep in his arms on the couch. He wished he could go back to those simpler times, before her mother passed, before … the thought trailed off, sadness sweeping into his soul like the gray and mottled clouds overhead.

Jasper wanted to kiss his daughter on her head, but traffic was starting to pick up as they neared their destination. A light sprinkle on his windshield turned to an instantaneous and torrential downpour.

He flicked on his lights and the wipers.

Jordyn stirred, but immediately closed her eyes, easing back to sleep amid the gentle thrumming.

As they took 275 over Old Tampa Bay, Jasper gently shook her. "We're almost there. You know where I'm looking?"

She wiped at her eyes, looked around, then closed them. "Near the historic district, I think."

He drove, following her psychic radar, hoping they weren't too late.

"Do you know if it's happened yet, or when it will?"

"No. Sorry." She shook her head.

Jasper drove faster until Jordyn pointed at a Budget Motel.

No Stopping

He swung into the lot. Looked at the pool where a couple families were swimming.

She followed his gaze, then glanced up at the second story walkway. "I think he's up there."

"Let's go," Jasper said as they got out of the car.

They took the stairs, Jordyn leading the way. She stopped at one of the rooms with a *Do Not Disturb* door hanger dangling from the lock.

Jordyn stared at the door, her eyes welling up and hands visibly shaking at her side. She whispered, "We're too late."

Jasper knocked on the door and waited, keeping his Mets hat low over his face, glancing at the pool to see if anybody was paying attention. Fortunately, no one seemed to be watching.

He faced the door, slipped on gloves, then reached into his jacket pocket for the tool Spider made from an Arduino board inside an iPhone case. The board was outfitted with a software script that would bypass electronic locks. While most of the upper-end motels had patched the exploit, places like this usually didn't.

Jasper inserted the barrel plug into the bottom of the lock then plugged the USB into the device.

Jordyn watched him, shifting from one foot to the other while staring at the door.

After the lock clicked open, Jasper opened the door.

His daughter gasped as they entered.

Cadillac lay on the closest bed, flat on his back, eyes wide open, a bullet through his forehead.

His girlfriend was on the floor in front of the bathroom, shot in the gut, eyes closed, blood pooled around her.

Jasper let the door close softly and whispered, "*Fuck.*"

He touched Keisha's neck, checking for her pulse.

But, of course, she was gone.

"Oh, God," Jordyn cried out. She was standing near the closed rear window, staring at the ground next to the second bed.

"What?"

She shook her head. "They killed two kids."

Jasper went over to check, to see if there was any chance the three-year-old boy or four-year-old girl were still alive.

His heart sunk.

What kind of fuckers would kill two kids? Why? They didn't even know anything.

Jasper understood killing Cadillac, and even his girlfriend, both of whom could expose BlackBriar. But they could've left the children alive. Someone would have taken them in.

Fuckers.

His daughter was bawling.

Jasper needed her to get it together. He grabbed her by the shoulders. "Jordyn."

She looked up at him through tears.

"Do you know who did this? I need you to tell me if you can."

She shook her head. "I … I don't want to touch them."

"Well, if you can see something any other way, go ahead."

Using the back of her hand, Jordyn touched the closest wall. Next, the bed. Then, the television. And finally, the dresser. Each time, she closed her eyes in furrowed concentration.

Jasper watched as she checked the room, searching for even the faintest of signals left behind by the killers. Sometimes he could see when she found one, though he wasn't sure if she was somehow broadcasting her vision or if he was picking up on the signals himself. He used to think he might have some of her gifts but now was no longer certain.

She shook her head after a whole lot of nothing. "Sorry."

"I need you to touch Cadillac. If any of them knew the killer, it would've probably been him."

"Please," she cried. "Please don't make me."

Jasper took her trembling hands in his. "Honey, I wouldn't ask you otherwise. But … these people, these kids, didn't deserve that. Help me find the monster who did this."

Jordyn squeezed her eyes shut, hard, gritting her teeth. "I hate this so much."

"I know, but you're helping them."

She opened her eyes and glared at him. "No, I'm helping *you*. You want to get even. I think we should just let this go and stop before someone else dies."

"Look at this," Jasper insisted. "Can we really let it go?"

She shook her head. "I don't want to see this. I have a horrible feeling."

"What do you mean?"

"I don't think this is the end of it. And if I touch him, this won't be the end of it for you. You're gonna keep chasing this until it finally kills you."

"Please."

Jordyn pulled away, went to Cadillac's large frame, stood over him. She glared at her father one final time to let him know she wasn't happy with his order, then she placed her left hand on his chest.

She fell back as if hit by something — an echo of a gunshot.

Jasper knew what it was because he felt it, too. He saw

the face that accompanied death, a man Cadillac knew as The Raven.

BlackBriar is cleaning house.

A glance at his daughter told him she was numb. Had witnessing their deaths fucked her up that much? Jordyn had seen some heinous shit before, but she was still a teenager. Despite being more mature than her peers, Jordyn was still a kid.

Worst. Parent. Ever.

But as her eyes began to well up, Jasper saw that something else was wrong. "What is it?"

"The dominoes." Jordyn said. "The first one has fallen."

Chapter 8 - Mallory Black

MAL GRABBED the Chromebook she'd been using for her recent vigilante work, untraceable to her. Using TOR, as she always did, she pulled up the doc to study her list of scumbags. She was still in Jacksonville, which put her closest to the guy she'd followed that night but didn't have a plan for, Dre Hamilton.

She read the file, refreshing her memory.

Hamilton was twenty-six when he'd raped a fifteen-year-old girl named Amber, whom he'd hired to watch his dogs. He'd gotten her drunk before taking advantage of her. The cops arrested him, but they'd bungled the evidence so he was released without consequence. Most rapists who got off on a technicality would be smart enough to thank their lucky stars and get the hell out of Dodge.

But Dre had other plans.

He became obsessed with Amber. Started harassing her, telling her he loved her and would wait for her to turn eighteen. He kept driving by her house and her bus stop, tried to talk to her every chance he got. When her mom went to the cops and filed an order of protection against him, he took to harassing her anonymously.

One night, someone sent Amber's mother — and all her friends and family — photos and videos from her webcam. The files were humiliating enough to make the girl hang herself.

Amber's mother, suspecting Dre, went on a tirade, telling anyone who would listen he was responsible for her daughter's death. The fucker sued her in civil court for defamation of character. She lost it and tried attacking him in court. Now she was the one in jail for attempting to harm him.

Mal had looked into the case, but, like the cops, she had no proof of what Dre had done. And despite wanting justice — and believing the guy was guilty as fuck — she needed some kind of proof before cutting off his dick.

She found his small two-bedroom 1950's ranch house at the end of a quiet dead-end street, backing up to the woods. Passed it slowly, seeing no car parked in his carport.

The lights were off.

Mal drove a few streets over to a 7-11, parked in the far corner of the lot. She pulled her hat over her head, slipped on gloves, and made sure her gear was safely stowed in her leather jacket. Then she hoofed it back to Dre's place, approaching through the side yard, careful to make sure no neighbors were outside.

The street was dead.

She went to the back of the house and tapped on the sliding glass door to see if anybody or anything responded. Dre had posted on LiveLyfe last week that his dog had died, and it *will be a while before my heart heals enough for another.*

Mal lifted the sliding glass door off the tracks. It was an

older model with no security bar or device to prevent entry. She was inside within seconds.

Didn't even need her bump key.

After retrieving her flashlight, she began looking around, searching for evidence that Dre Hamilton was exactly the guilty piece of shit she believed him to be. The house smelled faintly musty, and there was a reek coming from the kitchen. Despite the unpleasant odors and an overflowing garbage can, the place was relatively clean.

The house had two bedrooms, and both doors were closed. She opened the one closest to the rear and found a gaming room with a PC and three monitors on an arm above the desk. His gaming chair was worn. Bits of fabric had flaked and gathered beneath the chair on a thick black floor mat.

Mal turned on the PC. While it booted up, she checked Dre's bedroom.

The room had a king-sized bed, perfectly made. Nothing fancy, no extra pillows or shams or the slightest of feminine touches. No paintings on the wall. Only a nightstand, a dresser, and a mirror above it. A small wooden box sat atop the dresser. In it was a smattering of change, a ring with a trio of keys, and a handful of condoms.

She searched the nightstand then the dresser, rooting through his belongings and ripping drawers out with no concern for the mess. A trashed house would be the least of his worries.

Not even five minutes into her search, Mal found a shoebox hidden beneath the bottom dresser drawer. And in it was the proof she needed— a pair of girl's underwear, several photos of Amber, and a few other photos of girls who looked underage, each in various stages of undress. All of them were doing things to themselves. The photos looked like they were taken via their laptops.

The last item in the box was a folded piece of notebook paper.

Mal opened it.

PLEASE, Dre. Don't show anybody else.
Please.
Just leave me and my family alone.
—A

RAGE AND INDIGNATION, a thirst for vengeance like fingers at her throat.

Got you, fucker.

Mal started returning stuff to where it'd come from, wishing she'd been more careful. Then she went to his office, turned off the computer, then waited for the rapist to come home.

MAL HID BEHIND THE HOUSE, just outside the sliding glass door.

She was dressed in all black, from ski mask to boots. She'd look more than suspicious if anyone saw her, but Dre's house backed up to the woods, and there was a tall wooden fence dividing him from his only neighbor's house.

She had a gun, untraceable to her, and a pair of knives.

The gun was a last resort, a cudgel to get him to stand down in case he tried to resist. Mal hoped he wouldn't put up too much of a fight. It was surprising how much she enjoyed separating a rapist from his dick.

It sickened her at first, but now, thinking about how Dre had terrorized a young girl before turning on her mother and destroying their family, nothing gave her greater pleasure than imagining the blade severing his offending member.

The best part had been the look in Eddie's eyes when he realized what was about to happen — his total and utter realization that he had no control, that the evil fucker who'd lorded his power over unconscious women had become the helpless victim. It gave Mal a rush that might have been better than her pills.

Come on, Dre, where the fuck are you?

It was getting cold, and now she was shivering.

Forty minutes passed. Mal bounced up and down to stay warm as she wondered if she should come back another night.

Then she heard a car pulling up in the front yard.

She readied herself, stretching her limbs to pump warmth into her extremities.

The light came on, bleeding through the verticals.

She heard several male voices, talking, then laughing.

Fuck, he's got company!

Someone yelled, "What the fuck?"

Mal flashed over the scene in her mind, wondering if she'd left something out. Then she remembered — she'd left the door to the gaming room open.

Lights flickered on above her.

Fuck!

She bolted toward the woods.

Seconds later, still ten yards from the tree line, Mal heard the sliding glass door slamming hard in its tracks, the wrestling of verticals, and a man shouting, "Hey!"

Mal ran as fast as she could without looking back.

A gunshot thundered behind her.

Fuck, fuck, fuck!

She didn't dare turn back as she raced into the woods

and tore through the darkness, ignoring the brush threatening to trip her and the uneven ground trying to topple her.

Footsteps and bellows thundered behind her.

At least three men, judging from the voices.

She raced deeper into the thicket, deeper into the darkness, her heart pounding and adrenaline pumping.

Another gunshot.

This one she heard whiz by.

Fuck! Fuck! Fuck!

She barely dodged a tree and stumbled forward, nearly losing her step.

Mal was no longer certain of her direction, only that she was running away from them.

"Get him!" shouted one of the men.

Well, at least they think I'm a guy. Makes it less likely this is traced back to me when they report it to the police. Assuming they don't catch, rape, and kill me.

Mal kept running, feet pumping, hands tearing at branches as they clawed at her face.

A branch would surely poke her eyes out, or she would run straight into—

Another gunshot.

Then a yell from behind her and to the right. Another behind and to the left.

They were splitting up. A terrifying thought, thinking how well they might know these woods.

Mal kept running straight, wondering how deep the forest went. It didn't seem that big when she'd driven through the neighborhood, but outside appearances were often deceiving. And the woods always seemed more sprawling in the dark.

She kept running until she no longer heard the yelling behind her.

Mal dared to glance back, but it was too dark to see anything.

When she turned forward, she glimpsed light ahead of her — someone's phone being used as a flashlight, not even twenty feet away.

She froze, hugged the nearest tree. Put it between herself and the light.

Footsteps drew nearer, crunching on dried leaves.

Her heart pounded. Surely they could hear it.

The glowing light crept to her right.

Any second, he'd be right beside her.

If he turned, he would see her for sure.

"You find him, Al?"

"No," shouted the guy right beside her.

The light brightened. Mal had to move, carefully.

She pressed her weight against the tree then stepped gingerly forward, trying to keep the trunk between her and Al until he passed.

The light was only inches away.

Mal heard him panting, heard his footsteps.

Heard him say, "Fucking bullshit."

The light was so close, he seemed to be walking toward her tree instead of past it.

She moved another inch, watching the light swell on either side of the tree, its shadow grew larger as he approached, concealing her within it.

Which way was he coming from?

If Mal stepped the wrong way, she'd run right into him.

She chose left just as he passed on the right, and would have exhaled with relief, but a branch snapped underfoot and the light swiveled toward her instead.

Fuck!

"I got him!" Al screamed.

Mal launched herself at the enemy, throat punching him right in the Adam's apple.

He fell to the ground, gasping as he clawed at his throat.

Mal ran again.

Footsteps approached.

Someone screamed, "Al?"

But Al couldn't answer yet.

She kept running, but moving fast meant abandoning silence.

Mal didn't care. She saw light through thinning branches ahead and was terrified she might run into someone's yard, so she veered left. The land swelled higher.

Running grew harder as the grade grew steeper, but the men continued yelling. They weren't about to surrender now, so she couldn't, either.

Her lungs were on fire, her legs were burning jelly. She wasn't sure how much more she had in her. But still she kept going.

Then Mal hit something hard with her face, with her entire body.

She fell backward down the hill, into the darkness.

Chapter 9 - Jasper Parish

JASPER HAD BEEN TRYING to reach Spider all morning. An uneasy dread had settled into his gut as he drove back to the Butler projects where she lived, whispering three simple words on repeat in his mind.

You're too late.

And now, just miles away from her apartment, that message had crept through his entire body like tendrils of disease threatening to decimate his hope.

He turned to Jordyn, who stared out the window. She hadn't said much of anything since they left the motel in St. Pete.

Since they'd left the bodies.

"You get any visions on her yet?"

Jordyn shook her head. "Sorry, Dad."

He nodded, driving faster as rain fell harder.

As they arrived at the apartment complex, red and blue lights reflected and distorted through the rivulets racing down his windshield.

Too late.

Butler PD and Creek County Sheriff vehicles packed the parking lot.

More than forty people were gathered outside the perimeter of the complex, watching, some of them staring down the cops and deputies with the same hate and distrust he'd felt on his own body before.

People here had a love-hate relationship with the police. Older folks tended to want the cops more involved in the community. More feet on the ground, more community outreach. Keeping the streets safe and getting drugs out of their neighborhood. While the younger generation — those most likely to be pulled over or randomly harassed — had nothing but contempt for a powerful force that seemed hell-bent on crushing them. This segment of the community saw *all* law enforcement officials as the problem. Jasper had lived both sides of that line and was intimately familiar with how few easy answers there were, despite what glad-handing politicians might promise or preach with their silver tongues.

He needed to find out what happened. Did they get to Spider?

Jasper turned on his scanner but wasn't getting any answers outside of multiple fatalities. No names yet.

He drove slowly through the neighborhood, searching for anyone who might know something.

Somebody *always* knew something.

Jasper was about to circle back past Spider's complex when he spotted a group of young men standing in front of Hightower Gardens — government housing comprised of single-story apartments packed so tightly together that one garishly faded color and cracked pavement yard blended right into the next.

One of them — a tall, thin young man in his early

No Stopping

twenties wearing a Heat jersey and a curly fade — nodded at Jasper.

Maybe he was one of the men hanging around Spider's place, or maybe the guy mistook Jasper for someone looking to buy drugs. Either way, he wasn't hostile, and that made him the most approachable person in the area.

Jasper pulled up to the men and lowered his window, keeping his hand on his gun, just in case they wanted to jack his ride.

Heat Jersey came to the car while the other guys hung back. He looked even younger up close. Had sleepy eyes and reeked of weed. He looked Jasper up and down. "You the Professor, right?"

Jasper nodded. "You know what happened to Spider?"

"No, but I was told if you came 'round to bring you to her. Open your back door."

"Bring me to who?" Jasper asked.

"You'll see."

Jasper turned to Jordyn, her eyes apprehensive and scared.

"What are you doing, Dad?"

He opened the back door, hoping he wasn't making a mistake.

"Yo, gotta take the man to see someone," Heat Jersey called out to his friends. "Hit me if anyone comes 'round."

The other five young men nodded as their buddy climbed into the back of Jasper's car.

He expected to feel the barrel of a gun press against the back of his head as the door closed, but Heat Jersey leaned forward between the seats and pointed north instead. The pungent skunk stung his nostrils.

This dude bathe in the shit?

"Go that way."

Jasper obeyed, his gun now transferred from his right to left hand. "What happened? What do you know?"

"Patience, Professor. She'll tell you soon enough."

Was he taking her to Spider? Had she gotten out of there in time?

Hope swelled in his chest, but Jasper knew not to expect much.

They drove out of Butler and into unincorporated Creek County, out in the sticks, where farmland and large swathes of nothing dotted either side of the old, cracked county road.

Jordyn was still in her seat, staring straight ahead. Without her uttering a word, Jasper knew what she was thinking.

This guy's taking us out to the middle of nowhere to kill us.

He met the man's gaze in the mirror. There was a look people had when they intended to kill you. Sometimes it was fear. Other times it was a cold, steely gaze. But this man's expression was neither. He had the sleepy eyes of the perpetually stoned, a casual coolness Jasper couldn't entirely read.

"Yo," Jasper said. "Where we headed? There ain't much out here but rednecks and trees."

"We're almost there." The young man leaned back and lit a joint.

Jasper would've normally told him to put it out, maybe even stopped the car to make his point, but he needed the information the kid was leading him to. Plus, if Heat Jersey intended to try to kill them at some point, his reflexes would be slowed enough that Jasper could drop him first.

The young man leaned forward, eyes squinting. "Up here, there's a dirt road. Turn right."

Jasper slowed down, turned the wheel with his right hand, kept his left hand on the gun.

No Stopping

The car jostled and jerked on the narrow one-lane dirt road. Jasper had to ease up on the trigger so as not to accidentally pull it. He slowed down — it was hard to navigate with only one hand on the wheel.

Pines and brush crowded the road as if the forest would swallow it. Jasper had never been down this way. Maybe nobody had in ages. They were like vestiges of some grand plans for the land, a city to be that had never been born, and now nature was reclaiming her roads by the inch.

Heat Jersey instructed Jasper to turn left down another dirt road a few minutes later.

He did, and they came up to an RV parked in the middle of a clearing.

Spider?

"Stop," Heat Jersey instructed as Jasper neared the vehicle. Then he got on his phone and dialed a number. "Yo, Professor is here … A'ight." "She'll see you now." He leaned back and took a long drag on his pre-roll.

Jasper killed the engine. He got out with Jordyn, taking his keys with him.

Heat Jersey didn't seem to mind.

Jordyn looked at Jasper as he knocked on the door, her worried optimism mirroring his own.

"Come in," said a woman whose voice didn't sound like Spider's.

And it wasn't Spider inside. It was Kim. Her bright pink-and-blue hair was covered with a black beanie. Her face was bruised, lip fat and bloodied. She sat at a table in the RV's kitchenette, a pistol, a laptop, and a pair of matching phones on the table in front of her

"Kim, what happened?"

"Fuckers took Spider, and they killed Tyrell, Sammy, Big G, Jayce, and Calvin."

Tyrell was the only name he recognized.

"Shit. I'm sorry. Who did this? Why did they take her?"

She glared at him. "I'm guessing some people *you* pissed off. A big Russian fucker, told me to give it to 'the Professor.'"

The Professor?

Only Spider, and her associates, knew him by that name. It was Spider's nickname for him, comparing him to Professor X like in the X-Men comics, as though Jasper was collecting mutant kids, or in her case, a brilliant hacker, to wage a war against the bad guys.

Kim handed Jasper one of the cell phones on the table, a cheap burner. "He told you to call the only number on there."

Jasper glanced from Kim to Jordyn then dialed.

A man answered — American, not Russian. "Yes?"

"What did you do with the girl?" Jasper asked.

"Ah, this must be the mysterious black man giving me *so* many headaches. Mexico, Anders, the Madam, and now my money man. What did I do to earn such dogged interest in me?"

Victor Forbes.

"Hurt her, and I'll destroy everything in your world."

"Oh, I have no doubt. But here's the deal, Professor. You're going to give me my money back — all of it."

"A trade, the money for the girl?"

"Yes. But not until she's finished decrypting the drive. *Then* you'll get her back — *if* I have my money. But if you try anything, or if you contact the police, the feds, or the fucking U.S. Army — she's dead. We clear?"

Jasper was about to try and bargain, or perhaps threaten the man, but Victor hung up before he could. Jasper dialed again.

No Stopping

"Do not call me," Victor said before the first ring had finished. "*I* call you."

"Damn it," Jasper hissed, checking to make sure the ringer was on before dropping the phone into his pocket.

"So, what the hell did you get Spider all mixed up in?" Kim asked. "Who the fuck are these people?"

Jasper sighed, closed his eyes, and contemplated the situation, searching for some answer. "The less you know the better."

Kim said, "Silence isn't an option."

"Dad?"

Jasper opened his eyes. He looked at Jordyn before turning to Kim.

And that's when he saw her aiming a gun at his skull.

"Talk, *Professor*."

Chapter 10 - Mallory Black

MAL WAS BACK in Mexico and didn't yet recognize her world as a dream.

She was cuffed to the bed, watching helplessly as Jasper fell to the ground.

Paul Dodd picked up the gun, laughing as he turned to Mal. "Well, looks like the cavalry ain't coming to save you this time."

Jessi was dead.

Now Jasper was gone, too.

Mal was beyond caring if she died. A part of her wanted the pain of living to end immediately.

"Do it," she said.

"What?"

"Kill me like you did my girl. Then, at least, I can be with her."

Dodd stared at Mal then shook his head. "I asked you to kill me last time, but noooo, you had to arrest me. You should have fucking ended me! Then none of this would've happened. I wouldn't have been raped, and they wouldn't be dead. But you couldn't do it. You had to be the hero."

No Stopping

"Fuck you."

"No, Mallory. Fuck you. And now I'm going to make you regret your entire pitiful life. I'll kill you, but only after you're begging for death. Only after you feel what Ashley felt."

This was the end. Dodd was going to torture then murder her.

But Lucia showed up. And soon, Mal had a gun on him.

Dodd begged, pleaded for his life. Offered up a list of Voluptatem's members.

Jasper, wounded but alive, begged her not to kill him. Said they could use the list to save others like Jessi, like Lucia.

But Mal was too consumed with everything Dodd had done — to her, Jessi, and Ashley worst of all.

"If I could take it all back, I would," Dodd cried, wiping at his tears.

"But you can't."

"Don't do it, Mallory," Jasper said from behind her.

"You wanted me to feel what my daughter felt, right?" She placed the gun against his head. "I asked you a question."

"Please ..." he cried.

"Don't do it, Mallory!"

She could hear Jasper moving, trying to crawl toward her.

"Answer the fucking question, Paul. Did you want me to feel what Ashley felt?"

Tears were streaming down her face.

Dodd nodded.

"Then I want the same for you."

She pulled the trigger and fell to her knees.

Then Mal was in the club, the rapist Eddie begging her

not to hurt him. And she could only think about all the women who never had a choice.

Fuck him.

She dug in with the knife.

Then Mal woke up, gasping for air, heart racing, wet cheeks and sunlight pouring onto her face. Her head was pounding. Her nose hurt like a bitch, same for her chest and shoulder.

She looked around, confused, then remembered.

The woods.

The men chasing her.

But she was alone at the bottom of a hill, surrounded by trees.

Mal sat up, pulled out her phone to look at the time. 11:10 AM.

She was under a long time and damned lucky no one found her.

After opening the camera app then flipping the screen, she assessed her appearance. Blood caked her nose, purple from impact. Her right cheek bone was the color of uncooked eggplant. Scratches and scrapes dug into her face.

"Damn." She stood and checked her GPS.

Her body throbbed with every new step on the journey back to her car.

HER HEAD POUNDED and her hands shook as she entered her hotel room. A cold sweat licked her back. She thought about the sweet kiss of her pills.

Don't do it.
You don't need them.

No Stopping

You fucked this operation up. You left the door open and almost got yourself killed.

You deserve the pain as a reminder not to do this stupid shit anymore.

Somehow, Mal managed to ride out the shakes and refuse her cravings.

Ibuprofen instead — a poor substitute, but at least it would cut into the pain a bit.

She took a long hot bath. While soaking, she checked the news on her phone, looking to see if there'd been anything on Eddie the Rapist. Or on last night's colossal fuck-up.

There was a story on the *Times-Union's* website about an unnamed man who'd been attacked. He claimed to have been drugged and couldn't provide further details. It was being treated as a sex crime, hence the victim's anonymity.

Mal laughed at the irony, that *she* could be charged with a sex crime against a rapist.

But he'd kept his mouth shut like a good boy.

But now sober, and in such excruciating pain from her impact with the tree, Mal was seeing her attack in a different light.

Gone was the anger that had fueled her rage. Now, as she sat in the spacious hotel room tub with jet of hot water massaging her back, she felt something close to remorse.

What the hell am I doing?

Mal closed her eyes and tried to clear her mind, desperate to think of anything else.

Then she returned to the dream, to Paul Dodd pumping her with heroin, above her on the bed, forcing her to play his sick and twisted game.

Ah, look who's growing up. Such a sweet little girl. Have you been wanting Daddy to touch you?

She shuddered from the memory, screaming before sinking under the surface of the tub's water.

The jet sprays muffled the world above. She opened her eyes, staring at the bathroom lights through the bubbling surface, wondering if she could drown herself. Would her body allow it?

What was the point in living? She'd lost everything that had ever meant anything.

Her chest tightened as Mal remembered being a kid and going underwater to see how long she could hold her breath at the bottom of the pool. Her record was 86 seconds.

How long until I drown?

The world was a cesspool full of wolves preying on sheep. And Mal could never stop them all.

Even if she spent every night for the rest of her life cutting the dicks off every rapist she managed to track, Mal still couldn't end the violence being done to innocents.

Her lungs burned as she struggled to hold her breath.

For every Jessi Price, how many would go unsaved? How many women and children getting raped or killed, not just here, but across the country, or in places around the world that she could never get to?

I can't ever get to all the bad guys.

Her eyes joined her lungs in burning as the world above her continued to froth and bubble.

Now, let us begin, Ashley ... Whose been a naughty birthday girl?

She thrust herself upward, drawing a deep breath, inhaling and hating herself for the very air she was so desperate to draw in.

Then she closed her eyes and allowed the tears to fall.

∽

No Stopping

DOWN IN THE hotel's restaurant, Mal took a tall booth in the back, away from most of the Saturday lunch crowd which was mostly families and loud talkers. The bar wasn't yet crowded.

She ate a burger and fries, nursed a frosty beer, and scrolled through the news. Former Sheriff Claude Barry's "guest editorial" — *Where are Calum Kozack and Brianna Gilchrest?* — caught her eye. He was demanding answers from Creek County Sheriff's Office.

Why was the newspaper printing this shit? The sort of hit piece that could be found on Cameron Ford's garbage blog, not a respectable newspaper.

Barry ended the piece by writing, *Oliver Kozack isn't just a parent. He's one of the most successful job creators in Creek County. If the Sheriff's Office can't keep his family safe or offer him justice, what hope do the rest of us have?*

It might as well have ended with, *Vote for me in November.*

Mal wanted to call her ex, Ray, to ask what he thought of the depths his former employer was sinking to, but she couldn't. He was trying to move on, and she had to let go.

Their marriage had been falling apart even before Ashley's death, but there was still a part of Mal that missed him and wished she could go back in time to preserve those moments when they were all together.

But Ashley was dead, and Ray was with someone else.

Mal was all alone.

A sudden crash of glass exploding made Mal yelp. Adrenaline pumping, she gripped the gun in her purse and scanned the room for danger.

The bartender had dropped a tray of glasses.

He and two men at the bar looked at Mal with widening eyes.

Maybe she'd yelped louder than she thought.

Or maybe I look like a fucking maniac.

She was shaking, fear a punch in her gut, tears welling in her eyes.

Why the hell am I so afraid?

Panic constricted her chest.

Her heart pumped fast enough to give her a heart attack.

She had to get out of the bar, *now*.

Mal dropped cash on the table, grabbed her phone and purse, then started toward the exit.

She stopped in her tracks.

Two familiar faces were on the other side of the door — the fucking parasitic blogger, Cameron Ford, walking with Claude Barry.

They were looking at each other, so Mal was still invisible.

She couldn't let them see her this freaked out. What if one or both of them said something to trigger her? Then she might very well end up putting one or both of them into the hospital.

The three of them were on a collision course. They'd pass one another in the doorway in moments.

To her left, a woman walked out of the restroom. Before the bathroom door swung shut, Mal dashed inside to the closest open stall. She slammed the door, engaged the lock, then collapsed on the toilet seat and started to cry.

She needed to calm the fuck down. More than that, she needed her pills.

Don't do it.

Don't do it.

One image invaded her thoughts, tormented her relentlessly — Dodd's beady, evil, child-raping, daughter-murdering eyes.

Even dead, the monster still haunted her memories.

No Stopping

How could she ever expect to escape her past when it felt just as real and threatening as her present?

Mal couldn't run, so she dug into her purse.

Don't do it.

Don't do it.

She found the bottle.

Don't do it.

But then, of course, she did.

Chapter 11 - Spider

SPIDER HATED THESE FUCKERS. If they hadn't put a chain on her wheelchair's arm, she would have tried to escape already. At least that's what she kept telling herself.

She'd been blindfolded when they brought her in, so she didn't know where she was or what the building was like. All she had to go on was the large room she was being held in. It was sparsely furnished with a sofa, an empty bookcase next to a desk, and two tables, one of which Spider was confined to. Though there was no bed, it was probably a bedroom because it had an adjoining bathroom. Well, it was the size of a bedroom, but it felt more like a basement without any windows. Not that she knew of too many basements in Florida.

She occasionally saw others in the hall outside her room — lots of men in black, like the SWAT uniforms the Butler PD wore whenever they rolled in to take down some smalltime dealer and make a show of force. But these men weren't cops. They were mostly German, mercenaries who'd come to her apartment to kidnap her and kill anyone trying to stop them.

No Stopping

Spider heard suppressed gunshots from the men in black, then explosive ones from her neighbors, friends, and protectors. The Germans must have killed a lot of her people to finally get her.

And now she was a prisoner of Victor Forbes, stuck in some room where she was being forced to finish cracking the encryption. She was running a brute force program on the drive. The rest was out of her control, as it would take as long as it took.

Forbes also ordered her to kill a website he didn't even have a URL for. According to him, the site wasn't live. Spider didn't buy that, figuring its content was just hidden from the public. That meant she needed to find, hack, and delete anything that might possibly expose the members of Voluptatem.

She had a trio of laptops belonging Wes Richardson, the man who had presumably set up the site. Spider was poring through their contents, those she wasn't brute-forcing, to reach the encrypted partitions, searching for something that might help her.

So far, nothing.

Spider liked a good challenge, just not like this. Not helping fuckers that killed her friends. Not for monsters running a pedophile ring. Not for dicktips that would likely put a bullet in her head the minute she finished her job — assuming she could.

What the hell did the Professor get me into? And is he going to be able to get me out?

Or ... is he among the bodies?

Clark, the other person in the room, cleared his throat from a seat at the table behind her. Spider's only Internet-enabled computer mirrored to the laptop in front of him. White dude. Mid-thirties. Short brown hair, crewcut, glasses. Handsome. Quiet. Wore a black suit and was obviously packing.

He was tasked with watching her, making sure she didn't try to use the computer to contact the authorities or anyone who might be trying to find her.

"Do you want a drink?"

"Yes, please."

"Be right back."

He left the room, leaving the door partially open.

Is this a test?

Spider didn't know, or care. She'd already tried to access the Internet via Richardson's computers, but he wasn't connected and she didn't know the router's password.

With Clark gone, Spider could open a command prompt and quickly find the saved password along with whichever connection she was using.

She closed the launcher, her heart at a gallop as she glanced at the door.

Spider strained to hear footsteps, but instead picked up on Clark saying something to one of the other men. She wasn't sure how large the room was, but he seemed far enough from the door.

She still had time.

She quickly entered the connection details into Richardson's computer and established a connection.

Bingo — online.

Footsteps as Clark returned.

She killed the wireless connection, just in case he happened to look at the screen. Then she kept searching through email as Clark approached from behind carrying a thermos and a can of soda. He set a Sprite on the table beside her and kept the coffee for himself. The man was always drinking coffee.

"Thank you." She cracked it open and took a sip. The can chilled her fingers. The bubbly liquid was cold on her tongue.

Clark returned to his seat. He spun the cap off his thermos, poured some coffee, then took a long swallow.

She avoided looking at him, certain he'd see her guilt if she did.

Okay, now what?

Spider had a back-up plan for instances like this, having put it into place after seeing the Professor's grand plan. She'd set up an encrypted dead drop site for her hacker friend Cyphillest to check on. She'd get the IP address, send a message to contact the Professor, then give it to him. He'd know how to track her, assuming he was still alive.

If not, she'd have Cyphillest send that same info to the cops and hope like hell they could save her. Or that they weren't compromised by their relationship to BlackBriar or Victor Forbes.

She'd give it ten, fifteen minutes. Maybe wait until Clark had to use the bathroom.

The next time he left the room, she'd connect and send the message. It would be encrypted traffic, so the contents would be disguised. But if someone was paying attention to network traffic, they could see that one of Richardson's devices had connected to the web. Then she'd be fucked.

But Spider couldn't worry about that. She had to hope they weren't paying attention, that they'd overlook shit because she was a teenager and only a girl.

Clark knew she was up to something. She could feel him staring at the back of her head.

She kept herself looking busy, going through Richardson's email, searching for anything from a web host provider or domain registry, doubting that she would ever find what she was looking for.

If Richardson was sophisticated enough to create, or hire someone to create, a poison pill website for him, he probably used anonymous email clients and didn't leave shit on his computer to unravel his plans.

After twenty minutes of finding nothing, Clark's phone rang.

Please leave the room to take it. Please leave the room to take it.

He answered in an intimate sounding voice. "Hey … no. I'm going to be late."

I could scream for help. 'Hey, your boyfriend or husband kidnapped me!'

"What? No, I don't know. Sorry." His voice lowered.

Clark was aware of her listening, maybe he was protecting whomever was on the other line from her curiosity.

Now. Send the message now.

Spider enabled the Internet connection on Richardson's laptop, watched as the little icon showing her now online. She opened another command prompt window, grabbed the IP address, copied it over, then closed the window.

"How did it go?" Clark asked the person on the other line. His voice sounded different,

Her heart was racing, sure he was watching.

She kept her head the same as it had been, hoping her body was shielding the screen. She couldn't look to see if Clark could see what was on it. He would notice if she tried.

Spider went to the website, pasted the IP address, then started to type her message as something sharp pressed into her head.

Fuck!

No Stopping

"I wouldn't do that," Clark said in his southern drawl, the barrel pressing into her forehead.

She turned, about to play dumb, but his knowing eyes were a warning.

"Okay," she said, chagrined.

"Close it."

Spider closed the browser.

"Turn off the wi-fi."

She did.

He holstered the gun in his jacket, leaned on her table, and met Spider's eyes with a deadly stare.

"Let's walk through your little scenario, shall we? Let's say you do manage to contact someone to get you. What exactly do you think will happen then? Mr. Forbes has taken *many* precautions. It's his job, and mine by extension, to evaluate every possible scenario and mitigate anything you might do to try and escape. He won't let you leave until the job is done. Anyone you send here will be dead. That I can guarantee you. This place is fortified. If someone *does* manage to get through all the guards out there, they still have to get through me. And" — Clark gave her a slippery smile that sent a chill right through her — "that ain't going to happen. Now, all things being equal, I don't *want* to kill you, but I'll do that before letting you walk out of here. Do you understand, ma'am?"

Spider nodded.

"Good. This is your one and only warning."

He sat back behind her and picked up the phone. "Sorry about that. Now, what were you saying?"

Spider wanted to vomit.

Chapter 12 - Jasper Parish

KIM WAS HIGH AS FUCK, smoking copious amounts of weed as Jasper told his tale. She stared at him with zero expression and took another epic hit from the bong.

"You serious?" she finally asked, a cloud of smoke escaping her lungs.

"Yes, that's everything."

"What the fuck?"

"What the fuck, indeed."

"So? How you gonna get her back?"

"First I need to find out where he's got her."

"And how you gonna do that, Professor?"

"Do you have anything of hers?"

"What do you mean?"

"I need something of hers, like an article of clothing, jewelry that had some meaning, something I can get a signal from."

"A signal?" she took another hit. "So, Spider wasn't kidding about that psychic shit?"

"Oh, did I leave that part out of my story?"

"Yeah, kind of. What kind of psychic? Like, you can

No Stopping

see the future an' shit? Can you tell me what happens to me? When will I die? Maybe you can get me some lottery numbers? Tell me who's gonna win this weekend's games?"

Jasper didn't tell her his daughter received most of the psychic flashes, not him He had to protect Jordyn from people who might want to abuse her abilities. Best to let everyone think it all went through him.

"It doesn't work like that. I don't control what I see. But sometimes, if I have a personal item, I can get a flash of where someone is or what they're doing."

"Shit, I don't have anything. And the cops got her place on lockdown."

"I'll need to get inside."

"I can have someone get in for you."

"Best I go myself. The more people touching an item, the more clouded the link."

"What happens when you find out where she is?"

"Then I go and get her."

"You heard what kinda army those fuckers rolled in with, right? I'm only alive because they told me to give you that phone."

"I'll figure something out. I always do."

"I don't think you understand what I'm sayin'. I'm offering our services. Lotta people 'round here like that kid. Would die for her, even. Others, well, they wanna settle the score against the fuckers who came into our place and killed our brothers and sisters. The rest, well, they'll play for pay. You got enough scratch, I can round up an army to take those fuckers out."

"How much will you need?"

"Whatchya got?"

Jasper told her about the Pentz money then said he could get his hands on more cash if needed. Kim promised an army.

"I need to head back to town, make some calls," Jasper said once the deal was made.

"Sure you don't want a hit?" Kim said, again offering the bong.

"No, thank you."

Then Jasper left the RV.

11:21 PM

Jasper and Jordyn drove slowly past Spider's apartment building, no longer an active crime scene.

There were people hanging outside in the parking lot, blasting music, smoking ganja, drinking, and generally airing their return to business as usual despite what had happened last night. Wooden planks covered the front doors, probably where windows had been shot out of the complex. There was likely damage inside as well.

Jordyn stared out the window. "How can they just act like nothing happened? Someone was kidnapped. People were killed. Their friends or relatives are dead. But they're right back out there, acting like nothing happened."

Jasper looked at his daughter's crestfallen face.

"Maybe shit's been bad for so long that it's just another night to them. Maybe this is their way of dealing with the grief, to not let it bring them down. A sort of *Fuck You* to their enemy."

"How can this be anyone's normal?"

Jasper didn't have an answer, at least not one that made any sense.

He passed the parking lot as he drove around the neighborhood, looking to see if there were any cops.

No Stopping

An unmarked patrol car sat across the street from the apartment complex. Jasper didn't go slow enough to draw attention and wasn't even sure if there was a cop inside.

Butler P.D. was a small organization. They didn't have an abundance of cops to work the case, let alone sit on the building to see who might return. It could be Creek County Sheriff's Office, but Butler and Creek had an uneasy relationship. Butler cops didn't care for their better paid and larger Creek County deputy brethren. And Creek County deputies looked down on Butler as the sort of place you went as a rookie, a half-ass cop not good enough to get into CCSO, or a fuck-up who got fired from CCSO.

While CCSO aided in operations and worked within the county, Butler P.D. was determined to solve their own damned cases, especially ones this big. So, the car sitting on the apartments was likely one of only a few officers working tonight.

A distraction would definitely pull them away from the apartments. Jasper called Kim and asked if she could do the honors.

"How big you want it?" she asked.

"Not so big that Creek County sends all their deputies, but big enough to get the cops off Spider's place."

"One massive distraction coming up." Kim laughed before hanging up.

Jasper hoped she wasn't too high for his request.

He drove out of the neighborhood, just long enough to wait for a call on the Butler police radio — a suspected burglary in progress on the other side of town. A few minutes later, he drove past where the unmarked car had been.

It was gone.

Jasper headed to Spider's place. He took the rear

entrance to the parking lot and avoided the rowdy crowds milling out front.

The hallways were filled with the sounds of televisions and music, plus people talking, yelling, and fucking. Jasper and Jordyn ignored the noise as they made their way to Spider's apartment.

The walls were perforated with bullet holes. Blood had been mostly scrubbed away, but the reek of bleach still lingered behind.

Spider's apartment was an active crime scene, and the only place with police tape on the door.

Jasper pulled out his knife. He sliced through the yellow tape, picked the lock, then opened the door.

The place was a disaster. Shelves toppled, bullet holes pocking the walls, couch cushions ripped apart, stuffing littering the floor. Blood soaked the carpet just past the threshold. The cleaning crew for the crime scene had yet to arrive.

Jordyn closed her eyes and winced. "They shot Tyrell here."

Jasper saw a flash of memory, Tyrell attempting to push the men in black out. He hadn't wanted to fire his weapon. But they had no such worries.

He went down before he could get off a shot.

Kim screamed, reached for her gun.

A man blasted a hole in the couch next to her with a shotgun.

She froze, terrified.

The men stormed into the computer room, grabbed Spider by the back of her head, and confirmed their target.

In Spider's bedroom, Jordyn found a small glass unicorn on the dresser. She picked it up and examined it.

Jasper stood beside her, looking at the delicate item.

No Stopping

Given to Spider as a gift on her seventh birthday from her mother who'd told her that nothing was impossible if you really believed.

Jordyn echoed what Spider's mom had said, then followed with, "And this is what *believing* gets you."

"You get a bead on her?" Jasper asked.

Jordyn closed her eyes as she focused. "She's in a room. A man is with her, watching her."

"Where is it?"

Jordyn concentrated harder. Jasper saw a flash of the man's face, but it wasn't solid. More of an *idea* of a face, nothing Jasper could draw for a sketch or use for any legitimate search.

"No." She shook her head. "Not yet. But this is the strongest thing in her room. I think we should take it. Hopefully something will come to me."

"Okay." Jasper slipped the unicorn into his jacket pocket.

He was about to search the computer room when he heard somebody moving behind him.

"Hands where I can see 'em," barked a man from behind him.

Jasper raised his hands and slowly turned to find a gun in his face, a uniformed Butler officer — short and stocky, dark-haired, with tattoos running up his forearms and a nasty expression.

"W-what are you doing in here?" The officer's eyes were all over the place. He was scared, and a frightened cop with a drawn gun was a dangerous thing indeed.

"Felicia is my niece," Jasper lied. "I'm looking for her."

"Get against the wall, hands on your head, fingers laced together."

Shit!

Jasper weighed his options. He could make a move, but

the nervous cop would have an itchy trigger finger. He'd probably get shot if he tried anything.

Jordyn was still in the bedroom. Jasper hoped she managed to hide and wouldn't come out and get blasted by Officer Skittish.

"Can we just—"

"Hands on your fucking head!" the cop bellowed, his gun in Jasper's face.

A little closer and maybe he could disarm the guy.

Jasper slowly turned to the wall, raising his hands and braiding fingers behind his head as the officer had ordered.

The cop called it in, letting dispatch know he had a black male suspect in custody.

Backups would be there soon.

The first cuff violently kissed Jasper's wrist. His heart raced, his mind screamed, *Do something. Do something now!*

The window to act was closing. In seconds, his right arm would be brought down then both hands would be cuffed. He'd be shoved into the back of a squad car. Processed fifteen or twenty minutes after that, with his photograph and fingerprints run through the database.

Jasper's life and anonymity would be finished forever.

The world would know Jasper Parish was still alive. The law would start looking at him for deaths and unexplained disappearances. He'd rot in prison while awaiting the chair.

What'll happen to Jordyn?

Everything Jasper had worked so hard for would be erased if he didn't act.

His heart felt like it was going to explode.

The cop brought down Jasper's cuffed arm.

Now! Do it!

Jasper went to make his move.

No Stopping

The cop shoved him forward into the wall and drew his weapon. "Down on the fucking ground!"

Fuck!

Jasper began to lower himself.

A woman said, "Put the motherfucking gun down or you're dead, bitch."

Jasper turned to see a young black woman aiming a .45 at the cop. She wore a hoodie and a skull mask pulled up over her mouth.

The cop was shaking and terrified, probably about to try and talk his way out of it.

But the moment he opened his mouth, she shut it by pressing the barrel of her gun to his temple. "Don't make me ask twice."

He dropped his gun.

"On the ground," she said.

Jasper stood and grabbed the keys to his cuffs. He unlocked himself, then restrained the officer before grabbing his gun and radio.

"Let's go," his savior said.

Jasper didn't need to be told twice.

Chapter 13 - Mallory Black

MAL WOKE up at four in the afternoon still hurting from her face meeting with a tree.

She'd had a nightmare but thankfully couldn't remember it. She was pissed at herself for using again, and decided she needed another NA meeting tonight.

After popping three ibuprofen pills into her mouth, she chased them with the last gulp of ice water left in her flask.

Mal went to the bathroom then into the kitchen area of her room. She looked in her hotel fridge for anything that might be worth heating up but only had a carton of week-old Chinese food, a freezer-burned pint of peanut butter chocolate ice cream, and a bottle of vodka.

The microwave clock showed it was dinnertime. If she ordered from the hotel's restaurant, it would probably take forever. If she wanted food, she'd have to go out, or at least down to the bar of the restaurant and order there.

She did *not* feel like getting dressed or leaving her room.

But Mal was starving and would eventually have to get dressed for her NA meeting, anyway.

She threw on sweats and a sweatshirt, secured her hair

in a ponytail, then pulled on a cap. Just before she stepped into the hall, she spotted the envelope on the floor in front of her door.

Someone had written in black marker, *Det. Black.*

An ominous feeling froze her heart.

Relax. It's probably just a message left at the front desk.

She picked up the envelope then ripped it open.

Inside was a piece of printer paper with the same black lettering.

Need to talk. URGENT.

—*J.*

Mal grabbed her burner phone then dialed the number below the message.

"Hello?" Jasper's voice brought her back to the last time she'd heard it.

Mexico.

He had again saved her life. And, in turn, she had left him out of the reports. If she wasn't working, then she had zero obligation to follow up on the missing persons' case. Or anything else she suspected him of.

The first time she'd heard his voice, it was a warning that her daughter was in danger — a warning she'd not acted on urgently enough and had lived to regret. He'd also warned her Jessi Price was in danger, right before armed men boarded the girl's school bus and kidnapped the girl, before taking her to Mexico.

What horrible news does he have now? Did something happen to Jessi again?

She spoke hesitantly, afraid of what he might say this time. "You left a message?"

"I need your help."

"What is it?" Mal asked.

"How close are you to Victor Forbes?"

"Why?"

Jasper explained Forbes was behind everything in Mexico and now he'd kidnapped a hacker friend of his, a young woman. Forbes, and BlackBriar he thought, were cleaning house and had already killed several people, including Cadillac.

"I need to know where I might find him," Jasper said.

"Well, last time we spoke, I ended up kidnapped, too. I'm thinking he's not exactly going to trust me. Why not go to the FBI?"

"He said he'd kill her. Besides, I don't trust law enforcement when it comes to Victor Forbes. He's probably got so many politicians on his list, they'd kill Spider regardless. Any chance you can trace a number for me? My guy's not answering."

"I'm on leave. I can't just get a number traced without raising a mess of red flags."

Jasper sighed. "They're going to kill her. I need some way to find her."

"Let me see what I can do. I'll call you back, soon as I can."

"Thank you," Jasper said.

"Yeah."

Her gut was on fire as she hung up the phone, torn between an inexplicable anger at Jasper and a need to help him. She thought of Victor Forbes, the way he'd grinned when she'd asked about Cadillac and his role in the Jessi Price kidnapping. Smiled and lied. Already plotting her abduction and sale to Dodd.

Fuck Forbes and fuck BlackBriar.

Mal couldn't call him, so she'd do the next best thing.

No Stopping

She grabbed her regular phone then pulled up her contact info for Tim Brentwood, the narcotics officer in Jacksonville with whom she'd had a little thing. He'd tried reaching out to her a few times since Mexico, but she'd blown him off every time. Mal loathed the thought of requesting a favor from someone she'd ghosted, but if she was going to eat shit pie, then she might as well grab a fork.

Tim picked up on the first ring. She could hear sports in the background. He probably just got off work and was watching TV. "Hey, stranger. How's it going?"

Mal could work him but didn't think she needed to. Tim was a good guy and would probably help her. "Can I come by?"

"Now?"

"Uh-huh. I need a favor. And ... well, it's kinda big."

His voice went from flirtatious to concerned. He was smart enough not to inquire over the phone. "Sure."

"Can you text me your address?"

"Yeah, see you soon."

MAL WAS in Tim's Jacksonville apartment, sitting on his couch and nursing a bottle of Bud. He was right beside her, and he'd muted the football game, which was more than most of the guys she'd had flings with would have done.

She briefly updated him on Mexico. Mal hated telling stories about herself that engendered pity. She never wanted anyone feeling anything remotely close to sorry for her. But in this instance, it would likely help her request.

It's not manipulation if it's for a good reason.

"Damn." Tim wrapped an arm around her shoulder. She flinched.

He noticed and withdrew his hand.

"Sorry, I've been skittish ever since."

"No, I'm sorry. Is there anything I can do? You mentioned a favor?"

"You know Victor Forbes?"

"Yeah, BlackBriar. Why?" His brow furrowed.

"He's in this shit."

"What?"

"I went to him asking about one of the men who took Jessi Price. He lied right to my face then orchestrated my kidnapping."

"Victor Forbes is involved? No way." Tim shook his head. "He trains half our people. I've hung out with him, gone to games, and—" He paused, probably realizing how he must sound to Mal, defending the guy. "You sure?"

"Absolutely." She nodded. "And there's more."

Mal told him about the flash drive, about Spider's abduction. About people being murdered. About Cadillac and his family being killed and part of a cover-up. She finished telling him all the shit Jasper had told her then added, "He'll gun-shy and move the girl if I call him. I need to know where he is, but I'm off-duty and can't get a trace without raising—"

"So you want me to get a location? Without a warrant?"

"You know anyone who can help you … on the down-low?"

"Fuck," he sighed. "I dunno."

"You dunno if you *can*, or you dunno if you *will?*"

Tim stared at her, his handsome face troubled. She felt bad bringing this to his doorstep, asking for a favor that could get him fired. Or worse.

Mal could feel him wanting to say yes, but Tim was obviously worried about his job. It wouldn't take much to

No Stopping

push him over the edge. And, in the moment, that meant manipulating him.

She shook her head. "Never mind. I'll find another way. Maybe I'll just call him."

His jaw tightened. "No. That's a horrible idea."

"Well, I need to do something. He's going to delete the whole list, and a bunch of people are going to get away with some seriously heinous shit. They're probably going to kill a teenage girl."

She was laying it on thick, but Mal meant every word.

He nodded. "I might know someone who can help."

And this is the moment he drops his principles to help. Damn it, I'm a piece of shit.

"Thank you so much." She gave him a hug.

"You're welcome, Mal."

Such a piece of shit.

She gave him the numbers.

"Have you eaten yet?"

"No," she said, wanting to stay but knowing he'd want to fuck if she did. "But I can't stay. I've got a meeting I need to—"

"A meeting? At this hour?"

"NA."

"Ah, okay." No interrogation or pity party. Tim understood.

He asked her if she had a CloakPigeon account so he could reach her on encrypted channels.

Then she left, feeling awful for getting him to go outside the law like he probably was.

Mal desperately wanted to use. But instead, she drove to the NA meeting, hoping for strength.

At the very least, maybe she wouldn't feel so alone.

Chapter 14 - Mallory Black

THIS TIME, Mal wasn't late.

She sat in the church classroom waiting for the NA meeting to start, wondering if Maggie would be there. Some people went once a week. Others, especially new people and those who had relapsed, attended more often.

Mal checked her messages while she waited, hoping to have something from Tim. Nothing yet.

She thumbed through her news feed and saw Gloria had responded to Claude Barry's opinion piece, issuing a press release saying there hadn't been any new information on the missing Kozack and Gilchrest cases. Both were open but cold.

A matter-of-fact response. Mal scrolled to the comments section, a cesspool of haters and racists wishing for "the good ole days" of Barry's reign. It was hard to read the comments without wanting to respond with a few indisputable facts, but she resisted.

Mal was in the middle of reading one particularly infuriating comment from a Barry supporter, or proxy, someone claimed the seat beside her. She looked up, saw it

No Stopping

was Maggie, then turned off her phone. Glad the woman wasn't ignoring her, she offered a smile. "Hi. I'm sorry about the other night. I overstepped and—"

"It's okay. I've thought a lot about it, actually. You're right. I *do* need to do something."

"How's it going?" Mal asked.

"Not good. I tried talking to Tommy, and he wasn't hearing it. I told him I don't think we're good for each other, sorta broaching the subject. I explained that if he wants to stay together, I really need some support. Told him he should come to an NA meeting with me. But he hated that and said he didn't need to be in a room with a bunch of losers. Apparently, he can handle his pills just fine and isn't an addict."

"So, he's in denial," Mal managed before the meeting got started.

Maggie answered with what sounded like a bottomless sigh.

It was a solid meeting but dragged on for too long. Mal didn't share, but found comfort in the words of others who were struggling. A woman in her late fifties talked about dealing with abuse she suffered as a child that still haunted her today. That made Mal wonder how long *she* would suffer from her recent trauma. Gloria had suggested getting therapy, and Mal would be required to at least see the Sheriff Department's shrink before returning to work, but the thought of discussing what happened — with Ashley, Mexico, or any of it — felt like a fate worse than death.

Maggie had more pressing issues. Maybe helping her would be a way for Mal to work through her own shit.

After the meeting, she gave her number to Maggie, just in case Tommy was waiting outside. "You ever need to talk about anything, hit me up. Any time, day or night."

Maggie thanked her, then they left. Of course Tommy was waiting outside. And not just in his car. He was standing under the awning.

Immediately, Maggie's demeanor changed. Her shoulders slumped as the light in her eyes faded to a dull and distant echo.

Tommy gave his wife a hug. "Hey," he said to her, then he nodded at Mal.

He was tall and too skinny. Had a greasy brown mullet and dark circles under his eyes. The kind of guy that looked like he hung out way too much in bars bitching about his life but doing nothing to actually fix it. Poorly drawn tattoos lined every available inch of his arms and neck, including one that said *Fuck Life* on his left forearm.

Classy guy.

"So, you Maggie's new NA friend?" He gave her a knowing, overly familiar look.

What, exactly, had Maggie told him?

"You must be Tommy."

"Yeah, and … I didn't catch your name."

She didn't want to give her real name to this dirtbag. But Mal had given her name to Maggie and didn't want to cause any problems. She shook his hand. "Mal."

"*Mal*," he repeated, as if he didn't believe her. "How'd the meeting go?"

"It went well." Maggie nodded. "The usual."

"Ah, cool," Tommy said, his eyes wild and movements fidgety. He wiped at his nose and turned to Maggie, "Hey hon, you mind if I talk to Mal alone for a sec?"

Her face melted. "Tommy, you—"

"I just *wanna talk*." His voice rose in pitch. "Go wait in the car. *Now*."

Maggie gave Mal a helpless glance full of apology before slinking off toward Tommy's car.

No Stopping

Now alone with her, Tommy met her gaze with a ferocity he no longer bothered to hide. "You the one putting ideas in my wife's head about how she should leave me?"

Mal wanted to say *fuck you, buddy, it's none of your business*, but doing so might only make things worse for Maggie when they got home.

"I didn't say anything."

Tommy stared, his nostrils flaring. "Well, *alls* I know is that before she met you, she wasn't trying to get me to go to fucking NA meetings, actin' like she's gonna leave."

Mal had busted a number of guys like this for beating their wives, kids, and even their dogs. Guys who failed to take any responsibility for their actions and blamed the world for every morsel of shit they were forced to swallow. "A meeting might help. They saved my life. I was a wreck before I started coming."

"Well, *I* don't need 'em, and I'd thank you to mind your own fucking business when it comes to *my* marriage."

"I'm not sure what you think I said, but I assure you I didn't mean to interfere. I'm new here, so I don't have many friends."

Mal could get her mouth to lie, but she hated this prick enough that the disdain was surely there in her expression.

Tommy sneered, "What's yer deal, anyway?"

"My *deal?*"

"Yeah, you some kinda dyke or somethin', prowlin' NA meetings looking for sad bitches to draft into your feminazi group?"

"Why, do *dykes* threaten you?" Mal couldn't resist pushing his buttons, but she already regretted it, knowing Maggie would likely have to pay for her smartass comments.

He bristled, straightening his posture. "I ain't threatened by no bitch. Just stop fillin' Maggie's head with *your* man-hating bullshit."

Mal resisted all her urges — the urge to tell him he was a sad, pathetic excuse for a man, the urge to knock him flat on his ass, and the urge that was almost a compulsion to tell this asshole he should do his wife and daughter both a favor and put a gun in his mouth and pull the trigger. Preferably somewhere far from home so they didn't have to clean his mess.

Tommy walked away without another word.

Mal watched him climb into his Camaro. He slammed the door then revved his engine like an asshole before tearing out of the parking lot.

Mal was shaking as Tommy drove.

Louis ran up to her. "Everything okay?"

"Yeah, just met Maggie's lovely husband."

Louis rolled his eyes with a sigh.

"Maggie wanted me to call her, but Tommy showed up and interrupted before we exchanged contact info. You don't happen to have her number, do you?"

Louis looked at Mal, trying to decide if he should trust her. After a stilted moment, he said, "Okay." He checked his phone then gave her the number.

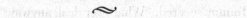

MAL WAS DYING for her pills, but she refused to let that asshole murder her sobriety.

Maybe she'd use tomorrow. But tonight, she refused to give in, even if anger was her only motivation.

She wasn't even sure why she was so worked up. It wasn't like she hadn't seen this movie a hundred times on the job — an abused woman too afraid to leave her shitty

No Stopping

man. No one could save a person who wasn't ready to save themselves.

Yet, Maggie *did* seem ready and wanting tonight.

Mal couldn't give up on her now. She'd also seen how this movie ended when the woman stayed too long — violence, death, murder of the whole damned family sometimes followed by suicide. There was a certain kind of pathetic man for whom a simple angry outburst wasn't enough. They had to let the world know just how deeply they had been wronged. As if they alone were the victims, that their pain weighed more than the world's.

They needed to prove that they mattered.

But in the end, the world never mourned them. They grieved for the victims, the women and children who paid for their lack of self-esteem and their woe-is-me victim mentality.

These losers weren't worth the spit on their graves. Or even headstones. No one should ever remember the names of these walking husks of shit.

Men like Tommy only changed when someone forced them to. If Maggie stayed with him, he had no reason to be a decent father and husband.

When Mal got home, she drank straight from the vodka bottle in her freezer. Not to get drunk, just to dull the edges. Then she opened her laptop and hit a couple of her data services, using Maggie's number to discover her full name and address.

Along with Tommy's arrest record.

"Hello, Thomas Milner." Mal pulled up his mugshot from a possession arrest six years back.

His rap sheet wasn't too bad. Possession of a controlled substance but not enough to put him away. He also had a DUI and a battery in a bar brawl from three years ago.

Small-time shit, nothing she could immediately exploit.

But then Mal saw Tommy hadn't worked in more than seven months.

How are you all living off a cashier's salary?

What sorts of other activities was Tommy engaging in to make his money? Maybe they were living off of savings or an inheritance. But Mal had a feeling a little digging might reveal something to jam Tommy up, to remove Maggie's man from her life — long enough for her and her kid to escape and start over somewhere, free from his overbearing menace.

Mal's CloakPigeon app beeped with a message from Tim.

Can we talk?

She called him.

"Hey," he said.

"What's up?"

"I got something on your guy."

"Oh?"

"A tip from someone who knows Oliver Kozack. Says he's gonna try and squeeze BlackBriar, lowball them on a new contract."

"*Kozack?*" All she could think about was Kozack's missing son.

"Yeah, BlackBriar does their security. And now Kozack sees the chance to land a better deal."

"So, he doesn't have a problem hiring a company associated with a pedophile ring, provided he can shake them down for lower rates? Do you know where and when the meeting is?"

Tim told her and she thanked him.

Before she could hang up, Tim said, "Hey."

"Yeah?"

His voice was somber. "Are you okay?"

"Yeah, I'm good," she lied.

Mal didn't know him well enough to vent to, and she sure as hell didn't like pity parties.

"You sure? I know you went through a lot of shit with Mexico and … well, all that. I just want you to know I'm here if you ever want to talk."

She was quiet, a part of her longing for release, for *someone* to confide in. Breaking down to Mike would only worry him. Maybe talking to someone she didn't know as well could offer her solace.

But now wasn't the time. A kidnapped girl's life was in danger, and the world didn't have time for her tears.

"I appreciate the offer. Maybe I'll take you up on it once all this shit blows over. Thanks, Tim."

"Anytime, Mallory."

She hung up.

Time to call Jasper back.

Chapter 15 - Spider

SPIDER WOKE up to the sound of a closing door.

Clark came in carrying two cups of coffee and a box of donuts. He set them on the table. "How are you?"

Before she could answer, he lifted her from her sleeping bag on the floor then eased her into the wheelchair.

"I need to pee," she said.

After he uncuffed her wheelchair, she rolled to the only other door she was allowed through. Once finished, Spider wheeled to her table. "When are you going to let me shower?"

"When the boss says you can. Now, eat."

Spider was hungry, but she ignored the box of donuts and coffee at her station. She had slept like shit and wasn't in the mood for token acts of kindness from her captors.

"Come on, I got those for you," Clark said through a mouthful of cruller.

"Gee, you shouldn't have."

"You're welcome."

The donuts smelled good enough to get her stomach growling.

"You're hungry. Eat."

"Why does it matter? You all are going to kill me, anyway."

"Where'd you get that idea?"

Spider turned and met his gaze to see if he actually believed his own bullshit. To her surprise, he looked almost genuine. "Well, first of all, I've seen your face. And your boss's. I also know your names. That's Kidnapping 101 — be able to identify your captors and you're a dead man walking. Plus, you killed a bunch of people already, and you're also involved in a pedophile sex ring, so forgive me if I'm not feeling too fucking hopeful."

"No need for the salty language."

Spider laughed. "*Salty language?* Of all the *shit* I just said, you're lecturing me about the F-word. Damn. Er, I mean, *fuuuuuuck*."

Clark rolled his eyes, took a sip of coffee, then looked back down at his phone. "Fine. Suit yourself. Starve."

She would, damn it.

She refused to eat his donuts.

Even though they smelled delicious.

The program she'd used to brute force the encrypted partition on one of laptops finally paid off.

The folder contained hundreds of photos, PDFs, and videos.

She clicked on one of the images and opened a nightmare.

"Jesus," she said, quickly closing the image.

"What?"

"Oh, nothing. Just your guy Richardson's stash of kiddie porn. Want I should make a copy of his collection for your enjoyment?"

"I ain't into that shit."

"You just work for people that are."

"No, the people I work for aren't into that, either."

"So, y'all just work for pedophiles then?"

"You're lecturing me on who I work for?" Clark's voice rose slightly higher than his usual drawl. "You work for drug dealers and gangbangers."

"At least they ain't kiddy rapists."

"No, and I'm sure all their clients are of legal age, right?"

Spider finally looked back at him. And she saw it, the first sign of annoyance. Good, she was getting to him.

She could press harder or back off a bit and let him come around on his own. What would the Professor do? He knew how to work people.

So did Tyrell.

She flashed on seeing Tyrell gasping on her living room floor, blood gurgling from his mouth as she was dragged out by BlackBriar's men. Their gazes had met, and he'd seemed so frightened. But even more than that, Tyrell seemed sorry that he hadn't protected her.

Tears welled in her eyes.

The door opened.

Victor Forbes entered wearing a charcoal gray suit, red shirt, and bright yellow tie. He smiled like he wasn't a sack of excrement.

The air changed. It had been tense from the beginning, but Spider was getting used to Clark, even if she was scared he'd put a bullet in her if she tried to escape. But Victor thinned the oxygen. It was suddenly a struggle to breathe. Her chest tightened with anxiety.

"Morning, boss," Clark said, standing as he entered.

"Morning. How are we on the flash drive?"

Spider wasn't sure if she should answer or if Victor was expecting a status report from his underling. But then he turned to her, expectantly.

No Stopping

"Still working on brute-forcing the flash drive. No way to know how long it'll take."

"And the website?" A frown teased the corners of his mouth.

"I decrypted one of the partitioned drives on one of the laptops, so I'll try that password on the flash drive then add it to the brute-force dictionary to try variations. As for the drive itself, I just got it open, so I'm hoping we can find something linking us to the website. Once I have that, I can hack it and bring it down."

"Very good then." Victor eyed her up and down.

Something in his eyes unsettled her. Not just the alpha male arrogance she'd seen when he threw her in this room, but a sinister something else he was obviously waiting to unleash.

He leaned toward her then opened the box of donuts. Eleven left, assorted flavors. Glazed, jelly, and one chocolate frosted — her favorite.

"Ah, donuts." His fingers hovered above the assortment as he debated his selection.

He chose the last chocolate. When he took a bite, he stared at Spider as though he knew that was the one she wanted and chose it to fuck with her.

Then he headed toward the door. She couldn't wait for him to leave the room.

But he turned around, instead. Crammed the rest of the donut into his mouth and raised his index finger to tell her to hold on for a second. He swallowed, licked chocolate frosting off of his hand, then reached into his coat.

"I almost forgot." He retrieved a photo from an internal pocket then held it up for Spider to see. It was the man she knew only as Professor Xavier. Sometimes she'd call him "X." He was getting into a car.

"Is this your Professor?"

Too late to mask recognition. He would know it if she lied.

Spider nodded.

"Good." He returned to the table. "And have you remembered his name yet?"

"I told you, he never gave it to me. It's not like we're friends or anything."

"Right, right." Victor grabbed another donut from the box. "That's all right, we'll know it soon enough. I've got friends in law enforcement. Soon, we'll have a name to go with our mysterious friend's face."

He left the room.

Clark stared at Spider for a moment, though she couldn't infer what the hell his gaze meant.

Scared, she turned back to the laptop.

Professor was always super secretive, deeply concerned about safeguarding his identity.

If Victor got a name to match the face, how long would it be before BlackBriar stormed his place?

She grabbed a donut from the box. Jelly squirted into her mouth. "I'm not eating this for you."

Clark didn't respond.

Chapter 16 - Victor Forbes

VICTOR GOT a call from Molchalin saying that even though he was on leave, one of their biggest local clients, Oliver Kozack, refused to deal with Susan. If he couldn't meet with Victor, Oliver would know something was wrong and take his business elsewhere.

Maybe Oliver was getting gun shy about his association with BlackBriar after the whole Paraíso situation and Anders, or maybe he smelled blood in the water and wanted to renegotiate the contract now that a few other companies had stopped doing business with BlackBriar as well.

Victor didn't know. What he did know was they couldn't afford to lose White Label Empire, the largest business in Creek County, a factory that provided hundreds of jobs and served as a major artery for the east coast transportation of bullshit tchotchkes. BlackBriar offered round the clock security to their warehouse as well as their cybersecurity needs. Their contract was worth millions, but more importantly, they were a prestige client BlackBriar used to land other big fish.

Hey, White Label Empire uses us, so certainly we're good enough for your shitty little business.

That was just this morning's problem. There was, of course, the ticking clock that was the whole Voluptatem situation. Victor wasn't sure how long they had before the website went live. Before Madam Pandora died, she'd said Paul Dodd had a poison pill website that would require him to enter a password every month to keep it from launching and exposing Voluptatem to the world.

There were many unknowns. For one, nobody knew how much was pretense and subterfuge. What information had Richardson gotten on the group? And how had he managed to get it? Maybe this was nothing, but despite Victor's extremely lucky life, rarely was he fortunate enough to be on the winning side of a winner-take-all bluff.

The other big unknown was how much time they had before Dodd was supposed to stop the website from going live. The shit in Mexico was almost a month ago now. Maybe Dodd had already entered the code. Or maybe there was some grace period before the countdown began.

Victor hated not knowing. His job was about protecting his clients from any and all variables, about seeing the threats before they were there. And, for the first time ever, he felt truly fucking blind.

Worse than blind, he was relying on lesser-thans to save his ass.

In addition to Spider, he had a team of five of his most-trusted cyber people working on clones of both the flash drive and Richardson's laptops.

When Victor woke up, he checked his messages for updates from each team then had to stifle his rage at the lack of progress.

At least the worst hadn't happened … yet.

He showered, dressed, then drove to Oliver Kozack's ranch on the west side of Creek County. The Russian drove behind him in a black SUV, always keeping an eye on Victor — just in case he tried to run.

Well, at least he's not in here with me.

The drive, one of the few times he wasn't being watched, Victor finally had a chance to try calling his sister again.

But still no word.

Did they already have her?

They killed his mother already, so surely they must have gotten to Veronica.

She was supposed to be vacationing in Mexico with her girlfriend. He'd left encrypted messages for both Veronica and Jasmine. Neither had gotten back to him.

Veronica always returned his calls within a day. She knew the nature of his livelihood. Not the shady fuckers he worked for, but she was aware her brother had a dangerous business, and he'd always told her she needed to be ready to run at a moment's notice because of his enemies.

She thought he was paranoid and often laughed at his expense.

Was she laughing now? Or was she crying, stuck in some subterranean torture cell in Mexico or some other location.

Victor hated not knowing.

He hated not being able to protect her, especially since she'd protected him from their mother as they were growing up.

Just when my sister needs me most, I'm fucking useless.

~

Victor arrived at Kozack's ranch home at eleven.

They met in Oliver's massive garage. He was buffing his yellow Corvette Stingray, one of several luxury cars he owned that were easily the most expensive vehicles in Creek County's rural westside.

He greeted Victor with a firm handshake and a wide, toothy smile. "Just got this baby at auction. You like?"

"Quite nice. What year?"

"1967 Sunfire Yellow Corvette Stingray L88."

"Not sure I've ever seen one like this."

"Yeah, not many around. Only 216 of them ever made, and only twenty of those were made in 1967. The head of GM's performance division wanted a 'stock' vehicle that could run a good quarter mile, so they modified Chevy's 427 cubic inch V-8 to put out 580 horsepower. No AC, radio, or creature comforts to speak of. Basically a track car sold as a consumer car. Hell, GM even lied about the power so consumers wouldn't buy them and as many as possible would end up on the track."

"Very nice. How's she ride?" Victor asked with the appropriate amount of awe. Truth be told, he couldn't give two damns about Oliver's fancy cars, but he always had to act impressed.

"Four barrel carb with aluminum heads and a four-speed manual transmission. Dynotested at 600 horsepower. How do you think she rides? Like a fucking beast."

Oliver reminded Victor of a fading Hollywood actor, a leading man if he were twenty years younger. His dark, slicked back hair had surrendered to salt and pepper, but he had a perpetual tan, a strong jaw, and blue eyes that other people saw as friendly, though Victor found them off-putting.

Oliver was a few inches shorter than Victor, but he

No Stopping

seemed taller, with the confident air of a man used to getting exactly what he wanted in every possible context.

"Want to take her out for a spin?"

"Hell, yeah," Victor said, still acting impressed.

Oliver opened the passenger side door for Victor as if he was his date. He climbed in, careful not to scuff any of the handsome camel interior. A tight fit, way too much for Victor's comfort, but he kept it to himself.

Victor buckled his seatbelt. Oliver didn't bother.

He pulled out, the car's engine loud, powerful, and imposing. "Gotta love that sound."

Victor had to admit, the sound *was* pleasing, though it would probably be easier to appreciate if he wasn't strapped in and feeling every bit of the road roaring from under the car and into his teeth.

Oliver left the west side for US 1. He drove along the beach and sprawling stretches of road, and whenever he came up behind someone on a leisurely ride up the coast, he'd swerve violently around them.

As he drove, he asked about the "whole scandal in Mexico thing" and wondered if Victor had any knowledge of Anders's involvement in the sex club.

So far, no one knew the ring extended far beyond Mexico or Paraíso.

"It was a shock to us all. We take trust very seriously at BlackBriar, and to have that faith violated is like being stabbed." Victor couldn't let it seem like this sort of thing was completely missed, though. What would that say of the organization, that they didn't know a member of their group was recruiting ex-employees to kidnap a child and a cop?

He lowered his voice to deliver the next piece of information. "Between you and me, there are some elements that don't add up."

"What are you saying?" Oliver asked, one of his bushy eyebrows arching upward.

"Well, there are certain elements of the media, and the government, that want to paint companies like ours with a broad, and perhaps artificial, brush."

"Fake news?"

"Yes. Being as big as you are, with the most important business in Creek County, surely you've run into your fair share of people who think you've accumulated too much power. They fail to see all the good you do for the community, all the jobs you provide. They've got other agendas, trying to appease special interests that line their pockets. Whatever happened to man earning his keep with the sweat of his own labor? These parasites all want to take what's ours."

"Yes! Exactly. People are so damned shortsighted. They can never see the big picture."

"Indeed," Victor agreed, smiling broadly. Now he was singing Oliver's tune, the song of the mighty man too good for the unappreciative masses.

Victor let that sit as Oliver drove in silence, enjoying the scenery, the sea looking gray beneath under a cloudy sky. He didn't want to say too much and appear defensive, so he'd play this next part by ear, see where Oliver took the conversation.

Then Oliver took it somewhere Victor hadn't expected. "How would someone even go about arranging a kidnapping?"

He could barely mask his surprise. "What?"

"If someone wanted to kidnap a person of note, how would they go about arranging it?"

Victor knew Oliver's son had vanished a while ago, along with a girl he may have been seeing. It would be too mawkish bringing that up. Too manipulative exploiting his missing son. Even if Victor had managed to sway him, Oliver would eventually see the ploy for what it was, and he would want to burn whomever tried to use his tragedy against him.

"I'm sorry," Victor said, "we're not in that business."

"Of course you're not, but people hire you to keep high priority targets safe. BlackBriar has escorted people out of country and retrieved kidnapping victims from the cartels and mobs, correct?"

"Yes. Why do you ask?"

"Oh, come on, we both know why I'm asking. Don't pretend you don't know what happened to my boy."

"You believe he's been kidnapped?"

"I do."

"Has anyone reached out to you for a ransom?"

"No."

Victor didn't have the heart to tell him that if it had been this long, his son was probably dead. Someone worth as much as Kozack, the kidnappers would've reached out immediately. More likely, he took off to avoid trouble or got himself involved in something he shouldn't have. Or maybe Oliver pissed off the wrong people. The Russian mob usually stayed under the radar, but they were active in North Florida. Maybe Oliver stepped on a few toes or was involved in some illegal business that infringed on someone else's illegal business.

He eyed the man, wondering what else he might be involved in. Victor knew most of the area's criminals and serviced a fair number of them. Kozack was rumored to be involved with some of the drug runners on the west side, but Victor had never heard it from a reputable source.

Oliver sighed. "He was either kidnapped or killed."

"Have you hired a PI?"

"A few, yes. And the goddamned sheriff's office is ignoring the case. This has got to be the worst sheriff we've ever had. Barry would never have let this shit happen on his watch."

"Agreed. Hopefully, he'll be back in office after the election."

"Oh, he will," Oliver said with an assurance that seemed oddly confident. Victor wondered what this man knew — was there some fix in play? Did they have dirt on Sheriff Bell?

Victor wanted to ask but couldn't divert the conversation from the man's missing kid. "Is there anything I can do to help?"

"Yeah, you can find my fucking son," Oliver said with an uneasy laugh.

Victor had to be careful. If he could help, great. But if he volunteered yet couldn't do anything, or if the kid was dead, then maybe Oliver would associate that failure with BlackBriar. Still, he had to say something.

"I'm sure you've got the best people on this, but I'd be happy to take a look at what you've got, maybe we'll fine a blind spot or see something your people missed."

Oliver looked at him with a genuine expression of gratitude. "You'd do that for me?"

"I can't imagine how you and Mrs. Kozack have handled this tragedy yourselves. I never had a child of my own, but I do have a sister who I love dearly. I don't know how I'd handle it if she went missing, but I do know I'd move Heaven and Earth to find her."

"Thank you, Victor, that means a lot to me."

And though they didn't talk business the rest of the drive, Victor's mission had been a success. BlackBriar would continue providing services to White Label Empire.

No Stopping

Now all he had to do was find the man's missing son, prevent the pedo ring from becoming news, and make sure his sister was safe.

Even if he did have to move Heaven and Earth to do it all, Victor was used to long odds.

Chapter 17 - Jasper Parish

JASPER WOKE up early in the morning to meet with Kim at the RV, about a mile northwest of Oliver Kozack's house — a massive estate on a ranch with no other homes around for a few hundred acres.

Kim wasn't alone when he got there. A black Escalade was parked in front of the RV. And standing guard outside the door was one of the three men who had approached him at Spider's apartment — one of Logic's men.

The man nodded Jasper through.

Kim and Logic were sitting at a booth, both smoking joints.

"So, we meet again, *Professor*."

Jasper had a bad feeling. He wasn't sure why Logic was here but figured it was probably to shake him down. Maybe he heard about the cash Jasper had at his disposal and wanted to relieve him of it.

He looked back at Jordyn, "Wait in the car."

Logic looked at him oddly, then asked, "Who you talking to?"

Jasper ignored him. "To what do I owe the pleasure?"

No Stopping

Logic, still seated and perfectly calm, said, "Well, Kim here has told me you're the one who got us all involved in your shit and got Spider taken by these dudes."

Jasper nodded, readying his right hand to reach for the gun in his jacket. He didn't think Logic was here to kill him, but he didn't know shit about the man, other than he was probably the area's primary dealer and one of Spider's criminal clients. He really wished she would've taken him up on his offers to work for him exclusively and get the hell out of Butler.

Logic took a hit. "So, again, I'm wonderin' who the hell you are. Like, what's your deal, man? Why you goin' after these folks? You some kinda real-life Black Batman or some shit?"

"No, not Batman. Just someone trying to help. These people kidnapped children, enslaved them."

"So, why you gettin' involved? What do you care if some kids get kidnapped? You know these kids?"

"No."

"Then what's it to you?" His eyes narrowed on Jasper. "Oh, hell. You're a cop, aren't you?"

Kim raised her eyebrows, looking like she might reach for the gun on the table in front of her.

"No. Just a pissed off man doing what the cops can't do."

"So, Black Batman, not Professor X ... what's this I hear about psychic powers?"

Jasper was pissed — not only at Kim for telling Logic, but also at Spider for letting Kim know in the first place. Still, in the end, it was his fault. *He'd* told Spider to convince her to work with him. Jasper had overestimated her loyalty. She was still a teenager, and kids needed to spill their secrets to someone.

And now these people, these dealers, wanted to exploit

Jordyn's abilities — exactly the kind of thing he was trying so hard to prevent.

"I get flashes sometimes. Nothing constant, nothing all that useful."

Logic smiled, seeing right through Jasper's lie. "Oh, I don't know about that. I mean, Black Batman has to fund his operation somehow, right? So, what is it? You bet sports? Pick lotto numbers?"

"I don't get visions like that. Mostly I see bad people doing bad shit, and ... well, I take their money."

Logic stood up and moved quickly toward Jasper, his face going from friendly to fierce.

Jasper resisted the urge to reach for his gun.

"So, how 'bout me, then?" Logic yelled. "You gonna take *my* money?"

Jasper kept his cool and responded slowly. "That depends. You raping or killing kids?"

"Hell, no."

"Then you're not my enemy."

Logic backed off, but only a little, still glaring at Jasper like he was itching for a reason to put a few bullets into his body.

"You cost me a lot of good people."

"How so?" Jasper asked.

"My men were in the parking lot when those fuckers rolled in. You owe those people's families, way I see it."

"No, *BlackBriar* owes them. You want to get their money, help me get Spider."

"Kim says you've got money now, that you're willing to pay."

Kim was keeping quiet during the whole exchange, clearly working for Logic. Whatever deal he'd made with her was null. He needed to make that offer to Logic directly.

"You got some soldiers you can hire out, then I'll pay." He told him how much he could pay via Pentz, assuming Logic took the cryptocurrency.

"All right," he said with a nod. "Kim'll set you up with some people."

"How many?"

Logic chewed on it for a moment. "Six."

"I might need more than that."

"Then you'll need more money. This ain't no run-of-the-mill job you're asking for. These fuckers already killed enough of my people. You're gonna need to pay top shelf prices for men willing to assume that level of risk."

"Fair enough." Jasper nodded.

Logic nodded back, raised the hoodie over his head, then shoved his hands into his jacket pockets and headed outside, leaving Kim with Jasper alone.

She looked relieved to see Logic go. "Sorry about that. He's passionate about our neighborhood."

"I can appreciate that. So, I need someone to get me close to a car that's going to be at Oliver Kozack's place."

Jasper told her his plan and gave her the address.

Kim grabbed her tablet then pulled up a Google Maps overhead image of Kozack's property. She gave a furious shake of her head. "Ain't no way you're getting on that land, let alone to Victor's car long enough to put on a tracker. Not without someone spotting you. You can't wait for him to go somewhere else?"

"This is my only window. He'll make me if I follow him, especially out here in the sticks."

"Why not just pull the fucker over? We can bring him back here, *make* him talk."

"If it was just him, then sure. That would've been my first suggestion. But he's got bosses that probably have no problem letting him die and killing Spider just to cover their secrets. This is the best chance to get him without getting her getting killed."

"Fuckers."

Jasper stared at the overhead shot. The house was enormous. That might have dimmed the odds of someone being in the front of the place and looking out on the driveway when he arrived, but there was zero chance a property that size, on a spot of land so remote, didn't have surveillance cameras.

"We need a distraction." Jasper looked at his phone to check the time. "Too early for pizza."

"You want food? I've got some candy and chips and shit in the kitchen."

"No, I was thinking we could order pizza somewhere, then you, or someone you know, could deliver it to Kozack's house. I'd be in the car, just get me close enough to put the tracker on. Whoever is home will probably think it's a wrong address delivery. Wouldn't alert anyone."

"No pizza places are open now." Then her eyes lit up, "*But* ... I've got a friend who delivers groceries."

"Yes! You trust 'em?"

Kim looked at Jasper with mock indignation. "What kinda' friends you think I keep?"

Jasper kept quiet.

She laughed. "I'm just fuckin' with you. But, yeah, he's reliable."

JASPER RODE in the back of the delivery van, hoping Victor Forbes drove one of the cars registered to him according to the DMV database. Any other vehicle and his plan went to shit.

The van slowed down.

No Stopping

Kim's friend, JT, a baby-faced young black man with a thick beard and large afro, said, "I hear these people out here on the west side are in the KKK."

"Wouldn't surprise me," Jasper said.

"Great. Man, you should'a hired a white dude, or better yet, a white girl, to do this shit."

"Relax, it'll be fine."

"If you say so," JT said as the van slowed to a crawl. "Where should I park?"

Jasper looked through the front windows and saw the black SUV, its plate matching Victor's registered vehicle.

"Pull up in front of the van, and park at an angle so I have a clear shot to the passenger side rear wheel well."

"Gotchya."

"And take your time."

"Yes, sir," JT said, parking then getting out of the van and walking around to open the rear doors.

He grabbed two large bags with the delivery services logo that matched his green apron. "Here's hoping I don't get lynched or sent to the Sunken Place."

Jasper laughed.

As JT headed to the house, Jasper climbed up to the front passenger side seat then popped out of the van. He wore a green apron and pretended to be lighting a cigarette like he was on a smoke break as he walked to the passenger side rear wheel well.

Jasper dropped his cigarette, then placed the tracker as he bent to grab it. He put the cigarette into his mouth, then returned to the rear of the van, acting casual, just in case someone happened to be watching from one of the upper story windows or from a camera he couldn't see.

He got back into the van, glancing through the windshield as he did. JT was still on the porch talking to a dark-haired woman Jasper recognized from photos as Mrs. Kozack.

A shiver went through him as he eyed the front door. It felt weird being on the property of the parents of the young man he killed. On one hand, that young man was a monster responsible for his daughter's suicide. On the other, Jasper was the man who had murdered their son. For the first time, a wave of guilt washed over him.

This woman at the front door didn't even know her child was dead, let alone that his killer was on her property. The only person in the world who knew the answer to the question that kept her up at night — *Is my son alive?* — was right here under her nose.

Jasper looked down.

Jordyn appeared in the back of the van. "I told you not to kill them."

It was always weird to see her when he remembered she was dead. It made no logical sense, and Jasper had to reconcile the fact that he was fucking crazy or he saw ghosts. He wasn't sure which was worse.

JT headed to the van holding the bags of groceries, stifling a smirk.

As he loaded the bags in back, Jasper glanced at the front door to see it still open, and Calum Kozack's mother stood there, looking right at him. If she stared long enough, she might see the murder on his face.

Then she'd come running out, screaming, clawing at him, asking what he did to her baby.

Fuck, hurry up, JT.

JT closed the rear doors, got in the driver's seat, then waved at Mrs. Kozack as he backed out.

"Fucking bitch," he said under his breath through a smile, pulling out of the driveway.

"What happened?" Jasper asked.

No Stopping

"Ah, nothing. Just givin' me that dirty look rich people give when they're tired of your shit."

"So, she didn't suspect anything."

"Bitch is clueless."

Jasper sure as hell hoped so.

Chapter 18 - Mallory Black

M AL WOKE up from another nightmare by way of haunting from her past, shaking, migraine on its way, and starving for pills.

She barely resisted. Didn't know what her day looked like yet. Maybe Jasper had called with info or needing help with the Spider situation. Maybe Gloria wanted to show up and surprise her again. No need to ruin a day of sobriety.

One at a time.

She swallowed some ibuprofen with water then grabbed her phone to check for messages.

Three from Maggie. The first two, within minutes of each other, late last night, were hang-ups. The last one, at 7:05 this morning began with a long pause.

"It's Maggie. Um, I'm not doing so hot." Mal could tell she'd been crying. And was high. "Tommy ... he got a bit rough last night. A bit too hard. I was in a lot of pain, and ... he gave me some ... " she broke off into sniffles. "Well, I used. And, God I feel like such a fuck-up. Please, don't call me back. Tommy sometimes takes my phone and ...

well, I don't want him to answer if you call back. I'll try again tomorrow." Another long pause and crying. "Sorry."

Mal clenched her fist and curled her toes.

She wanted to call Maggie back, tell her to get her kid and get the fuck out of there immediately. They could stay with Mal. It wasn't like she was planning to go back there anytime soon. But if she called and the asshole answered, it'd probably trigger him again.

It was hard to be patient while waiting on others to find their senses, but she had no better option.

Mal paced her hotel room, helpless as she replayed Maggie's message. She sounded so hopeless. Was Maggie okay? What if she'd overdosed? What if Tommy had beaten her into paralysis, temporary or worse?

Fuck!

For a long time, Mal had used the pills to chase her sadness away. But now she needed them to battle the rage that had clawed its way into her life and lived like a bird in its nest.

Anger at the horrors Dodd had waged upon her daughter, on her, on Jessi Price, and on who knew how many other children. Anger at the predatory system allowing a place like Paraíso to exist yet alone thrive. Anger at the men who preyed on women and got away with it. Anger at herself for fucking up her attempt to get justice against Amber's rapist. Anger at the corrupt system that sought to give power back to Claude Barry while leaving the professional corpse of Gloria Bell behind it. And now, anger at yet another abusive husband destroying the lives of his wife and daughter.

All of this fury inside her, and the only ways she had to cope were sneaking out and mutilating rapists or taking drugs. One or both would get her killed.

She flashed back on Dodd's perverted, craven gaze as

he stared down at her when she had no hope of stopping him. Tommy's look wasn't perverted, but he wore that same disgusting sneer as Dodd and the rest, letting her know he wasn't afraid. An expression that dared her to do something.

Mal couldn't sit by and do nothing.

She *refused* to sit by and do nothing.

So, she showered, got dressed, then took a ride.

MAL DIDN'T WANT to drive by Maggie's place in her car, so she rented a Camry for a little trip to Jacksonville.

She drove slowly, studying Tommy and Maggie's house, a cozy white-and-blue bungalow tucked into a quiet suburban neighborhood. She'd expected something more rundown in a worse neighborhood. But the house had a white picket fence, a recently planted plum tree, and a tire swing in the yard.

But that didn't change a thing. A polished exterior could mask the rot inside fine.

Tommy's car was outside.

She growled as she passed it.

Then she saw the Camaro backing out of the driveway.

She hung a right onto a side street, slowing down and watching her rearview as it passed. Tommy appeared to be alone.

Mal threw her car into reverse then drove back to Maggie's.

She pulled up in the driveway, got out of her car, and knocked on the door.

No answer.

No Stopping

She knocked again, staring at the peephole and wondering if Maggie was looking through it.

Moments later, she heard Maggie's voice on the other side.

"Mallory?" She opened the door. "What ... how do you know where I live?"

She had a huge black eye and a swollen left cheek.

"What the fuck? Did Tommy do that?"

"Why are you here?"

"You left a message on my voicemail. It scared me. So, I looked you up."

"You *looked me up?* What?" Slurred speech, pupils large and dilated. High.

"Get your daughter. I'm getting you two out of here."

"What?"

"You can't stay here with him. He's beating you." Mal lightly grasped her arm. "Come on. I've got a place for you both to stay."

"No! I can't leave. He has Emma."

"What?"

"Yeah, he took her to the store because I was sleeping."

"Damn it. You can't stay here. What happened last night?"

"It doesn't matter. And where am I going to go?"

"I have a place you can stay."

"I can't just hide away. It's not like he'd stop looking for us."

"We can file an order of protection against him, initiate divorce proceedings. We can go to the cops right now and they can get photos of what happened."

She started shaking her head, slow at first, then fast. Tears streamed down her cheeks. "This is ... this is going too fast. I need time to think about it."

If Mal pushed Maggie too hard, she risked losing her. Women in abusive relationships were stuck until they wanted to leave. Force them and they're likely to drop the charges against the guy or even turn on you. A sick cycle and hard to see yourself in it.

Mal would have to be patient. Or find a way to get Tommy out of the picture so the choice would be made for Maggie and she could think clearly.

"You said he gave you pills?"

"Yeah. He felt bad after he hit me. Told me to take them, that it wasn't a relapse if I needed them."

"He made you need them. He's been trying to get you relapse for a while, right?"

"That's not why he hit me," she said, defensively.

"Where does he get *his* drugs? Is he a dealer?"

She looked at Mal suspiciously. "Oh, my God. Are you a cop?" Maggie covered her mouth, suddenly afraid she'd said too much.

"No. Well, not in Jacksonville. I'm not on the job. I had to leave following my own relapse and an abusive situation."

She didn't want Maggie making the connection. *Oh, you're that Mallory Black, the one who got kidnapped by the man that raped and killed your kid!* And it was easier for Maggie to connect if she thought their situations were similar — not many people could relate to a kidnapping.

Maggie stared at her, biting her nails, chin down. "What would the cops do, anyway?"

"You can get an order of protection that keeps him away while you file for divorce. The cops document your situation. Maybe they come and find drugs on him at home and arrest him."

"I don't want him arrested."

"I'm just saying, it's one way to get the time and space

you need. Maybe he can get help. Go to rehab then put his life back together, then you can consider being together again. But he's a fucking threat to you right now ... to you *and* Emma. Do it for her if you won't do it for yourself. It's only a matter of time before he hurts her, too."

"He wouldn't touch her."

"Drugs make people assholes. Some of them *violent* assholes. You said it yourself — you don't want Emma seeing him treat you like this. There's no way that doesn't harm her, right?"

Maggie nodded.

"When can you leave? There's got to be a time when he leaves you both alone."

She nodded. "He's in a pool league. Plays tonight with his boys. We'll be here from, like, eight to one or two, whenever he runs out of cash for beer or gets kicked out."

"Good. Get whatever you need to take, sentimental stuff, medicines, the absolute necessities. I can get you new shit, whatever you need. And I'll pick you up tonight. Call me when it's safe to come. Okay?"

Maggie didn't respond.

"I'm giving you a chance to get out of this life. I can help you."

"Why are you doing this?"

"Let's just say I've seen enough bad shit. And I'm in a position to help, so why not?"

"You really seem to have your shit together for an addict."

"On some things, yeah. Others, not so much. But if you let me help you, I swear I won't let you down."

Maggie burst into tears and pulled Mal into a hug. "Thank you."

Mal hugged her back, softly crying. This felt a hell of a

lot better than hunting down predators, and almost as good as the pills. Maybe she could do more good like this.

She'd flush the rest of her pills down the toilet the moment she got home.

Cold turkey. Mal would have to quit if she wanted to help others.

Chapter 19 - Jasper Parish

JASPER SAT in his car across the street from BlackBriar's corporate headquarters, its massive gate almost disappearing under the twenty-five stories of glass and steel, all of them lit and gleaming onto the St. John's River beyond.

Jordyn sat beside him holding his phone with the tracker app. The dot on the GPS map hadn't moved since Victor had come here after leaving Kozack's ranch.

Jasper followed at an extreme distance until they hit I-95 and he could keep Victor's black SUV in his line of sight. Followed him to BlackBriar where he'd been waiting ever since, minus a fast bathroom and food break.

"Maybe he's not leaving," Jordyn suggested.

He wished they could have followed Victor's car in, but the place was more secure than anything he'd ever broken into before or would feel comfortable attempting to breach. Plus, all the armed people working for him. Walking in would be a death sentence.

"Or maybe he took another car out. Maybe he found the tracker. Maybe they did a sweep as a security check and he took it off the car and left through another exit?"

"What if he has her in there?"

Jasper hadn't considered that. BlackBriar was a legit business, not some black site where they could stow a kidnap victim — *could they?*

"Do you think she's in there? You getting anything?"

Jasper handed her Spider's unicorn.

Jordyn closed her eyes, concentrated, then shook her head. "I see some past memories, but I'm not getting anything happening right now."

Jasper followed the SUV.

Its red tail lights were about five cars ahead in the left lane. He stayed in the center, allowing cars to weave in and out of traffic in front of him, laying back and avoiding detection.

"What are we going to do when we catch up to him?" Jordyn asked.

"Depends where they are. I'll get her myself if I can. If not, we call Kim's crew to storm the castle with us."

"Then what? Will you please stop this?"

"Stop what?"

"Your war on everything. Stand down. Retire. You're getting too old for this."

"Me? Too old?"

"Yeah. You almost died in Mexico. And don't even tell me you were fine."

"I was fine."

Jordyn didn't respond.

"What? You don't need to worry about me. I can take care of myself."

"Well, sorry for not wanting my father to be killed by the damned Mexican mob, cartel, or whatever the hell they were."

"Didn't *you* want to join me? Remember, back when you found out what I was doing? You were so excited! It was like Take Your Daughter to Work Day or something."

"That's before I saw what your 'work' was really like."

"What do you mean?" He turned on the wipers as drops of rain kissed the glass.

"Until I saw how much this changed you. A part of you enjoys this way too much. It's scary. And a bit sadistic."

"*Sadistic?* I'm killing bad people."

"Yeah, but you shouldn't enjoy it so much."

"I'm sorry if I enjoy stopping bad guys."

"But they're not all bad."

"Sure they are. I never killed someone who didn't deserve to be behind bars. We've studied each of them before—"

"Why not let the law handle it?"

"You know why! We've been over this. I handle the people the law allows to slip through the system. Or the ones who have somehow evaded capture. I only kill horrible people — murderers, rapists, child predators. How can that be bad? Why shouldn't I take enjoyment making the world a safer place?"

"A safer place? That's why you do it? Not as punishment?"

"It's not about the punishment. It's about stopping bad people from doing terrible shit. Period."

"Is that what it was with Calum and Brianna?"

"I didn't kill them. Well, not her."

"You let him do it, though! She didn't deserve to die. And how exactly did killing them make the world a safer place?"

"But ... she hurt ... *they* hurt you."

"*They* didn't kill me."

There it was, that awful thing he kept trying to forget. And Jordyn yet again reminding him of it.

A high-pitched whistling, like a tea kettle in his head. Pressure building to a terrible, swelling pain.

"Stop!" he shouted.

The car was silent, save for the falling rain and thrumming wipers.

"I killed myself, Dad. Not them."

His voice cracked. "They may as well have."

"Do you really think they were going to hurt someone else? Okay, yeah, I wanted Callum dead. I wished him dead many times. But Brianna didn't deserve to die. She was just a stupid kid."

"I did it for you."

"No, Dad. You did it for *you*. I begged you to let them go. I'm not sure how much longer until you become just as bad as the people you're hunting. Or … "

"Or what?"

"Nothing."

"Say it, Jordyn. *Or what?*"

"Or maybe you already are."

Ouch.

Jasper wanted to deny it, to argue, to accuse her of being ungrateful. But her disappointment was a sack of bricks and he needed every ounce of strength to hold it.

He drove in silence, feeling like the shithead he obviously was.

VICTOR'S SUV wove down several back roads, in and out of what appeared to be random neighborhoods.

"Where the hell is he going?" Jasper wondered, staying back a turn or a fair stretch of straight roads at all times.

"Do you think he knows we're following?" Jordyn's first words since their ugly little exchange.

No Stopping

"Sure seems like it. Unless he's being overly paranoid."

"He stopped." Jordyn pointed to the GPS showing Victor's dot on Harrison Street — a long, straight road they'd gone up and down at least eight times already. They were one right turn from swinging onto it themselves.

"Stopped?" Jasper was confused. There was nothing on either side of that road but woodlands.

"Could be he's dumping a body. Maybe Spider's?"

Jasper cut his headlights then turned on to Harrison. There were red lights ahead on the roadside, and the SUV door was wide open.

It was too dark to see if Victor had gotten out or was still inside the vehicle.

"Maybe he broke down," Jordyn said.

Jasper turned on his lights and started toward the SUV, which was about two hundred yards away. He slowed to twenty-miles per hour, well short of the posted forty-five.

He was so focused on the SUV and searching for Victor, he didn't see whatever he ran over until an explosion beneath him caught his attention.

Had to be a spike strip.

He screamed as the windshield shattered.

"Ambush!"

Jasper ducked, ordered Jordyn to do the same. He reached for his pistol, readied it as he peeked above the dashboard, expecting a second shot.

Nothing.

His phone rang, the one Victor had left for him.

He ducked as he answered.

A Russian man with a thick accent said, "You have a choice. Die now or stop trying to find the girl. When she's done, we will find you."

A red dot fell over his windshield.

"I want you to look up," ordered the man.

"Maybe when you're not aiming a rifle at me."

"I'm not aiming a rifle at you." The light disappeared.

Jasper looked up.

The back doors of the SUV were open and sitting in the back was the man, holding what appeared to be a machine gun.

Fuuuuuck.

Jasper had a pistol, but the SUV was too far for a precision shot. The man would turn their car to shredded cheese before he could try.

"Do you want to die tonight?" the man asked.

Jasper glared but could only make out the man's silhouette against the light behind him in the cabin of Victor's SUV.

"No," said Jasper reluctantly.

"Very well, then." The man hung up.

The doors of the SUV closed and the brake lights died as the vehicle moved forward.

Jasper didn't follow.

As the truck left, the dot on his screen stayed the same.

And sitting in the road next to where the SUV had been parked was a small cardboard box.

"What the fuck?" Jasper got out of his car and approached it.

"No," Jordyn said, following him. "Don't touch it. It could be a bomb."

"The Russian would have killed us if he wanted us dead."

Jasper knelt next to the box, then turned to Jordyn. "Maybe you should scoot back a bit … just in case."

She scowled, then moved way the hell back. "This good?"

Jasper nodded and reached out to open the box.

Big mistake.

Chapter 20 - Mallory Black

MAL WAS FEELING GOOD, despite still craving the pills after flushing her stash. Helping Maggie get her life back on track steered her mind from the addiction.

As she sat in Oasis waiting for Mike, who'd called earlier wanting to "talk about something," she wrote tips for Maggie in a notebook she planned on giving her. A cross between inspirational quotes and supplemental information she might need while escaping her husband's hold.

There was information about the women's shelter in Creek County, the local NA meeting places in case Tommy went looking at her old home group, and the names of a few divorce lawyers who specialized in difficult separations.

Maggie and Emma could stay at her house as long as they needed. She'd stick around for a bit, just in case Tommy somehow found her. She'd also help Maggie get on her feet, find another job cashiering or pursuing other ambitions. The big thing was breaking the addiction.

Helping Maggie felt an awful lot like helping herself.

Hitching her rehab to someone else's wasn't ideal. Relying on others always led to disappointment and stripped the onus to get better for herself. Besides, she shouldn't tie herself to a self-destructive anchor.

But maybe Maggie was ready to change.

And just maybe Mal needed someone to need her. She never considered herself the co-dependent type — quite the opposite — but right now she needed something bigger than herself to get better for. She couldn't give in to her worst tendencies if she was improving for Maggie and her kid.

"What the hell happened to your face?" Mike said.

"Nice to see you, too."

"Seriously, what happened? Did you get in another bar fight?"

"Would you believe me if I told you I ran into a tree?"

He stared at her for a moment before his smile finally cracked. "No."

"I was jogging and moved out of the way for this woman and her child on a bike and SMACK, right into a tree."

"Damn," Mike said, seeming to believe her.

He asked Mal if they could eat in her room. They ordered for delivery then went upstairs and took adjacent seats on the L-shaped couch.

Mike set Manila folders filled with documents on the coffee table.

"What's going on?" Mal asked.

"That's everything I've got on Calum and Brianna. No matter how I spin it, I see no evidence that points at anything other than your buddy, Jasper Parish. I need to bring him in for a talk."

She shook her head. As much as she hated doing that to her partner, Mal had to hold the lie.

"He died in Mexico."

"Yeah, Gloria told me. And, sorry, I don't believe you."

"What?"

"I don't know what his hold over you is, but he's not a good person, Mallory."

"He risked his life — not once, but twice — to save me and Jessi Price. Or do you still think he was involved with the kidnapping?"

Mike sighed. "And you're still going with the 'psychic' angle? Your guy killed Richardson and probably that lawyer. At worst, he's involved with these scumbags and cleaning up his own mess. At best, the guy's a vigilante."

"I trust my gut, Mike, and my gut says he isn't a bad guy."

"Isn't?" Mike asked.

"Huh?"

"You meant *wasn't* a bad guy, right? Because he's dead."

Mike stared through Mal's deception.

"Fuck, Mike. Dead, alive, I don't know. And if he *is* alive, I sure as hell don't know where he is."

"So, you haven't seen him at all since Mexico?" Mike questioned her like a suspect in the box.

Mal was nervous. Had Mike seen her with Jasper? Had he been following her? And if he was, what else had he seen her do?

"No." She met his eyes, challenging him to call her bluff.

Instead he looked down at the folders. Picked two photos from inside one then dropped them in front of Mal on the table.

"Jasper Parish blamed these two individuals for the suicide of his daughter. And these two just happen to go missing. Poof, off the damned map. Let's do the math, Mal. You have two missing kids and an unstable vigilante who blames these same kids for his daughter's death. You gonna' try and tell me it's all some big coincidence?"

Mike was right. And Mal was impeding the investigation by withholding information. But at the same time, she couldn't burn the person who had saved her. Twice. Jasper had also been in Mexico when she murdered Dodd in cold blood. If she betrayed him, why wouldn't he do the same to her?

She had to try and sway her partner not to go down this path. "If we put it out there that we even think he's alive, do you know what Barry, Ford, and all those fuckers will do? They'll bury Gloria in the election."

"So, we hold up justice to make sure Gloria gets re-elected?"

She didn't respond, despite his staring.

"Jesus, Mal, I thought you were above all the politics."

"What does Gloria want you to do? Do you really think she wants you to *find* Jasper and bring him in? Wants it out there that the department fucked up the arson investigation then sat by while a vigilante picked people off?"

"She put me on the case. She wants the truth, no matter the cost."

"Then you really don't know Gloria."

"If she really *would* want me to bury this, then how is she any different than the guy she replaced?"

Mal didn't have an answer.

Mike grabbed his files, shoved them into his satchel, then stood. "I've got to go."

"We didn't eat." Mal stood and reached out to stop Mike before he got to the door.

He turned around and eyed her like a stranger. Then he headed out as a young woman rolled up with their dinner waiting under silver lids.

"I've lost my appetite," he said without turning back.

No Stopping

"Mike!"

He kept walking.

"Should I—"

"Just bring it inside." Then Mal chased Mike to the elevator.

He paced in front of the doors, angry enough to explode.

"Please, come back. Eat. We'll talk."

"No, Mal. I'm not trying to be dramatic, but I can't be in the same room with you right now."

The elevator opened.

He stepped inside. "You change your mind and want to tell me where I can find your friend, give me a call."

The door slid shut.

She slumped back to her room.

The staffer smiled awkwardly and apologetically as she handed Mal the bill. "I can come back for this later."

"No." Mal gave her signature and a generous tip.

She wanted to scream. Or hit something.

Wanted to use.

Somehow, she avoided all those and bit into her burger with rage.

It was eight-forty-five and Maggie still hadn't called.

And Mal still didn't want to leave a voice mail

Maybe Tommy didn't go to his pool league.

Even if that is the case, she should've messaged me to let me know.

Something's wrong.

Something's gotta be wrong.

He found out. Maybe he beat her real bad.

Or worse.

Mal had to find out, so she left her hotel and drove to Jacksonville.

She arrived at around nine-thirty. No car in the driveway.

She parked in front of the house, got out, and ran to the front door and knocked softly.

No response.

She knocked louder, hoping Emma wasn't asleep.

Maggie finally opened the door in her pajamas. Emma wasn't in the living room. Neither were any packed bags. Maggie had two swollen eyes.

What the hell?

Her gut filled with acid. "You two ready to go?"

Maggie looked down, shame on her face. "I can't go now."

"What?"

"I thought about it, I really did. And thank you for the offer, but what kind of wife or mother am I if I don't stick with him when he's trying?"

"He's *not* trying. He fucking hit you!"

"We talked today, before he went to his pool league—"

"You told him you were leaving?"

"No. He came to me, apologizing. Got me flowers and everything."

"Oh, *flowers*! Well, shit, Maggie, why didn't you say so?"

"You don't know him. You don't know what he's been through."

"You're right. I don't know him, but I've seen enough men like him bury women like you."

Maggie looked as if Mal had smacked her across the face.

Good, she needs to see how serious this is! Maybe she'll come to her senses.

"I'm sorry, Mal. I can't do it. Not now."

No Stopping

"You can't leave if he kills you."

"He's not going to kill me, Maggie. It isn't as bad as you think it is."

Mal wanted to stay and maybe persuade her, but it was pointless. She was a stranger. Even if they were close friends, Maggie still wasn't ready to leave.

"You have my number if you change your mind."

She got in her car and drove away, resisting the urge to peel out or sock her steering wheel. She had to control her anger before it led her to do something stupid.

The thought of Maggie staying with her personal abuser turned her stomach. She thought of all the men she'd seen victimizing their wives, kids, and girlfriends, so many of whom ended up hurt or dead.

She couldn't think of any of those men who had changed, none she'd met first hand. Sure, it was possible, but only if an abuser was ready to change.

I should've just gotten her to go with me earlier. We could've waited for Tommy to come home with Emma.

Mal had another thought, one she wasn't proud of. *What will I do now?*

This isn't about you, it's about Maggie. Fuck, Mal, get out of your own misery for a fucking second.

I know it's about Maggie. But I can't help but think how much I was looking forward to helping her.

To maybe have another child in the house?

Best to squash the thought before—

A honking horn and flashing lights snapped Mal's attention to the rearview.

A cop, maybe one she knew, trying to flag her down.

She slowed on instinct.

The car pulled around her, then stopped horizontally, occupying the entire two-lane road.

Tommy's Camaro.

He hopped out then raced toward her door.

Mal barely had time to reach for the gun in her glove compartment.

She slid her finger around the trigger as he reached her door but kept the gun low, not drawing it until she felt a more certain danger.

His hands were empty as he approached, his face twisted in anger.

He smacked her window three times.

Mal snapped. She threw open her door, forcing him to fall a step back.

She kept her gun behind her back, ready as he got in her face.

"What the hell are you trying to do to my wife?"

"What?"

"Why were you at our house?"

His eyes were red, bloodshot. His breath reeked of alcohol.

Best she provoke him to take it out on her, and maybe give herself an excuse to take this fucker down. Get him thrown in jail for battery on a sheriff's deputy. After she kicked his ass, of course.

She smiled. "I was trying to get her to leave you, Tommy."

He stepped back, his eyes wide and registering surprise.

"Yeah," Mal leaned forward, "I saw what you do to her. Big man laying hands on a woman so much smaller than him. Boy, you must have a *tiny* dick."

"Fuck you, dyke."

Mal stepped toward him, hoping he'd take a swing. "Wanna put me in my place, tough guy? Or do you only hit women dumb enough to marry you?"

He balled both fists at his side, jaw clenched as he stepped toward her.

No Stopping

"Come on, pussy. Do it."

Tommy somehow managed to stop himself, despite his drunken haze. He barked a bitter laugh. "Nah, I ain't gonna give you the pleasure, bitch. I see what you're trying to do."

Fuck!

"You stay the hell away from Maggie." He pointed a shaking finger at Mal. "You think for one fucking second I'm'a let you come between me and my family, you got another thing coming."

Tommy turned to walk away.

Fuck, fuck!

Mal had really thought the asshole was dumber than he was proving to be. Maybe he wasn't a fucking idiot. Maybe he was even capable of not being a total and utter piece of shit.

Maybe.

But then he turned around and started walking toward her.

Yes, do it! Do it!

He smiled again, his eyes still crazy, "And if you think for one good goddamn minute that I'm gonna let her take my daughter away from me, that ain't happening. I'll kill us all first."

His gaze locked with Mal's, and she knew he meant it. Dodd's eyes had the same disgusting gleam.

Tommy spun around.

Mal wanted to draw her weapon on him now.

Kill him.

Kill him now before he makes good on his promise.

But she couldn't shoot him in the back. It was one thing to kill Dodd even as he tried to turn himself in. Even if someone tried to convict her, no jury would put her away when they saw all she'd been through.

This wasn't the same.

This was a man telling her to stay away from his family. Yes, he threatened to kill his wife, his daughter, and probably Mal too, but that wasn't something she could prove, and nothing a jury would give a damn about. She'd be destroying her life and turning Tommy into a martyr if she shot him.

Maggie would see him as a victim, and tell her daughter about how Daddy was killed by this crazy cop lady she met in NA.

Mal could only watch him walk away and get in his car. Listen to him peeling out. Sneer as she stared at him flipping her off.

She got back in her car and put her gun in the glovebox.

Spent a minute hitting the steering wheel as she screamed.

Then she thought of a way to bring him down. A way to make him fuck his own life.

She just needed to give him a push.

Chapter 21 - Jasper Parish

"What is it?" Jordyn asked.

Jasper stared at the box, large enough to hold a football helmet, but it only held a single photograph of him in his car. Grainy, likely taken with a telephoto lens.

He wasn't sure if the picture had been taken earlier today or at some other time. Whatever the case, they had been watching him when he hadn't even known it — when *Jordyn* hadn't even sensed it.

Had they followed him?

Did they know who he was?

Or where he was staying?

Jasper paced the roadside, considering his next best move.

"What is it, Dad?" Her voice was nervous, bordering on scared.

"Nothing."

"Bullshit," Jordyn said, marching toward him. "What is it?"

He didn't want to show her. Didn't want her worrying. But *he* was worried, so he had to show her. It was only fair.

Jasper showed her the picture.

"What the hell? Are they following us?" Jordyn asked. "How did I not pick up on it? *Shit!* Why'd they put the pic in the box?"

"I'm guessing they wanted to send a message."

"What kind of message?"

"They want us to back off. They're telling me they know who I am. Even if they don't know yet, it's only a matter of time."

"And then what?" her voice hitched between the last two words.

"Then we need to run."

"We should run *now*, Dad."

"And leave Spider to them?"

Jordyn turned. Now *she* was pacing. A long growl preceded her scream.

"Shhhh, don't want to attract anyone." He looked at his car, all four tires flattened by a spike strip. Needed to wipe it down for prints and any other evidence that could possibly link it to him, then get the hell out of there and head for home.

He folded the photo, shoved it into his pocket. Kicked the box into the woods. Rushed back to the car then called Kim. "Hey, you got anyone who can come get a car with four flats? They can strip it or whatever."

"Yeah, I might be able to find someone."

"Good." He gave her the details then hung up.

Jordyn looked at her father. "What now?"

"Now we call for a ride and get to the garage."

THE GARAGE WAS Jasper's safehouse just outside Creek County — an old shop he'd bought under an alias that stored his cars, all purchases made under assumed names. There was an apartment above it where Jordyn was getting into one of the two beds while he checked the security feeds on the closed-circuit televisions.

Jasper figured they were safe here, that nobody had followed them, but he couldn't sleep before running through his security protocols, anyway.

A text came from Mallory. *Need to talk. Can you call?*

"Hey, it's me," Jasper said when she answered.

"My partner wants to ask you about a couple of people you might know something about. He suspects you're not dead. He might be closer to *sure of it.*"

Jasper sighed. "You told him?"

"No, but my partner knows when I'm lying."

"So, what are you suggesting? I'm in the middle of trying to help Spider, and there's some Russian dude trying to kill me. Are you suggesting I turn myself in?"

"So, that tip didn't help?"

"I got a tracker on his car but they found it. And ..." He was going to tell her they had his picture and it wouldn't be long before his face was out there. But he could still contain this. It wasn't in Victor's interest to flush him out, not while Jasper still had something he wanted.

"And what?" Mallory asked.

"And some Russian dude nearly killed me."

"So, you're no closer to finding her? Why not just tip off the feds?"

"Who knows how many feds or politicians are on that drive? How many people want this thing buried? I can't trust anybody else on this."

"I know a guy at the FBI, good, honest—"

"Only myself. Thanks for the help. I'll figure something else out."

"And *then* will you talk to Mike?"

"I'll think about it."

But she didn't hang up. And in her silence, Jasper sensed she wanted to say something else. "What is it?"

More silence, then in a trembling voice, perhaps even fueled by tears, Mallory said, "I get why you do it now."

"What?"

"The whole vigilante thing. I didn't understand it before. But I do now."

"This about Dodd? You feeling bad about what went down?" Jasper was careful not to say anything that might condemn her. The call was encrypted, but still, the caution was necessary. "Don't feel bad. Fucker deserved it. There were no other options."

"Sure there were. And I … well, I made the choice. Now I have to live with it."

Mallory was quiet again. Her voice reminded him of the people on the other end of a helpline, someone on the edge of suicide. She wasn't anywhere close to okay.

"Are you all right?"

Mallory laughed, sniffing back tears. "I'm fan-fucking-tastic, pal."

"It's not your fault what happened. I can't imagine the hell he put you both through. What he did to your daughter — I only wish I'd found him sooner."

"You and me both." Mallory choked on a sigh. "You ever feel guilty?"

Jasper wondered if she was recording the call, something she could use as a confession. He considered mentioning what she'd done in Mexico so they'd both be incriminated, but the pain in Mallory's voice was enough to cloud all her thoughts. He didn't want to throw her under the bus, even if she was trying to bring him in.

"Why would I feel guilty? I'm protecting people who

No Stopping

can't protect themselves, stopping the bad guys the law can't or won't stop."

Jordyn sat up in bed, staring at her father and shaking her head. "Be careful what you say, Dad."

Mallory didn't seem to be debating him like before. She was wrestling with her own regrets. And if she wasn't careful in the aftermath of what happened with Dodd, she'd end up in the darkest and most self-destructive of places.

"I've not hurt anyone who hasn't one thousand percent deserved it or who wouldn't have gone on to hurt others without my intervention," Jasper continued. "You think Paul Dodd would've stopped if he'd been arrested in Mexico? We both know his money and connections would've gotten him out. Especially down there, where they allowed a place like Paraíso to exist in the first place, and right under their noses. He would have escaped, then raped and murdered even more children. Him dying was a net positive for this world. Nobody mourns him, and nobody should feel bad about what happened. *Nobody*."

"What would you do if you *thought* someone was going to do something bad, but they didn't yet?" Mallory asked after a long silence. "Could you justify that?"

"Like I said before, I *know*."

"But what if you didn't."

"Then I wouldn't act. I'm not the crazy monster you think I am."

"Right. *You're a psychic.*"

"You still don't believe me?"

"Mike thinks you had something to do with Dodd."

"What do you think? You think I'd have something to do with that sick fuck?"

"I don't know what to think, anymore. You're asking me to believe something impossible to prove."

Jasper had a way to prove it, a way she wouldn't have any choice but to believe, but showing her might not be the best idea and could very well piss her off.

But she was in doubt, and he needed her to believe him.

"Do you remember buying that lottery ticket?" Jasper asked.

"What?"

"Your winning ticket. You don't remember buying it, do you?"

"Um … why?"

"I think you know why."

"No, I really don't know what you're getting at."

"I knew the numbers ahead of time. I bought the ticket and left it in your house."

"What?"

"I wanted to help you after what happened with Ashley. It was the only thing I could think to do to help from afar, after I saw how much everything was falling apart."

"You broke into my house and gave me a winning lottery ticket?" She laughed, clearly uncomfortable. "Bullshit."

"Hold on a minute …" Jasper went to his phone and pulled up the photo he'd taken of the winning ticket in his hand then sent it to her. "Check your phone."

"What the fuck? Why would you do that?"

"I was trying to help you."

"Help me or assuage your guilt?"

"What?"

"You trying to buy peace of mind for all the deaths you're responsible for?"

"*Peace of mind?* I don't know if you've been paying attention, but I don't feel remorse for any of them. *Period.*

No Stopping

And I'd do each and every one of them again if it meant keeping people like you, Jessi, and Ashley alive."

"Don't you say her name. Don't use her to justify what you've done."

Mallory hung up on him.

He called back, wondering why she was so mad and wanting to apologize. He knew she might get upset if he told her about the ticket, angry he'd broken in or maybe she'd consider it blood money, but this rage was born somewhere else, perhaps from her guilt over killing Paul Dodd.

Mallory didn't answer.

He texted back: *I'm sorry. I only want to help.*

No response.

Chapter 22 - Mallory Black

IT WAS TOO DAMNED early to be up, let alone looking to score.

But after a night without any shuteye, she sure as hell didn't feel like waiting.

Mal drove her rental into the Butler projects, ponytail tucked into her Marlins cap and oversized shades covering her face.

A few Butler PD cars were patrolling the streets. None of the corner boys were out slinging. This time of morning would normally have one cruiser on duty, definitely not the three she'd spotted already. She should have probably checked the news before driving over. Shit was clearly going down.

Everyone got antsy when the cops patrolled. Made it a lot harder for Mal to make the kind of deal she wanted to make.

She'd have to be careful. She could easily get pulled over. A white woman on this side of town driving around without any apparent direction meant only one thing. The

Butler cops knew her, and she could easily lie her way out of an awkward situation, but she preferred invisibility whenever possible.

Mal drove by Butler Veteran's Park, a large chunk of land located smack in the middle of the city, the kind of place people once brought their kids before the playgrounds were worn away to urban disease, before the basketball pavement cracked and the hoops lost their nets and chains. It was the kind of place clearly living on borrowed time, waiting for a repaving and conversion into an overflow parking lot for the Butler Courthouse a few blocks away.

The county's four courts were always packed, no matter the time of day, until after the park closed and the lights went off. Mal scanned the crowd searching for one dealer in particular — Logic, real name Pervis Evans. One of the bigger dealers. The police couldn't touch him because he was too damned careful. He was loved in the projects because he took care of his neighborhood, funding the families who needed him most, even if he was helping to decay it from the inside out.

No Logic, but Mal kept driving until she saw someone else who might be able to help her.

She parked then walked the cracked asphalt trail, overgrown with grass and weeds in too many places, until she came upon the table where an old black man was playing chess with a Hispanic teen.

"Hey, Doc," Mal said as she approached.

Real name, James Fowler. Native to Butler, Doc ran a barbershop until he retired six years ago. If there someone was worth knowing, he knew them. And nobody fucked with Doc. Not rival gangs, not thieves or muggers, and not the most desperate of crackheads looking to score. Doing so was sacrilege and would earn the offender any number of hard-ass gangsters out for their ass.

Doc looked up at Mal, rolled his eyes, then cast his gaze back down to the chessboard. The teen was a chubby kid, around twelve, in a black hoodie, green shorts, sandals, and giant glasses that doubled the size of his eyes. A faded red and blue skateboard lay on the ground right next to him.

"Can I get next?" Mal asked.

"Five bucks a game." Doc tapped the table where two five-dollar bills sat under a rock next to a bunch of white pieces, all belonging to the kid.

Mal reached into her pocket and dropped a twenty, the smallest bill she had, onto the table. "How about four games?"

The kid looked up at Mal, oblivious. "Wow, you must *really* like chess."

"Nah," Doc laughed. "She's just got a crush on me."

The kid eyed Mal like he thought Doc might be serious. "For real?"

"What? You think I don't have game anymore?"

"I dunno." The kid laughed. "She seems a bit *young* for you."

Mal smiled. "What can I say? I like men who were in the Civil War."

Doc rolled his eyes again then took the kid's last decent piece, a bishop. "Checkmate."

The kid looked stunned, "How'd ... aw, man."

"Come back tomorrow. We'll play for free."

"Really?"

"Yeah. You beat me, I'll give you today's fiver back."

"Really?" The kid was beaming. "All right, Doc, See ya."

No Stopping

He took off on his skateboard, his wheels crunching on the bumpy trail.

Mal sat. "Shit, Doc, now you're taking money from kids?"

"What do you want, *Detective?*"

"I'm sort of on the outs with the bosses right now. I'm not here as a detective."

"Have anything to do with that Mexico shit, or those bruises under your glasses, maybe that shit Cameron Ford's been bitching about on his idiotic website?"

"Just needed a break."

"Mm-hmm ... at least have the decency to look me in the eyes when you're lyin' to my face."

Mal took off her glasses then dropped them on the table next to her twenty.

Doc wrinkled his face in disgust. "Jesus, woman, put them back on. Who did that to you? Want me to sic some dudes on his ass?"

She returned the shades to her face with a smile. "Wasn't a him, was a tree."

"Uh-huh. So, what you doin' here?" Doc started returning his pieces to the board. "And damn, get your side ready. Bad enough I'm talking to a cop, don't need anyone seeing you not playin'."

Mal didn't need to look over at the basketball courts to know at least a few of the men had taken note of his playing partner. They couldn't recognize her with her hoodie and shades and hat, but they sure as hell knew Doc was playing with someone suspicious.

"Ladies first," he said after she'd set up her pieces.

Mal moved a pawn forward one spot . "I'm looking for Logic."

Doc moved one of his pawns two spots forward, no trepidation.

She hadn't played chess in forever, not since she refused to let her daughter win without earning it.

She thought of Ashley smiling the first time she'd beaten her mother, at only eight years old. She'd been so proud, but not half as proud as Mal had been of her baby girl.

"Why you lookin' for him?"

"I need a favor. And he owes me." Mal moved another pawn, already doubting her moves.

"Oh?" Doc moved a knight into play. "What kind of favor?"

"The kind it's best not to ask about." She countered by offering a pawn as sacrifice.

"He in trouble?"

"No, I swear. It's got nothing to do with the job."

"You know I ain't a snitch."

"And you know I've never lied to you."

"Fair enough." They traded pieces and a few more moves.

Mal didn't need to remind him she'd helped close a number of murders in the community, including a racially motivated atrocity. A double slaying a few years back where an angry redneck had murdered a mixed-race teenage couple making out in their car.

"Yeah, you always shot straight with me. Tell ya' what, you give me a number he can call you at, and I'll pass it on."

After Mal made a move, she reached into her hoodie, pulled out a notepad, then scribbled the number to her second phone.

"He'll remember me." She stood. "And thank you."

Doc tapped the table three times with him. "Where do you think you're going? You've got three more games to finish."

"Well," Mal said, looking down at their unfinished game. "Actually, four."

He moved his queen into position. "Checkmate. Now it's three."

Mal sat back on the bench and finished losing her twenty.

Chapter 23 - Victor Forbes

VICTOR WOKE up in the remote house with a throbbing back.

His room was nice, except for the bed. He had a private shower and bathroom, and, if you didn't count the cameras that were surely hidden in his room, he also had privacy. The rest of the house, or compound he supposed, sat on an acre and a half of woodlands on Creek County's westside.

The house was one of the ones Molchalin used to put up special guests of Voluptatem who came to the northeast coast for vacation. It was used to host sex parties for the most part, with members and underaged prostitutes. But right now, it was a prison for him and Spider. Plus, command central for this operation.

Molchalin had brought in his own crew from BlackBriar's European branch to watch over the house and Victor — men who owed no allegiance to his prisoner. Men who would kill him in a blink if he tried to escape. Clark was the only local he'd been able to bring with him — head of cybersecurity at BlackBriar's Jacksonville branch.

Victor showered then headed to the dining room where he sat across from Clark, who was eating eggs and fruit while reading the news on his tablet. The table wasn't large, but it still cost more than a new BMW on the lower end of the lot. Italian marble and stainless steel. Aluminum fusion leg polished and mirrored with an enameled crocodile pattern. The design was extraordinary, but Victor wasn't impressed. He preferred American wood and old-fashioned craftsmanship. But he'd also run security for parties in this place more times than he could count, so he understood why they would want furniture that was easy to wipe down.

A second man sat at the table a few chairs from Clark. A German named Franz, head of the European security team.

"Good morning." Victor poured himself a glass of water from the decanter on the table.

"Morning," Franz said with a barely a nod, looking at a German-language website and sipping his coffee.

"Good morning," Clark said in a friendlier greeting.

"Any news?" Victor asked.

"Nothing new," Clark said.

Jan, their resident chef from South Africa, came out of the kitchen with a wide smile.

"Good morning, Mr. Forbes. Per your request, I've prepared a fried egg with garlic and a side of hazelnuts and blackberries. But I hope you'll enjoy these croissants first." He placed a basket with warm croissants and honey butter in front of Victor. "Would you like some orange juice or milk?"

"This water is fine," Victor said.

Chef Jan returned to the kitchen, and Victor ignored the early morning carbs.

Victor turned to Clark. "Are you doing everything you can to sufficiently motivate her?"

"She's scared out of her mind. Does that count as sufficient motivation?"

"Did you tell her what happens to her if she doesn't get this?"

Clark swallowed the last of his orange juice then set his empty glass on the table. "She's doing what she can, same as our own people. No guarantees we'll get it in time."

Victor pounded his fist on the table, causing the plates and glasses on it to clank.

He felt Franz look up but didn't glance at the man. "Are *you* sufficiently motivated, Clark? Do I need to remind *you* what's at stake?"

"No, sir. Mr. Molchalin has already informed me."

Victor wasn't sure if Clark was name dropping to show his boss's boss had gone around him to speak with Clark directly or simply letting Victor know they were on the same page.

"Very well, then," Victor said with a smile, "if she doesn't have anything by the end of today, I want you to show her we mean business."

"Sir?" Clark asked.

"Cut off her left pinkie."

"But, sir, she needs to type."

"That's why we're leaving her other nine fingers."

"I don't think that's a—"

"I didn't ask what you think, did I?"

He stared at Victor but refused to challenge him. "Very well, sir."

Then Clark tucked the tablet under his arm and left his unfinished food on the table. Franz chuckled as he walked away.

Victor turned to him, wanting to smack the man across

No Stopping

his ugly, wide face. But Franz was a brick house. Even in his late forties, and looking one step down on the evolutionary chart of men, Victor knew it would be a mistake to get snappy with him.

Still, he couldn't say nothing. "What's so funny?"

"Ah, nothing," Franz answered dismissively. "You wouldn't get it."

"Try me." Victor glared at him.

Franz looked up from his tablet, only acknowledging Victor's presence enough to challenge him. "I wouldn't let my men talk back to me like that. You've got to show them who's boss. You let one talk to you like that, and suddenly you're everyone's bitch." An overly furry eyebrow arched as he smiled to show his atrocious dental work.

"I've got my men's loyalty," Victor said as Chef Jan served his breakfast.

Franz grabbed his tablet and coffee then stood. "Of course you do."

He left the room.

Victor looked down at his plate, troubled by the arrangement of the eggs and berries. It was as if the chef was in a rush and had thrown everything down without any care given to plating.

He looked up at Chef Jan. "What's this?"

"It's the —"

"I know what it is. I want to know why it looks like someone threw it all on the plate.

Chef Jan's lips curled down, red flashing in his cheeks. "I'm sorry, sir, I will make you another."

"I don't have time for you to make me another. Just make sure that lunch looks more presentable."

"Of course, sir. Please accept my apologies. Is there anything else I can get you?"

"No." Victor shoveled a forkful of eggs into his mouth,

disgusted with the lack of respect from everybody in this damned place.

He couldn't stop replaying the conversation with Clark on repeat.

Victor had personally brought Clark into BlackBriar. Recruited him from the Army and gave him a great paying job with a singular purpose. And *this* was how he repaid him? Questioning his boss in front of a lowly German thug?

Franz was right about one thing. Letting your underlings talk back was a slippery slope. Not only had Clark questioned his superior, he'd flaunted the fact that Mr. Molchalin had spoken to him directly.

You've got to show them who's boss. You let one talk to you like that, and suddenly you're everyone's bitch

Victor stood, determined to set things straight and show them all who was boss.

Chapter 24 - Spider

SPIDER WAS DYING for a scalding hot shower.

She hadn't bathed since she'd been brought here, despite the shower in the adjoining bathroom.

Now, she sat at her desk waiting for Clark to come back as her stomach continued to growl. She wished she'd eaten the dinner he brought last night and wondered if he'd bring donuts.

Funny how fast this was becoming her new normal — being held against her will, working to crack some sick pedophile's flash drive, and wondering if fried dough might be part of her morning.

She'd tried getting on the wi-fi, despite Clark's prior warnings, but she couldn't find a signal. They must've turned off the router while her overseer was at breakfast.

So, she kept poring through tons of email saved to the second of Wes's laptops, searching for any clue to the domain she was supposed to bring down.

Most of the emails detailed mundane information about his real estate holdings, alongside a few exchanges with men from dating sites. Spider tried not to let her emotions bury her hopes of escape.

But trying wasn't the same as doing.

And then, of course, there was Tyrell. Dead because of his loyalty to her. Spider thought she'd been doing something good by hiring him, offering a job to a friend who needed the money, who'd been caught up in the drug game too long. A job as her bodyguard was supposed to be safer. Spider didn't really have enemies. Despite working for dealers who might've been at odds with one another, her work didn't impact the others. She aided them all equally — hacking into places and helping them get out of jams, creating fake passports and credentials, getting schools to change grades for some of the younger ones to help them trade the hood for a decent college.

Spider was one of Butler's untouchables, so she never imagined she'd be putting Tyrell into any genuine danger.

And now he was dead because of her.

She thought of their last conversation. He was taking a culinary class at night school and was talking about getting out of here, heading to Orlando where his uncle's friend ran a restaurant. He dreamed of moving to Atlanta, a place he'd had fond memories of since he visited with his dad as a kid, and opening his own place.

I'm gonna call it Franklin's.

"What if there's already a place called Franklin's?" Spider had asked.

"Then I'll call it Franklin Thomas White's. Can't be too many places called that, can there?"

It seemed so hard to believe their conversation was only a few days old. She'd never look into his bright, happy eyes again. These bastards had killed him. And Spider wanted them all to pay.

She prayed the Professor was trying to find her and wasn't already dead.

When the door opened behind her, she turned.

Clark entered carrying his thermos in one hand and something wrapped in foil in the other.

He set it in front of her.

She opened the package to find a thick slice of banana walnut bread.

Spider took a bite, her mouth watering and her stomach rumbling in anticipation of more. "Thanks."

"You're welcome." He fished a bottle of cold water from his jacket pocket, set it next to her, then sat at his table, eyes down on his tablet.

"I could really use a shower." Spider reminded him without begging.

Clark said nothing, so she ate in silence, taking the occasional sip of water as she sifted through emails. She finally found one with a domain registration from three years ago.

"I need to get on the web."

"What is it?" Clark asked.

She called him over, showing him the website address she'd found registered to him: TheTruthRevealed.

"Shit." Clark grabbed his phone to turn on the router.

Her heart began to race. Maybe this was her chance to finally earn her freedom. Spider didn't want to help these fuckers, but she would if that meant getting the hell out of here.

She brought up the address, but it wasn't active, redirecting to a registry with a page saying that the domain was for sale.

"Damn," Clark said. "Maybe he let this one lapse, but he bought a dot org or another dot something. Check them all, see what you can find."

He dragged his chair over and sat beside her, watching as she worked. For the first time, it didn't feel like he was watching *over* her so much as working *with* her.

After twenty minutes, they found one active website, redirected to a conspiracy blog.

"This could be a placeholder," Spider suggested. "Assuming this is the same URL, once it's ready to go live, it'll forward to the actual site instead. But we have no way of knowing where it will be hosted until then. I can bring it down once we have that. Until then, I need to try and get into the registrar."

She did a Whois lookup to find out where the domain was originally bought, then searched through Wes's email for anything from them.

Nothing.

Spider went to the registrar and had an option to enter either an email or a login name along with a password. The website blocked her attempts with a time out before she could brute-force a password.

"I could make a script to run through different VPNs, but it's going to take some time."

"Let's do that." He got on the phone and relayed their findings to someone else.

As Clark finished the call, the door burst open. Victor stormed, his face flush as he looked from Spider to her boss. "What do we have?"

Clark updated him on the potential good news.

Spider expected him to be pleased, but instead Victor managed to look *more* annoyed.

"But you don't have anything for certain?"

"Well, no, sir," Clark said. "But it's something."

"No," Victor snapped, "it is not something. *Something* is when we've got the flash drive decrypted and the website is down. This is nothing!"

No Stopping

Clark started to say something, but Victor held up a finger. "I don't want to hear excuses. You're paid for results. If you can't give them to me, I'll have to do your job for you."

"What?" Clark said, uncharacteristically flustered.

Victor shoved him aside on his way toward Spider. He went around to her left then grabbed her arm.

"Wh-what are you doing?" she yelped.

He forced her fingers down flat on the table.

Spider tried to twist away from him, but being partially paralyzed, she couldn't exactly use her entire body to wriggle free.

"Stop!" Victor yelled, his voice taking on a terrifying tenor. He pushed down harder on her wrist.

She heard Clark say something, but it was lost in Victor's grunts as he pressed his body down on her arm, shielding her from seeing her hand.

"What are you doing?" Spider shrieked, her heart pounding fast.

He splayed her fingers apart.

She felt nauseated, her vision blurring at the edges as she realized what was about to happen.

"No!" she cried, struggling uselessly. In the months after her accident, Spider had refused to ever feel helpless again, but right now, her personal vow was only a joke.

The cold metal was sharp against her pinky.

She wailed, "Please, no."

"Stop!" Victor yelled again as he shoved the blade down. Then he stood back.

Spider stared in horror at her dismembered pinky finger, blood pooling around it on the table, and a bleeding stump from the second knuckle on her hand.

She felt dizzy. The darkness started at the edges of her vision, before blurring the world and everything in it.

Chapter 25 - Jasper Parish

JORDYN WOKE WITH A SCREAM.

Jasper grabbed his gun then searching for an intruder in the small room above the garage. But they were alone.

She sat up, sweating through her long-sleeved tee.

"What?" Jasper asked.

"He hurt her."

"Who?" But the answer was flooding his mind, alongside a perfect picture of unbridled brutality.

Victor Forbes over Spider, cutting off the tip of her finger. He could feel Spider's fear, followed by the cold shock and horror as she finally passed out.

And then, Jasper felt nothing. "Is she alive?"

"Y-yes," Jordyn said, shaking in her bed.

Jasper went to hug her. "It's okay, we're going to get her."

"*How?* Our one shot at finding her is gone." Jordyn stood and pushed past her father.

He thought she wanted to be alone, but she didn't leave. She went to her backpack, pulled out Spider's unicorn, then held it in her open palms, closing her eyes and focusing.

Jasper watched, hoping she'd get something this time. He always felt bad for Jordyn when her talents failed to manifest. And this time, Spider's life hung in the balance.

Forbes must've been frustrated to take such drastic action. If he was the evil fuck Jasper believed him to be, then how long did they have until he did something more? What if she couldn't decrypt the drive in time? Or what if she gave them what they wanted? What would they do, then?

Spider was dead unless Jasper got to her. BlackBriar was cleaning house, no reason to leave her alive.

Jordyn's eyes finally brightened, her cheeks pushing up with a huge smile.

"What is it?" Jasper asked.

"I feel something now. I don't know if it's her pain, or maybe that's she passed out, but ... yes, I feel something. We need to drive. If we get close enough, I think I can find her."

Jasper nodded.

Finally, some good fucking news.

THEY DROVE SLOWLY down a narrow road on the west side of Creek County, close to Kim's RV, assuming it was still parked there.

Jasper looked over at Jordyn as she stared out the window at the field of tall grass to their right. The field seemed to yawn on for a while before breaking into woodlands.

"What's back there?" Jordyn asked.

He slowed down and looked at his phone's screen.

"Nothing for about half a mile, then a residential neighborhood. Why? Sense something?"

She pursed her lips, then shook her head. "No. Keep going."

Jasper kept driving, feeling like he was going in circles. He looked over at Jordyn, trying to see if his daughter was losing the signal. She looked confused.

"It's okay if you lost it."

"No, no, I can sense something, like a name on the tip of your tongue. Just keep moving … there's a white van.

He turned west onto the main street, then continued toward the county line. They were surrounded by thousands of acres of forest dotted with the occasional road to nowhere or farms on either side.

They passed vehicles, mostly big rigs, work trucks, and pickups probably belonging to farmers. The dirty, dusty vehicles made the pristine white van more conspicuous.

Jasper found himself behind a big, slow-moving tractor trailer as they neared a long bend in the road. He couldn't pass without crossing a double line or risking getting pulled over or spotted by the van. But the longer he stayed behind the truck, the farther ahead the van would be, and the more likely he was to miss it if the vehicle turned onto a side street.

He merged left to pass the big rig.

And his windshield filled with a red blur coming right at him.

Jordyn yelped.

Jasper swung his car back into the right lane, heart pounding at nearly running head on into a cherry red Mustang, with several motorcycles behind it.

"What the hell, it's not bike week yet."

The truck slowed even more. Jasper was practically

riding its ass as a growing number of bikers prevented him from passing the truck.

"Damn it!" He slammed the steering wheel with his palm, stuck behind the big truck on a long run of road.

And still the truck decelerated.

"Oh, come the fuck on!"

More motorcycles passed on the left.

Jasper tapped his fingertips anxiously on the steering wheel. "Come on, come on."

The motorcycles finally all passed.

He merged and accelerated. Of course, the truck sped up, as if trying to keep him from passing it.

"Fuck you, buddy." Jasper slammed his foot on the pedal to overtake the truck.

He swung back into the right lane just ahead of yet another wave of bikers.

But the white van was gone.

"What the—?"

The closest vehicle was a silver sedan about a half mile ahead. Jasper couldn't be sure if the van had sped up to put distance between them, or if it had turned off one of the side roads.

"Fuck!" Jasper noticed a few small roads ahead that the van could have turned on to, or any number of the side roads he'd already passed.

He slowed down, glancing into the woods as he approached. He saw dust in the distance, maybe from the van. He took a sharp right, nearly missing his turn before sliding off-road. He slammed on his brakes, rocketing right for the trees.

Jasper braced for impact but the car stopped short.

The trucker brayed his horn behind them.

Jasper got back onto the dirt path then gunned the engine, eager to catch up to the trail of dust in the distance, hoping it was the van. He looked over at Jordyn. "Is it them?"

"Yes," she said confidently.

He breathed a sigh of relief, now certain they were still on the right trail. He had to slow down, lest he kick up clouds of dirt that might draw unwanted attention.

Jasper followed the van until it turned down another sideroad.

He stopped, giving it time to get further ahead, now certain he wasn't going to lose it.

"What the hell is out here?" Jasper pulled up the GPS on his phone.

No street view, obviously. So he looked to the satellite and saw a massive house a few hundred yards down the road. There was a gate, a large circular driveway, and a huge pool in the back — a mansion in the middle of the woods.

He went to the county appraiser's website to pull up title info and a sketch of the property, but there was nothing listed for anything remotely close to the location.

Without proper roads or utilities, Jasper wondered how anyone got permission to build a house here. And what purpose did a house like this in the middle of the woods serve, anyway? Maybe it was a secret sex club like that one in Mexico. Or a black site.

The CIA, and other agencies working on their behalf, had black sites out of the country. Was it possible Black-Briar had one here?

Jasper slowly drove past the road where the van had turned.

He saw the van going through an open gate with a guard shack and kept going, hoping no one had seen him drive by.

"What are we going to do?" Jordyn asked.

No Stopping

Jasper drove a bit further before turning down another dirt road. He kept east, until he figured he was about parallel with the property, then went to the trunk.

"What you doing?" Jordyn asked, getting out of the still idling car.

Jasper pulled out the quad drone then set it on the ground.

"A drone?"

"We need to see what we're walking into."

Minutes later, he was staring at the drone's cam feed. It showed several guards stationed around the property. Five on the roof, all with rifles at the ready, plus about a dozen cars and vans. The infrared camera revealed another dozen people inside the house. A large stone wall surrounded the property, with a guard stationed at the front gate.

"What is it?" Jordyn asked, seeing his expression.

"A small army."

"How are we gonna get in there?"

"By assembling an army of our own."

Chapter 26 - Mallory Black

WHEN MAL STEPPED into the Otis R. Jenkins Boxing Gym, everyone stopped and stared.

The gym, named after Butler's first black mayor in 1976, was the kind of place that offered local kids an escape from the rampant, crushing poverty through boxing and self-discipline. The gym was run by Eddie Jenkins, son of Otis, and a great boxing coach who'd steered a number of kids off of the streets and into the profession.

Even in his fifties, Eddie was a mountain of a man. He was in one of the rings nearest the entrance showing a scrawny teen girl how to move her feet before throwing a punch.

"No, no, no. You gotta do it like this." He demonstrated, impressing Mal with his agility. She'd never seen Eddie fight, but he had gone pro before life got in the way and he returned to Butler to take care of his mother and the gym.

He glanced at Mal, the question evident in his eyes. *What's this cop doing here?*

Eddie had never run afoul of the law, at least not that

No Stopping

she knew of, but he had been suspected of harboring many of the young men who had and helping them get out of town. He drew the line at hiding anyone who hurt a kid. That was how Mal had first met him in person, when he'd approached her one day a few years back to tell her where to find a guy who'd killed a kid in a drive-by.

Eddie told the girl to hold on as he stepped out of the ring. He approached Mal.

"How can I help you today, Detective?"

Mal had forgotten how massive he was. While his arms were still muscular, his new gut nudged the cotton on his faded yellow Otis R. Jenkins Boxing Gym T-shirt.

"I need to talk with Logic. He asked me to meet him here."

"He asked *you*?" Eddie's thin eyebrows arched up.

"Yes." She offered no explanation.

"All right. Follow me."

Eddie led her past the four rings that made up most of the main room, past the exercise bikes and weights where a smattering of teens eyed her suspiciously, then toward the rear doors.

There were a few rooms in the back where kids could do homework or play games after school. Eddie's office was way in the back. That's where she found Logic sitting a desk, typing onto a laptop.

His enforcer, Tracy Mack, sat beside him. He was a pit bull of a man. Had tattoos all over his body, including several on his face, as if he went into a tat shop and told them, *make me look as mean and ugly as possible*. The man was also Logic's cousin.

Tracy glanced at Mal with his sleepy, yet sinister, stare.

"Okay, give me a few," Logic told his enforcer. "But first, I need you to pat her down."

Mal had left her phone and gun in the car. She

stretched out her arms, preparing for a pat down, hoping Tracy wouldn't use it as an opportunity to feel her up.

But he didn't. Tracy pulled the paper bag from her hoodie pocket, looked at the cash inside, then handed it back to her.

"She's clean." He followed Eddie out of the office then closed the door behind them.

Logic was thin and short at five-foot-six, with thick black-framed glasses. He was wearing a purple hoodie and blue jeans, probably in fashion among his crowd. He was in his early twenties, despite looking no more than sixteen. Bullied as kid for being a nerd, he teamed up with his cousin and the two combined their intellect and brawn to corner the drug business, first in Creek County, then well into Jacksonville.

He closed his laptop and met her gaze. "What can I do you for, Ms. Black?"

"I need a favor."

He laughed when she explained it.

"I'm serious," Mal said.

"So, you want an amount that would land someone a felony for intent to distribute?"

"I'm not looking to jam you up."

"I know."

Logic said it so matter-of-factly, she wondered how he could be so sure.

"So, who are you trying to set up?"

"I didn't say what I wanted it for."

"Is for personal use? I can tell *you* use, but nah, I don't think this is for you."

"Can you help me or not?" Mal dropped the bag of cash on the center of his desk. "I'm paying double the going rate."

Logic looked inside the bag. Expressionless, he closed it

then slid it back to the center of his desk. "You wanna set someone up, why not just use something y'all already took off my guys?"

"This is personal. I'm not working now."

"This got to do with that shit down in Mexico?"

The event had made national news, and Logic was the kind of guy who made it his business to know everything, but Mal was still surprised to hear him bring it up.

"Sort of. Listen, you know I don't work narcotics, and I don't ask you about your business. I need your discretion. Let's just say I'm doing something the department can't do, trying to protect a little kid from some heinous fucking people. If I go through legal channels, it'll blow up. Destroy lives."

Logic stared at her.

Mal grew ever more certain he'd tell her to get the fuck out with every second passed.

"Okay. This make us even, then?"

"You don't owe me anything. I was just doing my job."

"Yeah, well, I wish more of y'all would focus on the *real shit* and not be chasing my associates."

"Like I said, I don't work narcotics."

Logic nodded. "But, are we even? You see, I don't like owing folks, especially cops."

"Yes, we're even."

"I don't know. Something this size you want to keep on the down-low, maybe you oughta owe me now."

"I'm paying you."

"I'd rather have a favor than cash."

She smiled. "I'm not a crooked cop. I'm not going to taint evidence, tell you when drug busts are coming, or help you break the law."

"Not that kind of favor."

"Then what?"

"I don't know yet." Logic smiled, though a part of her felt like he did know.

"I can't commit to something without any details. I don't even know if I'm going back on the job. Retirement is agreeing with me."

"People like you, they always go back."

"People like me? What does that mean?"

"You care too much."

Mal laughed. "You think you know me now, that it?"

Logic smiled. "It's my job to know people. So, we have a deal?"

"I'm not agreeing to something unless you tell me what I'm agreeing to."

"Then I can't help you." Logic pushed Mal's money to the edge of his desk.

She considered calling his bluff but needed her plan in play.

"Fine. But I'm not going to taint evidence, rat out snitches, murder anyone, tell you about drug busts, or do anything that fucks with the sheriff's office. I'm *not* a crooked cop."

"You said that." Logic smiled again. "But you ain't exactly straight. Wouldn't be here if you was."

"I told you my stipulations. As long as it's close to the line, but doesn't cross it, and I can do it, then I'll help you."

"Okay," he said after another long moment. "I can live with that. So, we have a deal?"

She nodded.

"I'll get you what you need."

"Thank you."

Logic told her where to make the pickup, at a park near the beach, way outside of Butler.

"Oh, one other thing … "

"Yes?" She turned back at the door.

No Stopping

"You know anything about the shit that went down a couple nights ago? Dudes in black, looked like cops but they weren't, rolled up and killed some of my affiliates, kidnapped a girl named Spider."

"Saw it on the news, but beyond that, no. Why?"

"Was hoping you could maybe verify what I'm hearing. Some of my folks saying it's a dude named Victor Forbes, runs that BlackBriar company."

She nodded. "I heard some similar rumblings."

"And why aren't the police going after those people?"

"Fuck if I know."

"What *can* you tell me?"

"Only that they're bad people. And if you have a chance at helping get that girl back, you'd be doing something the cops probably can't do."

Logic nodded. "Yeah, we're working on something with someone now."

She wondered if that someone was Jasper.

He must've caught the look in her eye. He tilted his head ever so slightly. "You know something more about it, don't you?"

"I need to go. Thanks again."

Logic called out, "You're a terrible liar, Detective."

Mal didn't respond. She just left to pick up her drugs.

Chapter 27 - Spider

SPIDER WAS sixteen in her dream, and still Felicia, living in the foster home with Bill and Mary Smith. Her fourth foster home since the crash killed both her parents and crippled her four years earlier. The final one, she hoped.

The parents were nice, an older couple who had taken in three kids, including Spider and twin autistic seven-year-old boys. The Smiths were incredibly patient, and with Mrs. Smith homeschooled Felicia. Everything was perfect.

Until that day at the mall.

Parents weren't the problem this time.

It was the Smith's birth daughter, Callie, who'd just turned seventeen.

Spider's dream returned her to the moment when everything went to shit. The Smiths had dropped Callie and Felicia off at the mall. Callie seemed to genuinely like her. Pretty, blonde, and popular. Plus, money. The whole cliché. Everything Felicia wasn't and never could be.

They were at the food court with Callie's friends, Stacy and Scott, rich popular kids with nice clothes and perfect teeth like Callie.

No Stopping

Felicia felt out of place with her kinky hair, ugly too-dark jeans, and faded pink top, plus that wheelchair and zigzagging scar that ruined her forehead. But she eventually learned to feel at home with the group. *Almost* like she belonged.

They were laughing and talking about school. For the first time since the accident, she didn't feel like a freak in a wheelchair. She sort of felt like a normal kid.

That was rare because Felicia had kinda always felt a bit like a freak. Into computers and reading unlike most girls she'd known growing up, she'd been a geek who never really fit in with anybody, except for a lone friend here or there, and that was before the accident.

But with Callie, Stacy, and Scott, they gelled like they belonged together.

I have a group of friends!

Felicia felt happy enough to cry. She would, later that night. But for an entirely different reason.

Callie and Stacy looked around the food court, trying to decide what to get before settling on Papa John's. Scott wanted Taco Bell, and since Felicia hadn't had tacos in forever, she went with him.

He offered to push her, but she could help herself.

The Taco Bell line was way shorter than the one at Papa John's, so they got back to the table well before the girls. Scott started asking Felicia questions about herself.

The conversation was awkward at first. She wasn't sure what to say and what she should probably keep to herself. It had been so long since someone cared enough to ask. Soon, they were talking like old friends. Then, to her surprise, Scott seemed to be flirting with her.

So, Felicia flirted back. It was the first time she'd felt pretty since the accident that left her scarred and partially paralyzed. She could barely believe how well things were going. It was like she was in a dream where she hadn't lost her family at twelve and could lead a normal teenager's life.

She tried not to make too much of his flirting. Maybe he was only being nice. Plus, Felicia didn't want to set herself up for disappointment by actually thinking she had a chance with a guy like Scott.

Then he shocked her by asking if she wanted to go with him to spring dance.

"Dance?" She laughed and looked down at her wheelchair. "I don't know how to tell you, but … " *No, no self-pity. Make a joke. Think of something funny, damn it!* "I'm so good on the dance floor, I'd probably embarrass you."

She loved the sound of his laugh, so she listened to its music before she continued.

"No, seriously, people would be pointing at you, asking if you had some motor skill disorder or something."

Scott kept laughing, and Felicia basked in her triumph.

"I'll take my chances. Just say yes. We'll have fun."

And before she could even doubt herself, the *yes* was out of her mouth.

Her lowest valley had been the accident, now this was her Everest. Felicia couldn't imagine being happier than she was in that moment. But the joy was short-lived.

Callie started acting different once she and Stacy came back with their pizza and Scott announced they were going to the dance together.

Felicia wondered if Callie had a thing for Scott. She hadn't said anything. And she was *always* talking about boys she thought were cute.

Callie barely spoke on the way home. Just the bare minimum of words necessary not to alert her mom that something was wrong.

At dinner, she barely looked at Felicia.

No Stopping

Later that night, when Callie was going to bed, Felicia knocked on her door.

Callie opened it, headphones on, phone in her hand. "Yeah?"

"Can I come in?"

"Sure." Callie walked back to her bed as Felicia closed the door.

Callie hopped into her bed, sitting cross-legged, not even looking at Felicia as she swiped at her phone.

"Are you mad at me?"

"Why would I be mad at you?" Callie didn't look up.

"I dunno, but you've been weird ever since lunch."

"Weird? Oh, you mean because you stole Scott?"

"What? *Stole him?* Are you two going out?"

"No, but last week he told Stacy he was thinking of asking me to the dance. Then *boom*, he asks you today! So, what the fuck, Felicia?"

"Oh, my God. I'm *soooooo* sorry. I didn't know you liked him."

"Mm-hmm." Still wouldn't meet her gaze.

"I swear, I didn't know. I'll tell him no."

"Um, no, you will not. He'll know I said something to you."

"I'll tell him I can't go. I'll say I like someone else or something. Whatever you want me to say. I would never want to come between you two."

Callie gave her a cold and vicious laugh. "Don't worry, it doesn't really matter."

"What do you mean?"

"It's not like he *really* likes you. He feels sorry for you. You're not his type, honey. For one, you're crippled. And, for two, this." She waved her hand over her forehead.

"What?" Felicia asked, knowing exactly what she

meant. It was just hard to believe that Callie would say something so mean.

She laughed again. "It's not like anyone could ever really think you're pretty. The kids call you Scarface behind your back."

Felicia felt like she'd been smacked across the face. She fought the tears as they stung her eyes.

Callie finally looked at her. "What?"

Felicia had never seen someone eye her with such disdain. Fear, yes. Pity, sure. But never with this kind of contempt, like Felicia wasn't worthy of having friends, let alone a boyfriend. That slap was more like a knife in her heart.

Then Callie drove the dagger deeper. "Oh, you didn't know? Yeah, sorry. *Nobody* likes you. They feel bad for you. They're only nice to you because I'm your foster sister."

The dream changed locations.

Felicia was glad not to relive what happened next, her freaking out and trashing Callie's room.

But then came another memory, talking to Mr. Smith downstairs later that night.

He was disappointed in Felicia, and that was almost as bad.

She tried to explain what had happened, but Mr. Smith wasn't hearing her.

I'm sorry for what Callie said, but you are responsible for your reactions.

Felicia had gone from one horror show to another, and this was the first time the parents actually seemed to care about her as more than a check from the government. She couldn't get kicked out of this foster home.

"I'm sorry," she cried. "It won't happen again."

"I'm afraid you're right about that. We have zero tolerance for violence in this house. I'm sorry, Felicia."

No Stopping

"*What?* You're sending me back into the system?"

He shook his head, barely looking at her. "I'm not the one sending you back. You decided this with your behavior."

On one hand, she felt horrible that she'd made him so disappointed. But on the other, Felicia hated that he didn't even see her side of things. That he wasn't giving her a second chance. That he was just going to give up on her, simple as that.

She thought he and his wife were different. Thought they cared.

Felicia cried, uncontrollably, apologizing over and over, begging for another chance. Not her proudest moment, but she loathed the thought of leaving. She even promised to find a way to make up with Callie, even though Callie had been so horrible to her.

"I want to tell you something my father told me when I was about your age. He said, 'Son, life isn't fair. In fact, it can be downright cruel. But no matter what life throws your way, you always have the power to choose how you respond. That is what makes the difference between winners and losers. Losers lash out and cry about the cruel injustices of the world. Winners figure out a way to roll with the punches and turn the situation in their favor.' I hope you can carry this lesson to your next house, and maybe have a better time of it. I'm sorry, Felicia."

He got up and left her alone in the living room, weeping and devastated. Mrs. Smith never even saw her off when the social worker came to pick her up the next day.

As Felicia got in the car, she looked up at Callie's window. Her former friend was standing there, shades open, glaring down with a naked expression.

Her dream shifted to the next house, the place with all

the terrible things. Atrocities that would alter her forever, and make Felicia surrender her birth name.

~

SPIDER WOKE up in her sleeping bag, staring at the bandage where the tip of her left pinky used to be. Her anger acquiesced to sadness.

She was alone in the room. Her wheelchair still at the desk.

Where's Clark?

Spider wasn't sure what time it was. It felt like early afternoon, and her internal clock was almost as reliant as the real thing. But right now, everything was fuzzy. She wasn't sure if she'd been drugged, suffered from shock or blood loss, or perhaps something even worse.

Where the hell is Clark?
Did Victor tell him to leave?
Am I being watched right now?

She had been scared of Clark but knew he wouldn't hurt her if she followed orders. But Victor was clearly a psychopath.

Spider felt sick to her stomach as she slowly sat up.

Despite common sense and a probably unrealistic belief in the Professor coming through for her, she had believed she would somehow persevere, same as she'd always done.

But it was harder to have faith with the throbbing pain of a missing finger.

She flinched as the door opened. Clark, carrying a water bottle and food. She was relieved to know he was still the one looking after her, even if he couldn't protect her from Victor.

Assuming he won't kill me on Victor's orders.

No Stopping

She shoved the thought from her mind as he asked how she was.

"What happened … after he cut my finger?"

"I cleaned and cauterized the wound. Does it hurt?"

"Yes," she said as he helped her into the wheelchair.

"Here." Clark reached into his pocket and pulled out a white bottle.

"What's this?"

"They'll help the pain." He unscrewed the cap, dropped a pair of pills into his palm. "It's five hundred milligram Percocets. All I have on me at the moment."

She'd avoided pain meds all through rehab following the accident. She'd been on morphine at the hospital and briefly took some medication upon her initial release, but she had pride in not needing them as her pain faded away. The pills helped, but they also made it easier to succumb. And the last thing Spider ever wanted to do was give up on herself.

"I don't want 'em," she said.

"They're safe."

Then a thought occurred to her. A way out of this mess if she wasn't going to get out alive. She held out her palm. "Okay."

He handed her the water and the pills.

Spider pretended to pop them in her mouth but slipped them into her pocket instead. She wasn't sure how many she'd need to overdose and die, but she might as well start saving up.

She wanted to cry, but then Bill Smith's lecture echoed in her mind.

Losers lash out and cry about the cruel injustices of the world, winners figure out a way to roll with the punches, to turn the situation in their favor.

She'd taken his advice to her next home. Hardened her soft parts and found a way to survive.

And she'd do the same here.

Just had to bide her time and figure a way out.

"Are you hungry?" Clark asked, his voice softer than before. "I brought you some muffins."

He feels bad. Find a way and use that against him.

"Yes." She met his gaze. "Thank you."

Chapter 28 - Victor Forbes

VICTOR WAS EATING lunch in the dining room, happy his meal was better than the slop he was served for breakfast and glad to see the kitchen was finally taking him seriously.

He thumbed through the news on his phone as he ate, praying there were no breaking headlines featuring the organization.

Nothing so far.

Franz made his way to the table then sat across from Victor.

There was the slightest shift in his demeanor. He no longer eyed Victor with the same smug expression. "So, you really did it, eh? You cut off that bitch's finger?"

The man's joy over such violence only proved him a cretin. But Victor had earned his respect, for whatever that was worth, so instead of dressing the man down like he might've otherwise done, Victor only nodded. "Let's just say she's been convinced of the job's importance."

"I'll bet she falls in line now. Your man, Clark, on the other hand ..."

"What?" Victor asked as Chef Jan brought Franz steak frites and a glass of ale.

"Oh, nothing."

Franz was obviously trying to get under his skin, but he was an idiot, and Victor played a better game of ball. "What is it?"

"Just whispers. You know, little birdies, I believe your saying is." Franz made a whistling sound and pantomimed flitting wings as he continued to whistle.

"What are the birdies saying?" Victor asked, hating himself for playing along. Even if he knew Franz was trying to outmaneuver him, he needed to know what the man was *trying* to do if he hoped to figure out the best way to handle him.

"He is telling some of the men how, um … *unstable* I think was the word he used. Yes, how unstable you are."

Victor took a bite of his roasted lamb without responding.

"I believe he thinks he'd be a better boss than you. But I disagree. It takes a certain kind of man to do the hard things, am I right? He could never hurt that girl. But you proved leadership. I can see why Mr. Molchalin appointed you as the head of this branch. Clark isn't half the man you are." Franz shook his head. "No way he could be boss."

Victor nodded.

Franz was trying to create tension between the two men, but why? Was he, or one of the other men, whispering bullshit into Clark's ears as well? Was this at the direction of Molchalin to ensure that Victor had no one on his side in the event that he needed to be eliminated? And if BlackBriar did kill him, would Franz be the one to do it? Or would they make Clark pull the trigger, as some sort of loyalty test?

His appetite gone, Victor took a swallow of his wine then pushed the plate away from him.

Franz looked at the mostly-full plate. "Are you finished?"

"Yeah. I try not to get too heavy a stomach when I'm working."

"Ah," Franz said, stabbing a fork into Victor's lamb. "Do you mind?"

"No."

Franz transferred the meat to his plate, next to the steak. "This lamb?"

Victor nodded.

So did Franz. "Not as good as the steak, but good."

Victor's phone buzzed.

It was the call he'd been waiting for — a deputy at the Jacksonville Sheriff's Office.

"Excuse me." Victor stood, taking his phone and the glass of wine.

He answered the call as he turned down the hall then ducked into the library for privacy. "Yes?"

"Hey, Mr. Forbes, it's Roy. I got that info you wanted. But one question … "

"Yes?" Victor said.

"When was that photo taken?"

"The other day. Why?"

"According to my source at Creek County Sheriff's Office, the man in that photo is dead."

"Oh?"

"Yeah. Name was Jasper Parish. Former cop from South Florida. His house burned down shortly after his daughter's suicide. Interesting thing is what he tried to do after she died."

"What's that?"

"He tried to get the sheriff's department to arrest

Calum Kozack, saying the guy raped his daughter and caused her to kill herself. But the DA, being a friend of Calum's daddy, didn't do dick."

Victor's wheels were furiously turning.

"Hey, Roy, did your source wanna know why you're asking?"

"I made up some shit, said it was an old case, didn't let on that the guy was still alive."

"Good. Don't say anything to anyone else, okay?"

"No problem, man. Mum's the word."

Victor hung up with a plan.

Chapter 29 - Mallory Black

MAL SAT in her rental at the red light, watching Tommy's Camaro idle two cars ahead of her.

Tonight, she would put her plan into action. Plant drugs in his car then leave an anonymous tip. Officers finding that quantity of pharmaceuticals in his vehicle would arrest him for violating of parole.

With her bastard of a husband back behind bars, Maggie might finally find the will to do what she should have done a long time ago — leave his ass and start over somewhere else.

The light turned green, and Mal followed him as he made his way to a pub in a strip mall. It shared a parking lot with an ancient Winn-Dixie, a thrift shop, a bail bondsman, a Subway, a payday lender, and a few other smaller shops. She parked in front of the Winn-Dixie but stayed in her car and watched as Tommy walked toward the pub with a pool cue case slung over his shoulder.

Her plan had a problem. The entire length of the pub's front was windowed, giving her a clear view of the crowd and pool tables, but also giving anyone inside a clear view of the parking lot.

Worse, the lot was well-lit in front of the pub, basically putting a spotlight right over Tommy's car.

Mal mulled her options.

She could wait until he drove home then plant the drugs there, but the odds of being seen by a neighbor were probably even greater.

Why does this dive have so many damned windows?

Mal watched as a car pulled up next to her and a young black woman got out with her little girl. She was coughing, a horrible croupy rasp, reminding Mal of several late-night hospital trips when Ashley was little and had the croup.

The woman glanced over at her. Too late, Mal realized she'd been staring. The woman hurried her kid away, as if the watching stranger might jump out and accost them.

She decided to leave for a bit, think about what she should do next somewhere else.

Mal pulled into a Burger King drive-thru. She ordered a Whopper, fries, and a Coke, then sat in the parking lot eating the greasy, lukewarm food, immediately regretting her decision. It reminded her of many such shitty meals with Mike as they sat in a car on a stake out, or while waiting for the techs to arrive at a crime scene. She missed her partner a lot.

She ate about a quarter of her food before wrapping it all up in the bag, getting out of the car, then tossing it into an overflowing garbage can outside.

Mal she got back in and drove around, sipping her soda until she finally called Mike, hoping a conversation might get her to stop lamenting their last conversation.

He answered after four rings.

"Hey, how's it going?" Mal asked.

"Okay. It's a bit early for a booty call, ain't it?"

"Fuck you," she joked. "I was just thinking of you."

"Missing me?"

"No, I was eating Burger King and regretting all the many life choices that led me to it, and thought of all the shitty meals we've scarfed down together."

"So, basically, you got indigestion and thought of me?"

"Basically."

"Awesome. So, you coming back?"

"Not yet."

"Call to give me some info on our mysterious friend?"

"Nothing new there, either."

"Um, okay. Well, thanks for calling."

"Don't be like that. Can't a friend just call to say hi?"

"A *friend* wouldn't choose to make another *friend's* investigation more difficult by withholding evidence."

A long sigh, then, "Can't we just talk without you giving me a guilt trip?"

"Okay, Mal, let's talk. How's it going, old pal? Awesome! Glad to hear. What's that? You're thinking of getting a dog? Well, I never pictured you as much of a dog person, but that really sounds excellent. How am I? Well, me and the wife are fine, except I'm working all damned day and night on a case no one but me and the parents of these missing kids seems to want solved. Yeah, that does suck, doesn't it?"

"You're such a drama queen," she teased, hoping to lighten the mood, if not the conversation.

"Okay, Mal, how are you?" Mike asked after a slight pause.

"Well, let's see, the man who raped and murdered my daughter had me kidnapped and pumped with heroin after I'd finally kicked my addiction, so now I spend my nights in NA meetings wishing like hell that I wasn't craving pills every second of every long ass day and wondering if I wouldn't have been better off if Paul Dodd had just killed me. And the only reason I can be glad I'm not dead is it also means Jessi Price is still alive."

Long silence on the other end.

Mal held back her tears. "I'm sorry. I didn't mean to—"

"No, you're right. *I'm* sorry. Is there anything I can do?"

She wanted to say yes, to come and sit with her, tell her everything would be fine, just like a friend was supposed to do. But she couldn't, not now when she had Tommy to deal with.

"Mal?"

"Sorry, just thinking. I'll be okay. Listen, I've gotta go. Thanks."

"Wait—"

Mal hung up. Not to be dramatic, she'd held in her tears as long as possible and didn't want her partner hearing her cry. So, she wept in the quiet of her car as rain plopped on the windshield, letting his next call tickle her voicemail.

She couldn't help but wonder how she'd fallen so far so quickly. Mal was well beyond 'going a bit outside the law.' And while she'd gone even further outside it when attacking Eddie the Rapist, this felt different, somehow more illicit.

Yes, Tommy was a piece of shit who hit his wife, but she refused to leave or turn him in. Who was Mal to make that decision for her, and by way of framing a man?

She was a cop, sworn to uphold, not break the law. This went against everything she was supposed to believe in, everything she'd dedicated most of her adult life to. Upholding the legal code and doing the right thing had always meant so much to her, enough that she'd missed many of Ashley's recitals and important moments. No first boyfriend or job, going off to college, or getting married and having a child of her own.

Her life had been stolen by Dodd. To uphold the law, she'd traded away so much of the only time she'd ever had with Ashley, and for what? Only to go full-on Death Wish?

Mal had affronted Ashley's memory and felt disgusted with herself.

Her tears fell harder.

Just take some pills and make the pain go away!
You sure as hell have enough of them!

An explosion of thunder made her jump with memories of Dodd, the gunshot, and a rising panic inside her. She could see his eyes as clear as if she were looking into them now — the way he stared at her like she was his possession. Looked at Jessi in the same exact way.

Like Tommy's eyes when he threatened Maggie.

Fuck you, Tommy. You don't own her.

She mopped at her tears, like the wipers on her windshield clearing the rain.

Mal could barely see through the window it was raining so hard.

Then it hit her — she could barely see out her window.

She finally had enough cover to plant the drugs in Tommy's car.

~

RAIN POUNDED as she climbed out of her car, heart racing and adrenaline pumping as she went to work.

She'd parked next to Tommy's Camaro so she didn't have far to go. It was easy to unlock with a slim Jim. He didn't even have an alarm. She opened his door and pressed her finger on the switch to keep his light from turning on.

Mal wasn't sure how long she had, so she hid the drugs behind the glove compartment, one of the first places cops would look, one Tommy wasn't likely to check.

She closed the compartment, used a rag to wipe the rainwater off the seat and the door. When it became obvious she couldn't get it all, she lowered the window an inch to explain the water.

Mal closed his door, peered over the Camaro to make sure nobody was looking, then got in her car. She drove away, laughing to herself.

Finally, something worked out!

The next day she would pay one of her old informants to place an anonymous call to the Jacksonville Crime Stoppers tip line to rat him out. A concerned mother who saw him dealing at a playground, maybe even say she's reported him to park officials and nobody had done shit so she was thinking about going to the news. That should light a fire under their asses.

With any luck, Tommy would be in jail by the end of the day.

Sure, Mal had violated her principles, and maybe tainted Ashley's memory, but the sacrifice meant Maggie and her daughter might stand a fighting chance.

Chapter 30 - Spider

SPIDER WAS FINDING it hard to work. Her finger was throbbing even more than yesterday, and she was still trying to abstain from Clark's painkillers.

She had collected six so far and hoped that would be enough to make him pass out. She would have had two more, but half an hour ago, just after a late dinner, she'd finally surrendered and swallowed a pair of them.

Now she was feeling fuzzy.

Clark was sitting beside her, looking over the code she'd written for a script to route brute-force attempts to the registrar from multiple IP addresses. BlackBriar had access to a bot network that could get the job done, but it wasn't a sure bet. Any number of things could go wrong. Even if they somehow managed to get login info for the domain she was trying to access, it still might not be the right one.

Victor would probably take another finger, or worse, if they botched this.

Clark looked over the code as she checked a fresh batch of email, on yet another account, searching for anything that might lead to the domain.

He sighed as he closed his eyes and squeezed his temples. It was the first sign of exhaustion, or any cracks, since Victor lopped off the end of her finger.

"You okay?"

"Just a headache." He unscrewed his thermos, refilled with coffee ten minutes earlier.

"Why don't you take one of your pills?"

"Nah, it'll be okay." He took a swig then returned to his monitor.

Clark looked so serious. For some reason, that made her start to giggle.

"What?" His brow furrowed.

"Nothing."

"What?" Clark repeated.

"Just … I dunno, you look *soooo* serious. You remind me of my Dad this one time when I was four or five and I said the F-word for the first time. He was mad at me, but then Mom started laughing and couldn't stop. They both tried to put on such serious faces, even though it was hilarious."

"You're high." He stared at Spider with barely any expression, sounding almost disappointed.

"You should try some, they'll help your headache. They're *really* good."

He rolled his eyes and ignored her, which only made her laugh harder. The left corner of his mouth twitched, ever so slightly, creating a dimple.

"Oh, my God, you have such cute dimples."

Clark ignored her, staring at the screen.

She reached up and went to touch his dimple to see if it would be hard or squishy.

He turned, eyes intense, and grabbed her wrist hard, scaring her. "Don't touch me!"

Spider pulled her hand away, feeling hurt. And scared. Suddenly, she was crying, way more than she should be.

The pills were making her too damned emotional. "I'm sorry."

He looked down at the table. "It's okay."

She wiped at her tears, embarrassed and hopeless. As she reached for the Sprite, an idea came to her. So she fumbled with the bottle then spilled it all over the table and her lap.

Clark leapt from his seat, checking to make sure the laptops were still dry. "Be careful!"

Spider cried again, or rather faked it. Time to set her plan in motion. "I'm sorry, I'm just … just feeling woozy. I … I need to puke." She rolled her wheelchair to the bathroom. After slammed the door behind her, she pretended to retch then flushed the toilet to disguise the lack of vomit hitting the water.

She kept making noises as she grabbed the pills from her pocket, wrapped in a piece of foil from one of Clark's muffins. She placed the foil on the toilet seat, then reached into her other pocket and grabbed the spoon she'd taken, mashing the pills and grinding the spoon back and forth on the foil as she kept pretending to vomit.

Clark came to the door after a few minutes. "You okay in there?"

Spider froze, hoping he wouldn't open the door and catch her grinding the pills to a powder.

"Yeah," she said, making herself sound as pathetic as possible.

She flushed again, then checked the powder, pressing her fingers into the foil to make sure they were ground to dust. Then she carefully folded the foil and slipped it into her pocket before tucking the spoon into her other one.

Spider went to the sink, splashed water over her eyes and face, then rolled to the door. She opened it to find Clark looking at her with either concern or suspicion.

Her heart raced. If he reached into her pocket and found the powder, he'd probably kill her himself. He'd warned her there would be no more warnings. And though he wasn't as cruel as Victor, the man clearly meant business.

She shook her head. "I'm sorry. I ... think I probably took one pill too many."

"It's okay. We'll just give you one at a time."

She made a disgusted face. "Now all I taste is vomit. Can I get another Sprite?"

He studied her again.

He's on to you. He's gonna call bullshit then search you!
You are SO fucked, kid.

"You want something for your stomach?"

"If there's any bread?"

"I'll check."

Spider only needed two more things to happen for her plan to work. For him to leave his thermos with her and for him to drink from it again when he returned — without tasting the medicine.

If any of those prerequisites went wrong, she was fucked.

Clark headed toward the door then paused in front of his seat.

Don't grab it. Don't grab it.

"Hey," she said, drawing his attention.

He looked at her, his expression still rattling her nerves. "Yes?"

"Can you see if they have that banana walnut bread?" Spider looked down as if her question was shameful, as if she was pushing her luck.

He almost smiled. "Okay."

And then he walked out the door, leaving his thermos behind.

No Stopping

Yes!

Spider waited for the door to swing shut then rolled to the table. She grabbed the foil packet and was transferring it to the other hand when it fell.

Fuck!

She reached down, but it had fallen under her wheelchair. Spider rolled back until she saw it beneath her but an angle that required her to adjust the chair before she could reach it. As she was leaning over, the door opened behind her.

Fuck, fuck!

Spider turned and looked up, feeling like she'd been caught red-handed, fully expecting to find Clark staring at her and the foil packet.

But it wasn't him.

It was one of the men whose names she didn't know. A young blond with frightening eyes.

"Where is Clark?" he asked in a thick German accent.

"Um," Spider was speechless, every word failing her.

The man stared into her deception, as if he could see the scheming all over her lying face.

"Um, he went to get a drink," Spider said, relieved that her tongue finally decided to obey.

He looked at her like she was stupid, shook his head, then left, letting the door close behind him.

She grabbed the foil packet, then reached for the thermos. She didn't have much time, especially if the German wanted Clark to do something for him now. Sometimes the men came to him about their phone and laptop tech issues, stupid shit that anybody with half a brain could figure out on their own.

Spider unscrewed the thermos then poured the powder in, hoping it would be enough to knock him out without killing him. She wouldn't mind Victor taking an eternal nap, but Clark had shown enough kindness to keep her from wanting him dead.

She stirred the still warm coffee, hoping its heat wouldn't destroy the efficacy of the pills — assuming they would do what she needed them to.

She twisted the thermos cap back on and put it back where she found it.

Just as Spider was slipping the spoon into her pocket, the door opened behind her.

She turned to see Clark carrying something wrapped in foil and another bottle of Sprite.

"Thank you." She smiled as he set them in front of her.

She saw a splash of coffee on the desk as she reached for them, then placed the foil-wrapped food on top of it, hoping he hadn't seen the coffee. She took the Sprite, opened the bottle, then drank nervously.

Clark sat next to where the coffee spot was hidden by the food.

She hoped he wouldn't move it or open it for her.

He returned to work instead. Spider sipped, waiting for him to take a swallow of coffee.

"You gonna eat?" Clark finally asked.

"Just waiting to make sure I'm not gonna puke again."

He reached for his thermos. "Okay."

Her heart went into overdrive as he unscrewed the cap and raised it to his mouth.

Oh, God, he's gonna smell it or taste it and he's gonna know. He'll say, "You tried to poison me after I got you banana walnut bread?" Then he'll pull out his gun and kill me.

Because they really don't need me now, do they?

He swallowed and winced.

Shit, shit, shit.

Then he looked at her, his eyes still suspicious.

"Did the German dude find you?"

No Stopping

He set the thermos down. "Yeah."

She went back to work, the next several minutes feeling like an eternity while waiting for him to either drink more coffee, pass out, or call her on the deception.

Clark cleared his throat. "Well, if you don't want this." He reached for the banana walnut bread.

Her hand shot out. She covered the splash with her sleeve then pressed hard against the table as she pulled her arm back, hoping to mop the coffee with her sleeve.

He opened the bread, tore off a small piece, then ate it. He smiled and passed the rest of it back to her.

"Thank you." She took a piece and put it in her mouth.

Spider could hardly taste anything over the metallic taste of fear on her tongue.

"Mm, this is good," he said. "Mind?"

She passed the bread back to him to have another bite.

He washed that bite down with more coffee.

Yes, buddy, drink up.

Spider kept working, waiting for something to happen.

After another forty minutes, she noticed that Clark was slumped over. She leaned toward him, making sure he was still breathing. He was, but it didn't seem like he'd be opening his eyes any time soon.

She could finally contact her hacker friends and ask for help.

But gunshots exploded outside before she could.

Chapter 31 - Jasper Parish

JASPER WAITED in the dark woods with Jordyn and four of Logic's soldiers for hire.

Four teams of five were stationed around the compound, waiting for the order to *GO* from the man next to Jasper. His name was Larry Coombs, ex-Army. He was in his forties, tall and thin, wiry yet athletic. His afro was short and graying. Wire-rimmed glasses gave him a professorial look.

"So," Jasper said as Larry waited on one of his men to report back to him, "how many of these guys have your kind of experience?"

Larry shook his head. "About six of 'em I brought in from around the state, a couple from Georgia. Rest are from the streets. Good with guns, but they don't necessarily have practice with shit like this."

Jasper was glad, and slightly surprised, to hear that there were six capable men ready and willing to take on a job like this with him, but he was concerned about the less skilled players. "I want to be sure they don't go in there guns blazing and get Spider killed."

"My guy sent a drone into the AC ducts and located her in the rear west bedroom on the bottom floor. We'll keep firefights to a minimum and try not to engage until we've secured the target. You and me will go in on the west flank after Carl and Jack take out the closest two guards."

Larry got on the radio with one of his men while Jordyn pulled Jasper aside. She looked pale, almost ghostly, especially under the icy moonlight.

"I have a bad feeling."

"What is it?" Jasper asked.

"Remember how I said the dominoes would fall and there'd be nothing we could do? I think this is it." Jordyn pulled her purple hoodie tighter then cradled herself. "Please be careful, Daddy."

She rarely added the *dy* to *Dad*. Only when feeling vulnerable. It reminded him of the times when Jordyn was little and she'd come to her parents' bedroom during a bad storm or after a nightmare. On one hand, he was overwhelmed by nostalgia when she called him "Daddy," but on the other, he hated to hear the fear in her voice.

"Don't worry, Jordyn, it'll all work out."

"You *don't* know that."

"No, but I do know shit isn't predestined. We can always change our fate. It's when we give up, when we don't fight — that's when fate wins. I refuse to give in and do nothing."

Jordyn shook her head then looked down, signaling that she was done discussing it.

She would sulk, instead. And as much as he loved his daughter and wanted to hug her and promise everything would be okay, they didn't have time for him to comfort her anxiety.

Larry was walking toward him.

"It's time," he said.

Chapter 32 - Mallory Black

MAL SAT in the NA meeting room curled into a ball in her seat, wearing blue jeans, a black shirt, and a green Army-styled jacket that went perfectly with her hat. She couldn't focus on a thing people were saying. She felt underwater as she waited for the door to open and for Maggie to step through it.

The meeting seemed to go on forever. By the end, Maggie still hadn't showed.

Mal ignored every attempt at small talk then traded the meeting room for the parking lot.

Headlights doused her. She looked up to see Tommy's Camaro.

The passenger side door opened, then Maggie got out.

Mal was confused as Maggie approached, eyes puffy and red.

"Tommy wants to talk to you."

Shit. This can't be good.

Mal glanced toward the car but couldn't see him beyond the glare from obnoxiously bright Xenons that practically blinded her.

No Stopping

"Wants to talk to both of us," Maggie added.

"Okay, have him step out of the car."

"He wants to talk somewhere more private, in the car."

He found the drugs.

Mal followed her to the car.

Maggie offered the front seat, but Mal insisted on sitting in back, so she could reach for her piece if Tommy tried anything.

She climbed into the back of the car.

"Where's Emma?" Mal asked as Maggie got in.

"Don't worry about her. My daughter ain't none of your concern." Tommy turned and glared at her, his eyes venomous, then past her as he peeled out of the lot.

Mal buckled her seatbelt and adjusted her jacket, putting her gun in easier reach.

Tommy glanced at her in the rearview. "I found your little present behind the glove compartment."

Fuck.

"So, thank you for that."

Mal stayed silent. No point in denying or arguing. She'd wait and see where the conversation was going.

"My only question is did my wife know what you were trying to do?"

Maggie stared straight ahead at the road, almost catatonic.

How much hell did Tommy put her through already tonight?

Mal had been so surprised to see Maggie approaching, she hadn't studied her face for bruises. And she was wearing a sweater, so Mal couldn't see her arms.

"No," Mal said.

"We've had a hell of a day, haven't we, honey?"

Maggie said nothing.

"First, cops show up at my house asking to search the place. And, of course, I can't say no 'cause I'm on parole.

But of course, you knew that, right? Then they searched the car. But, as you can see by us being together right now, they didn't find shit. Surprised?"

Still, Mal said nothing.

"Buddy of mine works security at the shopping center. He saw someone fucking around my car. My stereo was still there and no cash was missing, so I decided to do a little looking around. Lo and fucking behold, what do I find — imagine my surprise. At first, I thought it might be Christmas, but then I remembered there ain't no fuckin' Santa and ain't nobody ever given me shit for free. So, I realized someone was tryin' to set me up. And who else but another dirty fucking detective?"

Fuck. He knows who I am.

He glanced in the rearview with a smile. "Ah, yes, Mrs. Black, I do indeed know who you are. Surprised I didn't recognize you when we'd met before, seeing how famous you are. I followed your case. Hell, I even felt bad for what happened to your lil' girl, but … that was before we met. Now I see what a psycho bitch you are. Maybe it's a good thing your girl didn't grow up to be like you."

"Fuck you," Mal said through gritted teeth.

If Maggie wasn't in the car, she might've put a bullet through his head at the mention of Ashley.

"No, fuck *youuuu!*" Spittle flew from his mouth as he pounded the steering wheel.

Maggie jumped.

Mal stayed calm.

"Fuck you for trying to come between me and my family. What the hell is your deal, anyway?"

"*My deal?* My deal is I'm tired of seeing shitty guys like you abuse their wives and ruin their children's lives."

"You don't know the first thing about us!"

No Stopping

"You hit your wife and you're an addict. What more do I need to know?"

Tommy stared at Mal in the mirror, barely able to contain his rage. He might have already tried to hit her if he wasn't driving.

She welcomed such an attempt — any excuse to put him down like the rabid dog he was. In truth, she'd have more mercy for a mongrel than she did for him. A rabid dog couldn't help but turn on its people. An asshole like this had zero excuse. Mal could intimately understand bad breaks and addiction, but she could never — *would never* — understand a person who intentionally harmed those they claimed to love.

"Oh, *you're* judging *me*? I've got my shit under control. You're the weak one, in NA meetings because your life is so out of control."

"Yeah, you really have your shit together. Hitting your wife, sponging off her instead of getting a job. You're a model citizen."

Tommy met her gaze again. She smiled, really hoping he'd pull over and take a swing. But as good as it would feel to put him down, she wasn't thinking like a normal person right now. If she blew this bastard away in front of Maggie, it would fuck her up forever. Probably drive her into a worse bout with addiction. And who knew what would happen to their daughter?

Violence couldn't solve everything.

"I started thinking, you know what, I bet the media would love to know about this side of you. I saw all the articles and videos about you on that website. That one run by … what's his name? Oh, yeah, Cameron Ford. What did you do to piss *that guy* off? I wondered how much he'd pay for my story. *Corrupt Cop Frames Innocent Man.* Or maybe *Corrupt Dyke Cop Obsessed with Married Man's Wife*

Decides to Frame Him. Yeah, I like the sound of that second one better."

He had Mal's attention, but she masked her anxiety.

He turned to Maggie. "How much you think I could get for a story like that, honey?"

But Maggie didn't answer.

He reached over, grabbing her chin and turning it hard to face him. Mal wanted to break his fucking fingers.

"I don't know," Maggie finally said before he let her go. She faced forward again.

Tommy turned to Mal, smiling his big wolf smile, practically daring her to do something. "So, I started thinking about you and your lil' girl and how you probably don't need any more drama. Then I figured maybe you'd pay me *not* to tell my story."

"You've got to be fucking kidding me."

"Hey, don't act like you ain't got the money! I know you won the lotto. Rich, fucking rug muncher."

"Well, Tommy, since you're about as bad at math as you are at life choices, let's go over this. First off, when you take a lump settlement, you get significantly less. Then the government takes more than half in taxes. Like sixty-something percent. Then you subtract the money I've given to charities, or used to help victims of abuse, the cash I've lived on while I couldn't work, and—"

"You ain't poor."

Mal studied him through the mirror again. Along with the hate and fear in his eyes, she saw something else, sickeningly familiar, but in no way surprising.

Greed.

The man was thinking about dollar signs, not justice.

He didn't give a damn about how Mal had nearly ended his marriage. Sure, he was pissed she'd tried to set him up, but he was much more desperate for cash.

Paying a person off was like negotiating with terrorists. Still, it could buy her time to think of something else to extricate Maggie and Emma from this motherfucker's life.

"How much do you want?"

His eyes brightened. He had his fish on the hook and was ready to reel it in. But the wrong measure of greed could cost him everything. The asshole to be careful.

"Two-hundred grand."

"Ha!" Mal laughed. "You think you're gonna get even a tenth of that for your story? It's a fucking blog. Cameron Ford doesn't have the resources to pay you that much."

"No, but maybe I can get a book deal from some big *Jew York* publisher."

"And how long you think that'll take, Tommy? You really want to write a book and open your own life to that kind of scrutiny? No publisher in the world is gonna give you a dime before making sure you're a credible witness. And guess what? *You're not.* The media will eat you alive once they find out who you really are."

He was quiet, thinking, probably trying to figure out if he should make a counter offer.

Mal made one instead. "Tell you what, Tommy. I'll give you your two-hundred grand, but only under one condition."

His eyes flickered with hope then faded to skepticism. "Oh, yeah, and what's that?"

"What?"

"You hard of hearing?" She waited a beat. "Let them go. You can't possibly think this is gonna work out for you all, do you?"

"My wife loves me. Tell her, dear."

Maggie nodded. Hardly an overwhelming confirmation.

"She's terrified of you! She's dying to leave. You can't

be that dumb. It's the best thing for her and for Emma. Probably for you, too."

He turned to Maggie. "Is that true? I scare you?"

Maggie was quiet for a long moment, tears soaking her cheeks.

"Jesus Christ," he muttered.

Maggie finally spoke. "Yes, Tommy. You scare me. And you scare Emma. We don't feel safe."

He hit the steering wheel, so fast, so hard, and so abruptly, Maggie shrieked.

Mal gripped her gun. "See? You scare her. Let Maggie and Emma come with me. Give yourself six months to get your shit together. Use the money to check into a rehab or something. If you've changed after six months, maybe you all can try and make things work."

Tommy stared ahead, no emotion on his face. His eyes were dry, not crying like she'd expect from someone truly hurt by what Maggie had said. Maybe he was a sociopath, or so fucked on drugs he saw her only as an impediment to getting more. Maybe this was the push he needed to take the deal without feeling like the bad guy.

"So, you'll just give me the money? Then six months from now, you won't try and stop us from getting back together?"

"Not if you've gotten better. Believe it or not, this isn't about you, Tommy. I just want to see Maggie and Emma safe."

"Where am I supposed to go then?"

"You keep the house. I've got a place for them if they want it."

Tommy laughed, sounding disgusted. "Man, you really thought of everything, eh?"

"I'm only trying to help."

No Stopping

He laughed again, then turned to Maggie. "So, is that what you want then?"

But Maggie said nothing.

He pulled over on the side of the road and turned to Mal. "Can we have a moment to discuss this?"

She nodded then got out of the car.

They were on a quiet street. Mal could easily walk up to the car and put a bullet through Tommy's skull and nobody, except Maggie, would witness it.

She stared at the back windshield, seeing Tommy put his hand on the back of Maggie's neck. Was he was trying to scare her or was he actually being tender? Was a part of him still capable of being kind, or was this merely manipulation, a narcissist feigning the right emotions to grease their desires?

Maggie got out of the car. She walked up to Mal, still crying.

"He said okay. But he wants the money tonight."

Mal was going to press back, argue she didn't have that kind of money laying around. But the safe in her hotel told a different story, and right now, it was the one Maggie needed to hear most.

"Okay," she said. "Deal."

Chapter 33 - Jasper Parish

JASPER WATCHED through binoculars as someone from one of the other teams shot at a guard on the roof. The gunmen were all supposed to go down at once, but someone missed their shit.

Seconds later, the other guards on the roof started firing into the darkness.

The element of surprise had netted them only three of the guards. Now, stealth was out the window and the assault was on.

"Bring down the gate!" Larry commanded as one of his men drove a cargo truck through the front. He turned to Jasper. "Let's do this."

Jasper adjusted his ear protection and comms then followed Larry to the west side under the cover of rain and darkness, amid the misdirection of a bulk of their forces approaching from the east.

Two guards were looking that way when Jasper and Larry caught them by surprise.

The guard closest to Jasper heard him and turned, aiming his shotgun.

No Stopping

Jasper had his AR-15's barrel up faster and fired.

The man fell back, firing the shotgun blast into the stucco wall.

Jasper finished the man off as Larry felled the other guard. Then they breached a window on the side of the house.

Larry fired inside. A second later, he said, "Clear," then broke the rest of the window.

After he climbed through, Jasper followed him into the house then to a small library. The exit was closed. Larry motioned that he was going to clear the hallway, then left. The side of his head exploded in bone and blood as he caught a shotgun blast from a guard.

Fuck!

Jasper had barely known the guy, but he liked what he saw. Still, no time for grief. He aimed at the door just as Larry's killer stepped into view. Squeezed off several shots and ended the man before his AR-15 jammed.

No time to clear it. While Jasper couldn't hear footsteps above the echoing chaos of gunshots and screams, others were coming, and someone was shouting something in German.

Jasper dropped the rifle and reached for the pistol in his side holster.

Someone burst through the doorway, firing a shotgun.

They missed, just barely, wood and books taking damage to his left.

Jasper stumbled backward, raising his pistol in time to fire back. He found his target's chest and head, sending him to the ground.

Jasper fell to his knees, looked up to see if anyone else was coming, then grabbed the concussion grenade hanging from his belt. He tossed it into the hall.

After it detonated, Jasper stepped into a long corridor

with only a few doors on either side and one at the very back with a matching set of stunned BlackBriar men.

Jasper fired two more shots, both direct hits to the head, then he darted back into the library and reloaded.

Ducked back out and checked the hall.

No threats.

He headed toward the rear of the house, approaching the door he hoped would lead him to Spider. But he didn't open doors and clear each room like he normally would. He didn't know how much time he or Spider had. If someone was in there with her, every moment of delay might bring her closer to death.

Jasper raised his pistol as he approached.

A door burst open behind him. He spun around, ready to fire. But before he could squeeze off a shot and kill the giant Russian, the man violently twisted the gun from Jasper's hand.

His weapon hit the ground.

Jasper spotted the man's knife, too late. Still, he somehow managed to dodge the arcing blade. He had to take it from the Russian. He wouldn't get a second chance.

He brought his hand down on the man's wrist, keeping him from stabbing him. The Russian grunted and head-butted Jasper.

Pain splintered his skull, but he refused to bend.

Instead, he butted him back. The Russian's nose crunched on impact.

Hot blood sprayed all over Jasper's face. The Russian twisted his body, getting enough momentum to turn him around then slam him into the wall.

Jasper raised a knee. Missed the man's balls but found his gut.

The Russian wrenched his knife hand free. Came swinging again.

Jasper dodged, swiftly diving for the floor. He seized the pistol but had no time to turn. He could feel the Russian coming, blade arcing down toward Jasper's back or side as he dove.

The Russian landed on him, straddled him. Jasper rolled as best he could beneath his attacker. The knife barely missed, hitting the ground.

He raised the gun. The Russian grabbed his wrist as he fired. The shot went wide, pelting the wall.

Each man worked to wrest control from the other. Both sweated to stay alive.

Their gazes locked.

The Russian was taller and stronger than Jasper, but nowhere near as desperate. He had no higher purpose and was only trying to save himself.

But Jasper was on a mission. Adrenaline flooded through his system like a surge of electricity. He bucked, trying to knock the man off of him, but the guy weighed a thousand pounds.

Jasper struggled to turn the pistol, but the Russian moved his hand from Jasper's wrist to the barrel.

This was his only chance. Jasper let go of the gun, a dangerous move handing the gun over to his would-be killer.

The Russian's momentum caused the weapon to slip from his hand.

Jasper struck fast, his right hand finally free. He thrust two fingers at his enemy's eyes, twisted, then popped one right out of its socket.

The Russian screamed, forgetting his pistol, both hands now reaching toward the eye dangling from the hollow by its optical nerve.

Jasper grabbed the blade, raised it, then stabbed the

man repeatedly in his gut, like one prisoner shivving another.

He shoved the incapacitated and dying man backward before standing, grabbing his pistol, then putting a bullet through the Russian's skull.

Jasper turned his attention to the door at the end of the hall.

Chatter in his comms told him soldiers were communicating with one another. Some of them spoke like members of a well-trained unit while others were more colloquial.

"Yeah! Take that, motherfucker!"

Jasper aimed the gun at the door as he approached. He kicked it open then backed away, tossing his other concussion grenade inside before ducking out and hoping he hadn't hurt Spider too badly.

Her wheelchair was there, but the girl was gone.

Where had she — a bookcase had been moved aside to reveal a hidden room.

He cleared the adjoining bathroom before checking it out. It was empty, but there was an open hatch in the floor. "Damn it!"

Jasper raced over and looked down into a tunnel running under the house. "Anyone got eyes on the target?"

Several responses of *no* and *negative* bleated into his comm.

"I think they escaped," he said.

Kim and Logic appeared with his cousin, Tracy, and a few others moments later.

He didn't ask how many soldiers Logic had lost, nor did Logic update him on the obvious.

"I'm going down there," Jasper said. Then he did.

And everyone followed.

Chapter 34 - Mallory Black

MAL PULLED up to the house, hoping Maggie hadn't had another change of heart.

She hated paying off Tommy, but what good was money if she couldn't use it to help someone out of a situation? Besides, the money had apparently been a gift to her from Jasper. For a while after he told her, she thought about getting rid of it. A part of her felt like it was blood money from a serial killer, vigilante, or whatever the hell he was. Another part felt like the money was forever tied to Ashley, Jasper's attempt to make up for the fact that he hadn't been able to stop Dodd.

But then she considered the flip side. Mal had done a lot of good with the money. Helped people who really needed it. She could buy freedom for a woman like Maggie — someone who wanted to do good and needed another chance at life.

Victims like Maggie often felt trapped. They *wanted* to leave their toxic situations but doing so would be financial suicide. They might lose a spouse's healthcare or their kid would suffer. It was amazing how many miserable leashes a person could accumulate in their life, chains anchoring them to shitty situations, preventing them from living the life they wanted.

Most people could set themselves free if they saw those restraints for what they were — other people's anemic attempts to control them.

She wasn't sure what Tommy's household contributions were. The dickhead didn't have a job, so what the hell was the leash he used to keep his wife there? Mal doubted Maggie was making enough as a cashier, so Tommy must have been bringing in money somehow. Mal would make it so Maggie didn't need whatever Tommy's contribution was, whatever the current situation. She could use Jasper's money to offer Maggie and Emma a fresh start.

And who knew, maybe Tommy might get his shit together in six months.

Maybe Maggie wouldn't feel a need to take him back. Maybe she'd be strong enough to go on without him.

Or maybe Tommy would surprise everybody and actually fix his life.

But Mal knew people rarely changed for the better, especially when they had no motivation to do so. In reality, her giving Tommy money almost assured his self-destruction. And she would do what she could to protect Maggie from when he ran out of cash.

Mal wasn't sure what she'd do if he came for more money. She hated the variable hanging over her head. Part of her wondered if she shouldn't do something to nudge his self-destruction. She imagined herself standing over him as he overdosed.

Awful as it was to admit, Mal wouldn't help him. But was it truly terrible? She would never kill a venomous snake minding its business in the wild, but she sure as fuck would end one inside her house, threatening her family.

No Stopping

Tommy's a threat, just like that snake. And what do you to do a threat when it enters your house?

You exterminate it.

Now she was sounding like Jasper.

Cold rain chilled her as she got out of the car. She hurried to the door then knocked.

Tommy answered, looking oddly detached. Mal wondered if he was high or drunk as she silently handed him the envelope.

The asshole actually started counting the money in front of her.

Maggie appeared with two suitcases, eyes red and puffy again.

"Where's Emma?" Mal asked.

"At my friend's house. We didn't think she should be here for this. My friend will bring her over tomorrow." Maggie looked down and sheepishly away.

Mal could sense something wrong. Was the woman having second thoughts? Had Tommy threatened her? If she didn't drag Maggie out of there now, she might not be able to leave.

She grabbed both suitcases from Maggie.

Tommy finished counting and was suddenly all smiles. Probably already figuring out how much dope he could buy. He still had the stash Mal had planted on him, too. It was probably with a friend. No way the asshole flushed it.

"Yep, it's all here."

"I'll be waiting in the car," Mal said.

Tommy, still all smiles, said, "Pleasure doing business with you."

I hope he shoots this all into his veins and dies choking on his vomit.

Leaving them to their goodbyes, Mal rushed against the rain to put both suitcases in the trunk of her rental.

Once they were stowed, she hurried into the driver's seat then waited as the thrumming of the wipers added a beat to her anxiety.

Something felt off, but she couldn't place what.

She thumbed through her phone, checking for messages as she waited. One from Tim: *Hey there, how are you doing?*

She was about to text him back when Maggie rushed out the door then climbed into the passenger seat, wiping at her eyes.

"You did the right thing." Mal glanced at the front door to see if Tommy was standing there to wave goodbye.

He wasn't.

Probably inside counting his money again. Maybe calling his boys, or his dealer, planning a fuckhead fiesta.

"Why doesn't it *feel* right then?" Maggie asked.

Mal flipped on the heater and backed out of the driveway. "Probably because it's scary to leave the comfort of what you know, even when it's bad for you. But you *will* feel better, I promise."

"Thank you." She hugged herself.

"It's gotta be hard to start over, but I swear, it'll get easier. This was the best decision you could have possibly made for you and Emma."

Maggie stared out the window, looking lost, like she was already doubting her decision.

They drove in silence, with none of the questions Mal had expected her to ask. Nothing about the neighborhood or preschools. Not a word about Ashley. Her eyes on the wipers as if hypnotized. Mal wondered if she was high or in shock.

"How do you think Emma is going to take this?"

"I dunno," Maggie said.

"Is she going to miss him?"

No Stopping

"I think so, yeah. He doesn't spend a lot of quality time with her, and half the time when he *is* with her, he's shitty. But kids at that age love their dad no matter what. It's not like she knows better."

"Well, she will. She'll finally have a normal life."

More silence.

She wasn't sure if it was Maggie, the Kozack case Mike was working on, or perhaps even Jasper. But Mal could feel something like heat from the vents.

"So, have you thought about what you might do for a job?"

"I dunno yet. It's a long commute, and I don't have a car."

"I can help with the car. And I know the managers at a few different Publix, I can put in a good word for you. But you have to stay clean."

"Thank you. And yes, I will." Maggie shook her head. "I'll never touch the pills again."

Mal didn't believe her, though she wasn't exactly sure why. Addicts rarely made such declarations, at least not so fast or assuredly. They often talked about not wanting to, or lamented the daily battle. Maggie was acting like it was a cakewalk ahead of her, just like an addict.

Maybe she needed something to get through the night. It's hard leaving a husband who scares the hell out of you.

Mal wanted to ask if she was sober right now but decided against it.

Tomorrow was another day.

∽

MAL SHOWED MAGGIE AROUND, giving her a key to the house and the code to the security system before concluding their tour. They retired to the kitchen for coffee and conversation.

Maggie said, "I can't believe you don't stay here. It's such a beautiful house."

"It was hard after Ashley died, especially after her killer came here, tormenting me. I had to get out. Fortunately, I came into some money, so now I stay at a hotel most of the time."

"I'm sorry, I hope being here isn't bringing—"

"It's okay. There are good memories, too." Mal offered her a reassuring smile. "Like the time I was watching old eighties and nineties music videos on YouTube, trying to show Ashley what was cool when I was a kid, and she just looked so confused. It was hilarious. I never thought of myself as old. Even though I was a cop with a serious job, I always felt young at heart, like I had youthful taste. I never really loved the new stuff coming out, but I also didn't hate it. But the minute my daughter started having her own taste in music, mine felt antiquated and uncool."

"So, that's what I've got to look forward to? Becoming uncool as my parents?" Maggie laughed.

"Indeed."

"*Great.*" After a long and thoughtful moment, Maggie asked, "How often do you think of her?"

"Every day. I'm not sure what's worse, having a vivid dream where she's still alive and we're happy together only to wake up and feel the realization and hurt all over again, or lying in her bedroom and wishing I could brush her hair while telling her stories at night. All the time, I'll see a book or something in the store and think, *I should get that for Ashley*, or *I bet Ashley would love that*." Mal felt tears welling up, and she didn't want to give in and make this night about *her* pain. She finished with, "It fucking sucks."

No Stopping

Mal stood and went to the fridge for a bottle of water. She called from the kitchen, "Can I top you off?"

"No, I'm good."

Mal returned to her seat and tried to think of a way to lighten the mood. "So, any plans for tomorrow?"

"No, I wasn't sure if you were working."

"I'm on leave. Gonna hang out here as long as you guys want me to."

"Won't it be hard for you? I don't want you to feel obligated to—"

"Don't be silly. I only left because it was hard to be here alone with my thoughts. I think having other people, and another kid in the house, will help me. How do you think Emma will take this?"

"I have no idea."

"Are you scared she won't want to stay? That she'll miss her dad?"

"Yeah, but I think in time she'll get over him."

"Are they close?"

"No, not really. She loves him, but she's also always asking, 'Why is Daddy annoyed at me?'"

"Damn."

"This will be good for her in time. What about you?" Maggie asked. "Won't this cramp your style? Having a stranger and her kid crashing your space?"

"I can always go up to my office if I get sick of you.

Maggie laughed.

"Seriously, it'll be fine. I'm just hoping I can remember how to act around little kids."

"Well, she's quiet at first, so you'll have to carry the conversation. But you won't be able to shut her up once she gets to know you."

"I wouldn't have it any other way." And she meant it,

genuinely looking forward to having a little girl in her house again.

Mal didn't think she would ever be around kids again, after Ashely's murder, and certainly couldn't imagine bringing another one into the world. But maybe Maggie and Emma would help to heal her wounds and get her to a place where she would consider having another child.

She thought about Jessi and how much she'd come to care for her. They'd gone through hell, but Mal had helped her in the end. Katie was another story. Thinking about the teenager whose father was abusing Katie and her mother still brought only pain.

Mal had shot Katie's father in the line of duty, after he killed the girl's mother. Her attempts to save Katie and her mom from an awful situation had only made everything worse.

Katie blamed Mal for destroying her family. She'd gone to see the girl in the hospital after she'd emerged from her coma. Katie told her she wished they'd never met and Mal should have let her die. Now, the girl was in the foster system and had rebuffed every attempt to visit her.

Maybe everyone would have been better off if she'd left well enough alone. Sure, the girl was being abused, but at least her mom had still been alive.

Even now, Mal wondered if sometimes she hurt people more than helped them. Would Maggie regret taking her help? Would Tommy flip out and kill her and Emma?

Maggie stretched her arms with a yawn. "Well, hate to be a party pooper, but I'm beat."

Mal showed her to the master bedroom. It was hers and Emma's until she made the guest room into a space for the girl. She didn't want anyone in Ashley's room or for anyone to change it. But that's where Mal would sleep for now.

No Stopping

She brushed her teeth, got undressed, then climbed into Ashley's bed and snuggled with her daughter's old stuffies, inhaling her scent which still lingered on the pillow. She thought of better days, back when her baby girl was still alive, bright with smiles and giggles.

Those memories eventually sent her to sleep.

~

THE NIGHTMARES CAME — Paul Dodd tying her up on Ashley's bed and worse.

Mal woke up with a loud cry in a cold sweat. She couldn't be in Ashley's room anymore.

That monster had tainted the one sacred place left in her house. She sobbed, tearing the sheets and blankets from the bed, wailing *WHY?* on repeat before collapsing to the floor where she continued to tremble.

"I just want you back," she blubbered, "I just want you back."

She needed her pills. The only thing that dulled the pain and got her through moments like these. The only thing that made life without Ashley anywhere near bearable.

Just one pill. To get through the night.

The sound of a car door slamming yanked Mal out of her ugly little moment and back to the present.

Maybe Tommy found out where she lived and had come to harm Maggie. And probably her.

She looked out the window and saw his Camaro pulling out of her driveway.

What the fuck?

Mal grabbed her gun, bounded down the stairs, then ran out the front door.

The Camaro's headlights were already at the end of the street and turning.

A scream would be worthless, so Mal went back inside and slammed the door, fearing what she might find in Maggie's room.

Would she be dead?

Or … gone?

She raced back upstairs and found the room empty, bed neatly made with a sheet of legal pad sitting atop it.

Dear Mallory,

I'm going back to Tommy.

He made me lie to you until he got what he wanted.

He said not to come after us, or he'll go to the media. He also recorded you that night in the car.

Sorry.

I really wish we could've started over here, but it's a pipe dream. And if there's one thing I've learned in my life, the moment you start believing in pipe dreams is the moment someone will pull the world out from under you.

Sorry,
Maggie

Mal stared at the note in her trembling hand.

Then she screamed and turned her knuckles bloody.

Chapter 35 - Spider

THE VAN STOPPED. Spider's heartbeat kicked into overdrive.

They'd escaped through a tunnel before she was blindfolded then shoved into the back of a van. They'd only driven about ten minutes, so not too far. Now she was wondering why they'd stopped.

Were they already at their safehouse or whatever?

Or ... had they planned to kill her and dump her in the woods.

She'd heard Victor and Clark arguing in the front, but she'd only made out a few words:

"When she's done," Victor had said.

But *what* when she was done? Were they going to set her free or kill her?

Maybe they decided to take care of her now. Running would be easier without a cripple in the back of their van.

Spider sat up, wishing she could remove her blindfold, but her hands were cuffed behind her back.

Muffled voices preceded the sound of the rear doors opening.

"It's just me." Clark climbed into the van.

"Where are we?"

"Had to move locations. Everything will be fine."

"What happened back there?"

Victor's voice was angry and stressed to the point of breaking. "What happened? Your fucking 'Professor' attacked with his thug buddies. Killed a lot of good men tonight. And for what? Nothing!"

"What happened to him?" Spider asked.

"Get her set up," Victor said, without giving her an answer. "We've got work to do. This shit ends tonight."

Ends tonight? Is he expecting a miracle?

He'd severed the tip of her pinky. What else might he do to make her work faster?

Spider flinched as she felt hands at her shoulders.

Clark said, "I just need you to lie back so I can move you. I'll take off your blindfold once we're inside."

She allowed him to gently lay her back, his hand under her head.

She heard pacing, then a ringing phone.

"Yes, we're here," Victor said before walking off out of earshot.

Clark pulled Spider to the edge of the cargo bed then lifted her with a slight grunt.

She felt utterly helpless as he carried her.

"Where's my wheelchair?"

"Had to leave it behind."

Shit. That's not good. They're gonna kill me.

"We'll get you a new one. Not a problem."

Clark kept walking. Judging from the sounds of the building, it was indeed a house. The walls felt close, not far apart.

They ascended a flight of stairs. Clark lifted her in a modified fireman's carry. She felt embarrassed with his hand across the back of her thighs, especially since she couldn't feel how high it was.

He set her down in a swivel chair. "Hold on a moment."

Then she heard him walk out.

Spider rolled forward a bit and hit what felt like a desk.

She heard him returning and moved her chair back to where it had been. After what sounded like he put down bags, he walked over to her then removed her blindfold.

Spider was in a small bedroom with plain white walls scuffed with black marks. It was furnished with only a desk and a bed with a bare mattress, nothing else. The window was boarded up.

Clark met her gaze. "I'm going to remove your handcuffs. Don't do anything stupid."

"What the hell am I gonna do?"

He went behind her and unlocked her restraints. In a low voice, he said, "We'll just pretend you didn't drug me."

Shit. He knows it was me.

The cuffs came off.

He got in front of her again then kneeled. His stare was intense. She wanted to look away but didn't.

Clark looked at the door behind him to make sure nobody was coming, then with his voice still low, he said, "If I told him what you did, he would tell me to kill you."

"I'm sorry," Spider whispered. "But I know you all are going to kill me, anyway."

"Do your job, and I'll do whatever I can to make sure you live through this."

Spider wanted to believe him, but Victor was his boss. What could he do? It's not like Clark had stopped him from cutting off her finger.

Still, something in his eyes felt like a promise, and she

needed something to hang on to, even if that something was a lie.

"I'm going to set you up here, then you're going to finish this, okay?"

Spider nodded.

"I'll be working with you. We'll get this done together. Do you understand?"

"Yes, sir," she said with a nod.

They were up and running minutes later. Spider worked diligently, considering her next best move. She still wanted to reach out to her hacker friends, but she needed to get her location first, then hope the Professor was still alive or that cops would actually come to save her.

Would Clark leave her alone again? He had to go to the bathroom at some point. Would he kill the wi-fi connection every time he left her alone?

She was tracking down a few more domains when she heard Victor scream for Clark — a terrible bellow that had her heart pounding and adrenaline pumping.

Something happened.

Had the website gone live?

And if so, how long until they put a bullet in her skull?

Clark glanced at Spider. He looked like he was going to turn off her wi-fi but rushed out the door instead.

She went to work immediately, tracking down her IP address and location then bringing up the hacker forum in a separate window.

"We are fucked!" Victor screamed from the other room.

Clark said something inaudible.

Victor shouted again. "It's too fucking late!"

"We know the domain now," Clark tried to argue. "She can take it down."

No Stopping

"What part of *it's too fucking late* do you not understand?"

Spider got the info she needed then sent a message to her friends. Would they get it in time to even do anything?

Victor sounded seconds away from going nuclear.

Footsteps marched toward her door.

No, no, no, no!

Spider quickly closed out the windows as the door exploded open.

"You failed!" Victor screamed, jabbing a finger at her.

"What happened?"

"The website is live. It's too late."

"I can hack it," she pleaded. "Tell me the URL. I'll get in and—"

Victor yanked a pistol from his pocket then aimed the barrel at her forehead.

"No, just give me a chance!" Spider raised her hands in front of her face, as if they could stop a bullet.

Victor glared down the barrel at her, hate in his eyes. This wasn't her fault, but he needed somewhere to target his anger, and Spider might as well have been wearing a bull's-eye.

"Killing me won't change any of this. You'll just be adding murder to your charges," Spider said, trying to defend herself. "Please, let me help you."

"*Help me?* How are *you* going to *help* me?"

"Let me at the site. I'll—"

"No. It's over."

"Please," she begged again, now crying. "You don't have to do this. You're not a murderer, are you? Just leave me somewhere. I won't tell anyone anything. Just—"

"Enough!"

"Sir, she's right. There's no need to kill her. The genie is out of the bottle."

Hope swelled in her. Maybe Clark could convince Victor to free her.

"So, what?" Victor said, turning to Clark. "We set her free and expect her to pretend none of this ever happened? She's seen my face. She's seen *your* face."

"I won't tell anyone. I swear! I just wanna go home."

Clark said, "I trust her. She won't say anything. There's no need for her to, right?"

He looked at her, and she was starting to believe Clark could win him over.

"Right. I swear, just let me go. I won't tell anybody anything. I swear on my parents' lives."

Victor laughed at her then turned back to Clark. "Wow, are you *really* buying her Poor Lil' Girl act? She and her *Professor* stole my money. This girl isn't a saint, and she fucking drugged you. You think I didn't know about that? That I wasn't monitoring you both? You got sloppy and too trusting."

"Yeah, but she—"

"What, Clark? She *what?*"

"There's already enough of a shit storm coming for us. Why add to it? They don't have you for murder. And the stuff they do have us for, we can insist the bosses made us do it."

Victor's warped expression in response to Clark's suggestion that they rat out the bosses wasn't good. He put the gun to her forehead.

She let out a welp, followed by a series of pleas, but Victor ignored her and turned to Clark.

"I'm really starting to question your loyalty. You're going to betray the company that's put food on your table and given your life purpose?"

Clark's shoulders went back, his eyes narrowing on Victor. "Sir, my loyalty is to *you*, not this company. Especially not after they forced us into this shady shit. I don't think you knew what we were getting into. And I will continue to stay loyal, *to you*. But damn this company for what it's done. You want me to take the fall for you, I will. But, please, let her go. She's a kid, for Christ's sake."

Victor stared at Clark.

And, for the first time, he appeared to be swayed.

But then he said, "Loyal to me? Okay, Clark, prove it. Kill her."

No, no, no, no!

"Please, don't. Please." She hated begging, but everything was different with a gun to her head.

Victor offered his weapon to Clark. "Go ahead. Prove your loyalty."

"No." He shook his head, refusing the gun.

So Victor raised it. He fired several thunderous shots.

Clark's body jerked with each bullet that slammed into his torso. He stumbled then fell backward.

Spider screamed.

Victor turned to her. "Now, tell me who you messaged."

Chapter 36 - Jasper Parish

JASPER WAS DRIVING around the town in the pouring rain with Jordyn, waiting for her to pick up on a signal from Spider.

"Nothing yet?" he asked.

She shook her head, still turning the unicorn over and over in her hand.

"Keep trying." He kept driving aimlessly, staying in the unincorporated part of the county.

The longer he drove around, the he feared they were leaving town. And the longer he waited, the farther they got.

Logic and Kim were regrouping with the soldiers who survived the ambush. Logic said they'd contact Jasper if they'd heard anything. But that seemed increasingly less likely as minutes fell to an hour. Darkness would soon bleed into daylight. If he didn't find her soon, he might not find her alive.

If they'd at least seen a vehicle, he could've called Mallory and asked her to have one of her deputy pals to put out a BOLO or something. But right now, they had nothing beyond Jordyn's unreliable abilities.

She stared out the window, jaw clenched like something was wrong. Had she seen something and was afraid to tell him?

Is Spider dead?

"What is it?" Jasper asked.

"It's on you if something happens to her." When he didn't respond, she added, "You brought her into this. You put her on their radar."

"She works with me. This is what she's good at."

"So, what, you were just offering her an opportunity? Couldn't find another hacker? She was the *only* one? She's still a kid, Dad."

Jasper didn't like her accusatory tone.

"She already works for the dealers around her. Not like I twisted her arm. If anything, I was giving her this job so she could get out of this life."

"You could've just given her the money, no strings. Right?"

"I tried to give her money before, and she insisted on earning it. Remember?"

"You shouldn't have had her working on this."

"How the hell was I to know they'd find her?"

"You knew it was a possibility."

"Yeah, and I tried to get her to leave. She *chose* to stay."

"She didn't know what these people were capable of. You did. So, like I said, it's on you if she dies. Same for everyone else who died tonight. You just *haaaad* to get revenge, and—"

"This isn't about revenge."

"Whatever." Jordyn crossed her arms.

Jasper slapped the steering wheel. "Why are you doing this?"

"Doing *what?*" She kept staring out the window.

"Making me feel like shit. You think I'm not worried sick? You think I feel *good* about her being taken? I don't need you reminding me of what a shitty father I am."

She turned to him, confusion knitting her brow.

"Shitty *father?* What's that got to do with this? This is about Spider." Then, after a moment of silence, she said, "Oh, yeah."

And as she said it, Jasper remembered again, how he hadn't been there for Jordyn when she needed him most, and how alone she had been when taking her life.

Then she was gone again, only the unicorn sitting on her otherwise naked seat.

"Please come back," he said to no one.

Jasper drove in silence, his heart aching, praying he hadn't let another young woman down.

He'd failed to save his own daughter.

He'd failed to save Ashley.

He'd failed to keep Paul Dodd from taking Jessi and Mal a second time.

And now he was on the cusp of yet another failure. He couldn't afford to fuck up again. Well, that horse had left the barn already. What he couldn't do is allow Spider to die because of his sloppiness.

Jordyn was right.

Spider was only in this mess because of him. That's why it hurt so fucking much to hear Jordyn say it. She saw through his self-deception. No one else knew who and what he really was.

Jasper hated what she saw.

Hated himself.

His phone buzzed with a text.

He slowed down to look at the screen. The message was from an unknown number.

No Stopping

. . .

Friend of Spider's.
 She's in danger.
 Hurry.
 12251 NW 4th Street
 Creek County

Jasper plugged the address into his GPS. He was only a few blocks away — too far from Butler to wait for backup.

Might very well be walking into a trap but he couldn't ignore the text.

He considered forwarding the message to Kim but too many people had died tonight already. He couldn't add another name to the list.

Jasper would do it alone. Or die trying.

Chapter 37 - Jasper Parish

IT WAS AN UNASSUMING TWO-STORY HOUSE, backing up to a long fence and trees that served a barrier between the neighborhood and the strip mall behind it.

Jasper parked at the end of the street in the swale of an abandoned-looking house. Heavy rain served as decent cover for any neighbors who might glance over and wonder why there was a car where it probably shouldn't be. He watched the property through binoculars.

No car in the driveway. The lights were either off or the windows were covered with shutters or curtains. Jasper turned to the empty seat beside him.

"I could really use you now, Jordyn."

Still no response.

"I need you to help me see what I'm getting into. I might be walking into a trap."

But Jasper was on his own.

He holstered his gun and got out of the car.

Jasper didn't bother with a mask. He didn't want anything getting in the way of his visibility or hearing as the wind and rain were already doing a number on both.

Besides, he didn't plan on leaving any enemies alive who might be able to identify him.

He kept to the sidewalk as he ambled toward the house, alert for any movement. Jasper had to look everywhere. If this was a trap, a sniper could be in any of the houses, sitting in the dark, staring through a scope and waiting for the perfect shot.

Jasper reached the end of the block. He approached the house, scanning the windows, ensuring the curtains were closed and the lights were all off.

He circled to the sliding glass door in back, placed a leather-gloved palm against it, then slowly slid it open. But then he stopped.

It's a trap. No way they left the door open unless it's a trap.

His instincts screamed to leave, but he couldn't go anywhere without knowing if Spider was inside.

He slid the door another inch. Gun in hand, he pressed in, brushing the curtains aside, bracing for someone to hit him.

It was quiet inside, save for the low hum from an AC and some unnamed appliances. Soaking wet, he worried his shoes would squish on the floors. Fortunately, the house had carpet to absorb both the water and noise.

He swept the bottom floor but found nothing.

Climbed the stairs, stepping carefully. Of course, if this was a trap, they already knew he was in the house. Probably were watching from cameras, either in another room or remotely. Maybe they'd trigger a bomb once he reached the top floor.

Still, Jasper had to press forward.

The second story was dark, save for light bleeding from a room at the end of the hall.

There was also the sound of typing at the end of the hall.

Was it Spider, working for them? If so, where were her keepers?

Jasper had to pass three other doors before reaching his goal. He opened each one, slightly, gun raised, just to make sure nobody was inside them. Went room to room, finger on the trigger, ready to fire the second someone came at him or he found an enemy.

But the rooms were all empty, except for the neatly made and naked furniture. The place reminded him of a model home.

Now, only the door at the end of the hall remained.

Jasper drew his gun, aiming as he approached.

Best to go in bold. Use the element of surprise.

He kicked in the door.

Spider lay face down on the ground, blood pooling beneath her.

His heart stopped. Breath left his body as anguish rolled in. He fell to the ground, desperate for her pulse.

Faint, but there!

He turned her over and saw the gunshot to her belly. He ripped his shirt from the bottom, formed a makeshift rag, then pressed it against the wound.

Spider opened her eyes. They fluttered with barely enough strength to stay open, recognition barely there. She opened her mouth, but only blood dribbled from her lips.

Jasper grabbed his phone, dialed 9-1-1. Told the dispatcher to send help.

She closed her eyes again.

"No, no, no, stay with me, stay with me."

He remained on the line with dispatch, giving details. "Tell them she's bleeding out. They need to get here, stat."

Jordyn's accusation echoed in his mind as he answered the dispatcher's questions.

If something happens to her, this is on you.

No Stopping

But as her words haunted him, he heard the sound of typing again. His eyes found the phone under the table, playing the sound of deception.

Shit!

He spun around.

Victor charged, wielding a bat.

Jasper was too late to stop him.

Chapter 38 - Mallory Black

MAL COULDN'T SLEEP, so she returned to her hotel then got skunk drunk before finally crashing.

She woke to the obnoxiously loud chime of her phone.

Her head throbbed. She felt like shit, but at least she'd stayed away from the pills.

One small victory.

She grabbed her phone, squinted at the screen.

Tim never called in the morning.

"Hey."

"Hey, Mal. How long you been up?"

"Does 'I'm not up yet' count as an answer? Why?"

"I need to talk to you before you see the news. I'm downstairs."

"See *what* on the news?"

"Can I come up?"

"Yes." Fear fucked with her gut and doused her hangover in flames.

She got out of bed, threw on some sweats and a long-sleeved tee, not even bothering with a bra. Then she opened the door, waiting for Tim.

No Stopping

The elevator dinged. He got off, sorrow in his eyes.

He had bad news, and she was scared at what it might be. For a moment, Mal wondered if she was dreaming and Tim was here to tell her Ashley's body had been found.

Then she thought about Jessi Price. But how would Tim know before anyone else reached out? Maybe it was Jasper. Tim knew just enough about the situation, maybe he pieced together some stuff on his own and now the vigilante was dead.

"Hey, Mal," Tim said, hugging her for too long.

"What is it?"

"Let's go inside."

She let him into the room, then they sat on her couch. "Come on, Tim, you're starting to freak me the fuck out. What is it?"

"I was working a case, low-rent drug dealer named Tommy Wilkes."

Oh, fuck.

Tommy ratted me out! Tim is here to arrest me. Fuck, fuck, fuck, fuck.

Mal kept quiet, letting him talk.

"Anyway, I've had eyes on him ever since we got an anonymous tip. We knew he hid a large stash of drugs, just not where."

Fuck. Fuck. Fuck. Fuck.

"And I saw you there last night, leaving with Maggie and a suitcase. Were you two close?"

Where the hell is this going? How should I answer? Does he think we had the drugs in the suitcase, that I was somehow involved?

Mal wondered if Tim could see the fear in her eyes. If he could see her wheels turning as she anticipated his line of questioning and prepared her careful responses.

Of course he could. Tim had too much experience

dealing with addicts, liars, and criminals to miss the obvious. Even a cop could be lousy at hiding their lying eyes.

"How do you know her?" Tim asked.

She was suddenly cold and shivering.

"We met in NA. Tommy was abusing Maggie, and I offered her a place to stay, at my house. Brought her there last night, but then woke up to find them leaving. She left a note saying she was sorry, but she was going back."

Mal was leaving out major details, particularly the parts involving her paying off Tommy and planting drugs in his Camaro.

But Tim probably already knows both. That's why he's here.
You're FUCKED.

"Why are you asking me about this?" Mal hoped she looked more innocent than she probably sounded.

Tim reached for her hands then held them. Only then did she know why he was there. He wasn't there to bust her. He'd come to Mal's room because he was sorry for her loss.

"There's no easy way to say this, but this morning dispatch got a call from Maggie saying that her little girl had somehow found Tommy's pills and OD'd." Tim swallowed and squeezed her hands. "She's dead, Mal."

"No, no, no," Mal said, tears welling, heart cracking in two, lips trembling.

"She told dispatch she'd killed Tommy and was going to kill herself."

"No … " Her voice cracked, the dam breaking. "Is … is she dead?"

Tim nodded.

The dam finally broke. And so did Mal.

Chapter 39 - Victor Forbes

Victor still couldn't reach his sister.

He'd been calling ever since the news broke and had the distinct feeling he was too late. She was dead already.

He pulled up to the gate outside Kozack's ranch.

Oliver waited in the dark, bundled in a heavy coat, smoking a cigarette.

Victor rolled down the window.

"That's him?" Oliver peered into the van.

"Yes."

"Go on through. Pull the van into the workshop in back."

Victor could hardly see the workshop, save for the fuzzy lights cutting through the fog ahead. He drove through the open door, parked beside a tractor, then killed the engine. A glance behind him showed his captive was still unconscious. Victor had secured Jasper after knocking him out, then drugged the man to make sure he would never be a problem again. He climbed out of the van.

Oliver entered the workshop then closed the door. "You really stepped in it, eh?"

He wasn't in the mood for a lecture, but Oliver held the keys to his freedom— passage to Mexico and a quarter million in exchange for the man who murdered his son.

"Yes, and thanks for helping me out. I owe you."

Oliver didn't respond, stepping past Victor for another glance inside the van. "How do I know he's the one?"

"Because, as I told you on the phone, he's a dead man. He blamed your son for his daughter's suicide. Said he raped her. Went to the police, then faked his death after you pulled strings to snuff the investigation, biding time to exact vengeance."

"He tell you all that?" Oliver said, studying him.

But Victor had been reading people longer than most and knew with certainty Oliver had already bought his story. The man was desperate for answers, and Victor was handing them over. Now he was negotiating, hoping to whittle the price. Oliver had him over a barrel, powerless, now that he'd delivered Jasper.

BlackBriar issued a response claiming ignorance of the entire fiasco within an hour after the news broke. Whatever evidence there might have been of their involvement was surely gone. Anyone who might ask questions would have already been paid off. Victor was a man without a nation. The fall guy. He might never make it to a trial. BlackBriar could have him killed before he had a chance to testify against the people behind it all.

Oliver smiled. "Don't worry, I'm not trying to change the terms. Well, not entirely."

"Oh?" Victor braced for whatever he might say next.

"I just have to know — how many famous people were involved in that pedophile ring? Were all the names really released?"

"I haven't seen the list, but yes, there were quite a few influential people on it."

No Stopping

"Damn." Oliver shook his head. "And how did you all keep it secret for so long?"

Victor hadn't figured Oliver for a gossiper, but he was a powerful man who enjoyed having knowledge that others didn't. So, Victor would give him some meat to chew on.

He told him how they'd collected evidence to keep anyone from ever going to the authorities. If someone posed a threat, BlackBriar neutralized it.

"You had hit men? You *murdered* people?"

Victor nodded. "Find me an empire that doesn't have blood on its hands."

"Fair enough, but … didn't you ever feel weird protecting pedophiles?"

"Not my call. I was a good soldier, doing my duty. I thought I was doing good for the first couple years, believe it or not. Once I realized what was happening, I couldn't leave. Fuckers killed my mother, and probably my sister. They knew all my weaknesses."

"Damn." Oliver shook his head. "So, what will you do in Mexico?"

"Try and live a normal life." Victor wanted to end the conversation. "So, what's the arrangement? Is someone coming to pick me up? Are you taking me?"

Another voice answered, someone else in the workshop.

Victor turned around to see the former sheriff of Creek County, standing there with a shit-eating grin and a gun aimed at Victor.

"On your knees."

Victor turned, glaring at Oliver. "We had a deal!"

"On your fucking knees, boy!" Barry shouted.

Oliver smiled at Victor. "Sorry, Mr. Forbes, but it would be a federal crime to help you escape. I've worked too damned hard to lose everything aiding someone like you."

"You motherfucker," Victor growled.

Barry's foot found the back of Victor's knees, sending him to the ground. He was cuffed in seconds, faster than the fat old bastard should be able to move.

Victor swung his leg, knocking Barry back.

Barry's gun fell to the dirt.

Victor dove for it.

A gunshot boomed behind him. "Stop!"

Victor's hand fell just short of the pistol as he froze.

Oliver was aiming a pistol at him. "Go ahead, make me a hero."

Barry stood then finished cuffing Victor. Only after his hands were securely behind him did the former sheriff grab him by the back of his hair and smack him in the face.

"Don't you ever fucking try that shit again!"

This time, Victor didn't move.

Barry got on his phone and made another call. "Yes, I've got him. Come and get us. Just outside Kozack's place."

Victor glared at Oliver, who was lighting two cigars. Victor yelled, "He's got Jasper Parish in the back of his van! Ask him what he's gonna to do to him!"

"What's that?" Barry said. "I didn't hear ya', boy. Speak up."

"Fuck you."

Oliver looked down at Victor and blew a ring of smoke in his face. "You tell anyone else about Parish, and I'll make sure your sister is killed."

What?

Oliver winked and smiled.

No Stopping

Sirens brayed just outside.
Barry grabbed him by his cuffed hands. "Come on."
Victor had no choice but to obey.

Chapter 40 - Jasper Parish

Jasper knew he was dreaming, but he didn't want to wake up.

At least in his dreams, his wife and daughter were both alive.

And he was still a good man — an officer of the law.

Once upon a time, things had been normal.

They were driving to a restaurant in West Palm Beach that Carissa had wanted to try.

Jasper looked over at her, and they traded a smile. It ached like only a memory can.

"Dad?" Jordyn said from the back seat.

But Jasper couldn't talk. He stared into Carissa's crystalline eyes instead. He should be looking at the road, but he was trying to decipher something in her expression. Her eyes held a secret, and if he was patient enough to decode it, he might find his way back to them both.

"Dad," Jordyn repeated.

He kept staring, feeling his body moving through space and time.

An acrid odor burned his nostrils.

No Stopping

"Wake up, Dad!"

Jasper woke to the smell of gasoline. He was cold and soaked in fuel, arms bound behind his back. He opened his eyes, recoiled from the sting of gasoline and a bright light shining on him. With effort, he made out a room with metal walls, maybe a shed, and someone else silhouetted in the light before him, sitting in a chair about ten feet away.

Victor?

He remembered finding Spider bleeding to death. He had to get her help.

Jasper squinted, trying again to see past the blinding light. But that was impossible.

He closed his eyes, pulling at the cuffs binding his wrists behind him.

What does this fucker want? And why did he pour gas on me?

"Do you know who I am, Mr. Parish?"

How does he know my name?

Jasper blinked until he could see something beyond the blur and agony.

The man stepped closer, and he could finally see who was speaking.

Something died in his stomach.

"Oliver Kozack."

"So, you do," said the man.

Jasper heard the man shifting something back and forth in his hands. He opened his eyes again but couldn't see what Kozack was holding.

Something small.

A gun?

A knife?

He heard the man walk toward him.

His eyes shot open, afraid of what Kozack was going to do. Jasper looked to his left and right as his captor turned on a video camera perched on a tripod to his right.

Fucker wants a confession.

"I've brought you here to answer some questions."

"Why'd you pour gas on me?"

"Fail to answer my questions and I'll be forced to extract them." He tossed the item in his right hand over to his left.

Jasper finally saw what it was.

Kozack flipped the lid of his metal lighter open and closed. "Where is my son?"

"Who?" Jasper asked.

Kozack glared at him, shoved the lighter in his pocket, then walked over to a bench and returned with a hammer. He brought it down on Jasper's right knee cap.

Jasper screamed as pain exploded through his body.

Kozack stepped closer.

Jasper wanted him near enough that he could use his legs to attack.

But Kozack was smart enough to stay a safe distance away.

Jasper might've been able to launch himself forward, but the torment in his knee made that action impossible. Now, if he tried anything, he'd be lucky to not fall on his face.

He breathed through clenched teeth as Kozack walked toward him, keeping to his side, then pressing the cold metal hammer against Jasper's cheek, hard enough to hurt his teeth.

"I'm going to ask you again. I suggest you give me a better answer."

"I don't know," Jasper said.

"Wrong answer!" Kozack screamed, raised his hand, then brought the hammer down onto Jasper's other knee.

"Fuck!" Jasper roared.

Jordyn appeared. "Tell him, Dad."

No Stopping

"Get out, baby!" he shouted, not wanting Kozack to hurt her.

He wheeled, looked around, then turned back to Jasper. "Who the fuck are you talking to?"

Is he fucking with me?

Why isn't he attacking Jordyn?

"Get out," Jasper begged her.

"He can't see me, Dad. Remember?"

"Remember what?"

And then he did, and the old, familiar sadness washed over him.

He remembered the dream, driving Carissa and Jordyn to West Palm Beach.

God, how he wished he could be with them again.

Even if it meant death.

That would be preferable to a miserable existence like this.

Kozack smacked him across the face. "Hey, Crazy, who the hell are you talking to?"

But Jasper refused to answer.

"Please, Dad. Tell him. He's going to kill you."

"Good." Jasper smiled at Kozack. Then, despite the pain, he started laughing.

Kozack stared, perplexed by his response to torture.

"You can't kill me," Jasper whispered.

And Kozack said nothing, narrowing his eyes at Jasper before swinging the hammer at his face.

Jasper didn't flinch, and the hammer didn't connect.

He looked Kozack in the eyes and his smile widened. "You can't kill me. Go ahead. Try."

"Dad!" Jordyn cried.

"Do it!" Jasper yelled.

Kozack screamed back, "Where is my son?"

Jasper saw a way out of this. A way to end it all and

join his family again — assuming there was an afterlife and he wasn't already on the way to Hell for all he'd done.

Big assumptions, but worth the risk.

"He's dead," Jasper said.

Kozack stared at him, the first cracks in his bravery showing.

Another smile. "I killed him."

Kozack's lip began to tremble. "Why?"

"Because your son raped my daughter and recorded it. Had someone else rape her, too. Recorded that shit and put it out there for the world to see. After that, my daughter killed herself."

"No," Kozack said, shaking his head. "My son would never rape anyone. Your daughter was probably some whore looking for a payday. Fuck my son then try and blackmail him for my money."

Jasper shook his head, still smiling. "You don't really believe that. How many sexual assaults have you gotten him out of?"

"Fuck you," he spat.

"Your son was a monster."

"Fuck you!" Kozack yelled louder, stepped closer. Raised his hammer over Jasper's head, ready to strike him dead.

Jasper met his hateful gaze. "Your son was a monster, and I take monsters out of this world."

Kozack struck. But instead of hitting Jasper in the head, the hammer crunched into his shoulder.

The pain was ludicrous, nearly made him black out.

But a hard smack across the face from Kozack brought him back. "Where is my son's body?"

Jasper wanted him to finish. Wanted to push the fucker over the edge. He smiled, surely more of a grimace — the best he could do through the pain.

No Stopping

"I dunno. A bit of him here, a bit of him there. You'll never find enough to make a proper ID."

Kozack screamed and dropped the hammer. It fell to the concrete with a clang. He punched Jasper in the jaw, then the nose, then repeatedly in his face.

The agony was too much, but Jasper had to push Kozack into finishing him off.

"Dad, no! Stop it — *don't push him!*"

Oliver pummeled his chest and stomach, even hit Jasper in the balls.

His universe was a torment, but he had to hold on.

Kozack stepped away, staring down at his bloodied fists. "I'm going to kill you."

"Good idea." Jasper spat blood through broken teeth. He laughed again, his eyes so swollen he could hardly see Kozack. "That still won't make your son any less of a monster."

He heard the lighter's lid flip again.

Good.

He's gonna do it. Just another nudge.

"Do you know what Calum said to me before he died?"

Silence.

He could hear Kozack breathing. And crying.

"You wanna know?" Jasper asked again, still smiling.

"What?"

"He said he blamed you for raping my daughter. He told me you were such a disappointment as a father, such a fucking failure, that you ruined him. You made him into the monster I had to kill."

"You're lying." Kozack furiously shook his head. "He never said that."

Jasper had a flash, a memory, either from Calum or maybe his father.

"Don't do it, Dad," Jordyn said.

Jasper laughed. "You wanna know the moment you ruined your boy?"

Kozack said nothing.

Jasper could feel his fear in waves.

"Don't, Dad. Please."

"Callum was six or seven. He broke a window on one of your cars. You beat the hell out of him, but that wasn't what broke him. It was the next day, when you didn't even ask him if he was okay. Then the next week, when you wouldn't even look at him. Your son was sobbing when he told me all that and more, begging me to kill you instead of him. Since it was your fault for making him a monster."

Jasper couldn't see Kozack, but he could clearly hear his cries.

Jordyn came closer, touching her father's shoulders. She might have been looking up at him, but Jasper saw nothing.

He heard the lighter's lid flipping open again.

"He *begged* me to kill you before I finished him off. But you know what I said? I told him that his daddy was right, he *was* a fucking disappointment. All your boy could do was cry. I slit his fucking throat once I got tired of hearing it."

Kozack screamed and rushed him.

Jasper fell back and slammed his head on the concrete.

The world swam above him.

Jasper just had to let go and welcome his death.

He heard the lighter flick again, then Kozack's muffled voice. "You know what? I *was* going to kill you. I wanted revenge. But I don't want your pain to end. I want you to live with it like I do. Live with loss of your daughter, forever."

What is he doing?

Is he setting me free?

No Stopping

There was a pause, then a few beeps as Kozack called somebody. "Yes, Sheriff Barry. I'd like to turn in the murderer of my son and Brianna."

"Hey!" Jasper yelled.

Kozack ignored him.

"Kill me, you pussy!"

Still, Kozack said nothing.

"You're a pussy just like your fucking son!"

He heard Kozack's footsteps walking toward him.

Yes! Do it! Finish me!

Pain tore through his head, then Jasper saw the purity of darkness.

JASPER WAS DRIVING with his wife and daughter again.

The road was clear, the sun hanging bright ahead. Inviting rather than blinding, like a cartoon sun with a big smile, the kind he used to watch with Jordyn when she was still little.

He glanced over at Carissa. "I'm here, baby. I'm here."

Carissa leaned in and kissed him.

"Can we get ice cream after dinner?" Jordyn asked, leaning forward from the back seat.

Carissa said, "Of course."

Jordyn patted his shoulder. He touched her hand as he kept his attention on the road.

Carissa leaned into him, smelling like sweet peas.

They were finally together again.

He turned on the radio, hoping to find some music Jordyn and Carissa could sing along to. But there was no music. Only beeping.

Confused, Jasper reached to turn the station.

But the beeping only got louder.

He looked over at Carissa. "What's that?"

She appeared equally baffled. Then her face began to melt.

"Mom!" Jordyn cried out. Her face was dissolving, too.

The brightness was suddenly everywhere, the sun now blinding him.

Screaming, Jasper opened his eyes in the middle of a surgery, blinding light above.

The doctor yelled something to a nurse.

Then Jasper faded away.

Epilogue 1

Mal sat alone on the lounge chair of her hotel room balcony, staring at the moon above a glittering ocean.

The cool and salty night air blew her hair back. She loved watching the moonlight as it glistened on the waves.

Such a beautiful night to die.

She was sitting with a half-empty bottle in one hand, her bottle of pills in the other, trying to think of a single reason not to end it all.

Her phone rang, again.

Still Tim.

She let the call tickle her voicemail, wondering if her mailbox was full by now. It had been three days since he'd told her the news about Emma and Maggie, three days since she'd breathed a word to anyone other than room service.

The world was a shit show, and Mal was exhausted by it all. Tired of pretending life could promise more than suffering. She tried to think of anything good that she could hold on to. A lone example of things working out for the better.

Epilogue 1

Three days ago, the world found out about the pedophile network. Several high-profile politicians, businessmen, and actors had either been arrested or gone into hiding. A few had killed themselves. While that might have seemed like a victory in the battle between Good and Evil, it was chased by terrible news the very next day.

Victor Forbes had been caught, by none other than former Sheriff Claude Barry. To make matters worse, Forbes somehow 'hung himself' while in custody at Creek County Corrections.

A hit job for sure, and Gloria Bell's reelection bid was sure to be collateral damage. That corrupt fuck Claude Barry would be back in power.

Additionally, several people arrested as part of the network would probably go free as Forbes was one of the only people able to testify against them.

Good Guys take one step forward and ten giant steps backward.

And in the category of Not Sure If It's Good or Bad News, this afternoon, Barry also happened to nab another person on the Most Wanted List — *Jasper Parish*.

Yet another ding on the Sheriff's Office. Mal could only imagine the damage control Gloria and Mike must have done on her behalf. She'd ignored calls from both of them today, along with one from the front desk and a knock on her door.

Maybe someone would come by to question or arrest her.

Can't arrest me if I'm dead.

Another drink from the bottle.

Mal hated what her life had become. Hated herself for letting it get that way. Loathed herself for losing Ashley and for being so damned weak that pills were the only way to feel any happiness.

Epilogue 1

At one time, she'd thought she could do this. But now, she knew better.

She wasn't cut out for this world.

Mal had failed everybody who ever mattered to her. She couldn't even do the one real job she had in life — protecting her daughter. To hell with trying to protect Maggie and Emma.

There was no protection from the wolves of the world. She could run, or even hold them off for a bit. But she couldn't ever hide. Eventually, they found her, devouring her weakest parts until all that was left was a husk of who she used to be.

She opened the bottle

Fifteen pills inside. She'd counted them every few hours for the last three days.

Fifteen ought to do the job.

She tilted the bottle back and poured some in her mouth, using a gulp of wine to wash them down.

Mal was about to pour more down her throat when her phone rang.

Oh, come on, Tim. Just let it go.

She felt bad for the guy. Genuinely liked him. Maybe something could've come from it. But she was done. Mal glanced at the screen, maybe she'd say goodbye. But the Caller ID said something different.

It was Colleen Price, Jessi's mother.

Her heart started racing, fearful something had happened to Jessi.

"Hello?"

"Hi, Mallory. It's Colleen. How are you?"

Oh, just about to end my life, and yourself?

"Okay. You?"

"Jessi saw the news and she wanted to talk. Would that be all right?"

Epilogue 1

"Um ..."

"Just a few minutes."

Mal set the bottle of pills between her legs. "Okay."

She pressed the phone to her ear, waiting to hear Jessi's voice.

"Hello, Mrs. Mallory."

"Hi, Jessi. How are you."

"Okay. Did you see the news? About Mr. Jasper?"

"Yes. Yes, I did."

"Why did they arrest him? He's not a bad guy, is he?"

"I don't know, Jessi. I guess the courts will figure that out."

"But he saved us. Twice. Bad guys don't do that, do they?"

"It's complicated. Sometimes bad people do good things. Sometimes good people do bad things."

"But Paul, he was a bad person doing bad things. All the time."

"Yes, Jessi. He was a bad man."

"Do you think Mr. Jasper killed those people like they say he did?"

Jessi sounded like she desperately needed Jasper to be good. She wouldn't know how to think of him if he wasn't. Mal felt the same conflict about Jasper, even after all she'd done.

"Deep down, I think he is a good man who has been hurt a lot. And he helped us. Way I see it, that makes him more good than bad."

"That's how I see it, too," Jessi agreed.

Mal stared down at her bottle of pills through a long moment of silence. She felt more determined than ever to end things tonight. But what would that do to the girl if she did?

Jessi would know, either soon or when she got older,

Epilogue 1

that she was the last person Mal spoke to. What would that do to her already fragile psyche?

"I miss you, Mrs. Mallory."

Keep it together.

"I ... " Her voice cracked. "I miss you too, Jessi."

"Are you okay?"

Mal wiped at the tears and forced a laugh. "Yeah, of course. Are you?"

"I've been having nightmares a lot lately. The therapist says it'll be a while before I'm better."

"I'm sorry. I get them too."

More silence. Mal wasn't sure if Jessi was crying, too. And that only made her cry harder. She wanted to hug her, promise everything would be okay. But how could she lie to her like that when things weren't okay and they never would be again?

Mal heard Jessi cover the phone as she whispered something inaudible to her mom. When she got back on the line, she said, "Mrs. Mallory?"

"Yes?"

"Could I see you sometime?"

No, Jessi, you can't see me. Mrs. Mallory is going to take a bunch of pills and wine and never wake up again. Sorry. Nice knowing you. And good luck healing from all that other shit and now this, too.

"Sure," Mal lied.

"This Saturday? For lunch? Mom says she'll treat."

Mal couldn't help but laugh at the sweet offer of her mom treating, as if *that* would be the thing to make her accept the invitation.

Her tears flowed as she had flashes of Dodd standing over her, ready to kill her and Jessi.

Then she thought of Ashley when she was four or five, lying next to her in bed, asking Mommy to tell her a story

Epilogue 1

to help her fall back asleep because the dark was so scary. Bedtime stories were sweet, comforting lies, told in worlds where either there wasn't any real danger or the good guys and girls never left evil undefeated. Lies to help with falling asleep or living life without losing your mind.

"Can you, Mrs. Mallory?" Jessi repeated, sounding on the verge of tears.

It would break Jessi if she said no. She was in a vulnerable place, and, for whatever reason, be it their mutual survival or Jessi's need for someone strong —*ha!* — to help her through this, Mal had an obligation.

Jessi needed Mal to tell her a comforting lie and stave off the pain.

As much as she needed the agony to leave her, ending her life now would be selfish. It wouldn't just destroy her, it would ruin Jessie, her ex, and the memory of Ashley.

"I'd like that very much," Mal said, wiping her tears away.

"Thank you. I'm gonna go to bed now."

"Okay, honey. Sweet dreams."

Jessi's mom came back on the line. "Thank you for that. I'm not sure what's wrong, but she really needed to hear from you tonight."

"It's okay," Mal said through her tears. "I think I needed it, too."

Mal hung up, went to the bathroom, then threw up the pills and wine.

She had more to live for than herself. And for now, that would have to be enough.

Epilogue 2

"I'm not letting you do this." Jasper's lawyer, Lucas Cahill, sat beside him in the hospital room, shaking his head.

Cahill was a heavyset man in his fifties with gold wire-rimmed glasses and sandy-brown hair on the verge of graying. He often reminded Jasper of a man who might be running a small family ice cream shop, friendly looking, with a kind smile. But his blue eyes told a different story. The man had seen things and could be a honey-badger in the courtroom.

He was a mob lawyer Jasper had helped out of a jam in exchange for info on a mobster he didn't work for.

Jasper had just told him everything that had happened since he'd last seen him, and the man was now staring at Jasper with both dumfounded admiration and annoyance because Jasper had already spoken to deputies without his lawyer present, giving them a full statement or confession while out of his fucking gourd.

"I don't know what the hell you were thinking, talking to them." Cahill shook his head again. "I'll get it all thrown

Epilogue 2

out, don't worry, but you've been beaten half to death and are obviously over-medicated."

Jasper asked him to set up an estate providing money to a few important people in his life, and to set aside enough for Spider's medical bills. She'd miraculously survived the gunshot wounds but was in a coma, according to Cahill.

"So, let me get this straight … you want to confess, and not only to the murders of Calum Kozack and Brianna Gilchrest, but also to these other people?" He held up the sheet of paper where Jasper had written all of his victims' names. "People they ain't even lookin' at you for?"

"Yes, sir."

"As your lawyer, I'd highly advise against this. You'll never get out of prison if you cop to all this."

"I don't care."

"You don't care about freedom? If we're just talking the Kozack case, I can get you down to ten years, maybe less given the circumstances. They don't even have bodies. No bodies, no evidence, except your confession to Kozack, inadmissible and obtained under extreme duress. I ought to have Oliver Kozack brought up on charges. We can sue the fuck out of him."

"No. Kozack is in tight with the law here. No way that'll ever fly. Besides," Jasper shook his head, "I want a clean conscience."

"Yeah, well, you can have that on the beaches in the Bahamas, too. Say the word, and I'll get this dismissed. Even if you do confess, you've got a psychiatric disorder. We can get you off on insanity."

Jasper pounded his cuffed fist into the bed's metal railing. "I'm *not* insane."

Cahill smiled. "Okay, but clearly, you've got doctors saying—"

"I don't *care* what the doctors say. I am sane."

Epilogue 2

Cahill frowned. "I don't give a good goddamn if you're *one thousand* percent sane. You got doctors on the record stating otherwise, you take it, son. It's the difference between you doing time in a federal fucking prison and a psychiatric hospital."

"I don't want to be in a fucking mental facility."

"You know what happens to ex-cops in prison, right? They will kill you."

"I'd rather be dead than turned into a vegetable with all the damned drugs."

Cahill sighed. "Sounds to me like you *want* to be punished. I don't know what kind of shit's in that head of yours, but as your lawyer, I strongly advise you to talk to a therapist and take some time to think about this."

"I've made up my mind. I'm pleading guilty. I'll get a public defender if you—"

"No, no. I'll do it. But, please, think about it. Give it twenty-four hours."

"Fine. Twenty-four hours. But I'm telling you now, I'm not changing my mind."

Cahill gave Jasper one last look, then shook his head one final time before leaving the room.

He was all alone, if he didn't count the sheriff's deputy standing outside his door, which he didn't. Jasper wished he could see Jordyn, but it was probably best she didn't come. He didn't need her getting into any trouble. Best she lay low in the safehouse. He'd left enough cash for her to get by.

He turned on the TV, watching Sheriff Barry being interviewed about Victor Forbes's mysterious death. Then he was asked about Jasper.

"The fact that our own Sheriff's Office didn't know this man was still alive and hunting our citizens is terrifying to

Epilogue 2

me. Gloria Bell must be held accountable for her negligence."

Jasper's mind was too fuzzy from the drugs to follow the conversation. He knew just enough to be annoyed, so he killed the TV.

The door swung open after a knock, then Mallory entered. She turned and thanked the deputy at the door for letting her in — probably against the rules.

She held flowers, blue and yellow ones, maybe irises then set them on the table next to his bed. "How are you?"

He hated the way she looked at him, with way too much pity.

"Oh, just another day at the office. Yourself?"

"Okay."

"To what do I owe the pleasure? You here to make sure we keep our stories straight?"

Mallory shook her head. "I worried about that at first, but I couldn't give a shit now. Barry is going to get in, so it's all kind of fucked. Mostly I came to suggest you keep the confessions to yourself.'

"What?"

"They don't have bodies, they don't have cases."

Jasper stared at her, confused. "Weren't you trying to nab me for the same thing not too long ago?"

"Well, a lot's happened since then."

"Yeah, a lot of people have died. And, to be honest, I'm not sure how much more I can take. I … just want to stop the grind, stop the killing, and stop the death I bring to—"

"Jessi and I wouldn't be alive if not for you." Her eyes were wet.

"Are you going to cry, Detective?"

"No. Fuck no."

"Good," he teased. "I'd hate to lose respect for you."

Epilogue 2

She smiled.

"Thank you, I appreciate you coming down here, but … I'll be fine. I'm ready to pay for my crimes."

Mallory nodded. "I understand."

"But will you do me one favor?"

"What's that?"

"Can you look out for my daughter?"

Mal stared at Jasper for a long moment, then gave him a sad-looking smile. "I can do that."

"Thank you. I just want to stop all this before she pays for my sins. Before she gets k—"

Then he remembered, again.

And he felt like an idiot.

"I'm sorry. I … I get confused sometimes."

"It's okay." Mal squeezed his hand.

He blinked his stinging tears away. "The worst part is forgetting she died, then remembering. It's like I'm in this dream where everything is okay, then, BAM, reality hits. I'm awake, and she's gone again."

"I know the feeling all too well. I dream of Ashley all the time. And they're so real sometimes. It's great while I'm in them, just like old times, one big happy family." She let go of his hand to wipe a falling tear. "If that's the only way I can have her, the only way I can remember her as she was, then I'll take it. No matter how much it hurts to wake up."

"I just want to say sorry for all the shit you've been through, Mallory. I wish I could've stopped him before it all started. You don't deserve it."

"Thank you. And, I wish I'd taken the opportunity to take care of him sooner, too."

Jasper saw something in her eyes, a familiar pain he recognized immediately. "You've hurt people since then, haven't you?"

Epilogue 2

Mallory looked back at the door, making sure it was still closed, then back to Jasper. She nodded.

"Who?"

"Just some rapists. Hurt them, not killed them."

"Ah. Be careful, it's a slippery slope. You'll end up where I am before you know it, getting people hurt or killed by all the collateral damage."

"Good thing for me I don't have anybody close anymore." She gave him an awkward smile. "Were you serious about that lottery number?"

"Yes. Why?"

"So, who sees things, you or ... her?"

"Sometimes I do. But mostly her. When she's here."

"Can I ask you something?" She looked scared, desperate. Or maybe bereft of hope.

Broken.

"Sure, what is it?"

"Will I — Never mind. It's stupid."

"No, what is it? Ask."

Mallory turned away, wiped her cheeks, then looked back at him and laughed uncomfortably. "No, really, it's stupid. I don't even think I wanna know."

"What is it?" He met her gaze.

And in that moment, he felt their connection, their shared pain, and how they'd always be connected by their trauma. Friendship forged in misery.

"Will I ever ... will I ever be happy again? Is that something you can even tell?"

"I ... I don't know. I could try."

"You sure?"

"Give me your hand."

Mallory reached out, tentatively, and put her hand in his.

Her hand was smooth, cold.

Epilogue 2

He closed his eyes, waiting for something.

And then he got two flashes.

One of them bright enough to make him smile.

But the other was dark, and Jasper couldn't mask his face before it betrayed him.

"What is it?" She pulled her hand away. "What did you see?"

"You're going to have another child."

"What?"

"A daughter."

"What? I'm not even married. With who? When?"

"I don't know." Jasper shook his head. "It's not that specific. She's older ... maybe you adopted?"

"Why did you look so scared?"

"Because there's somebody out there even worse than Dodd. And he's going to come for you."

THE END

The story continues...

Need to know what happens next? Of course, you do. The series continues with *No Fear*.

GET NO FEAR TODAY

A quick favor...

If you liked *No Stopping*, then *would you kindly** consider taking a few minutes to leave a review on your favorite bookselling site. If you're a book blogger, we'd love any mentions on your blog or YouTube channel, also. Every bit of word-of-mouth helps to introduce us to new readers.

As always, thank you for reading,
   David Wright (and Nolon King)

(** Bonus points if you got the* Bioshock *reference.*)

About the Authors

Nolon King writes fast-paced psychological thrillers set in the glitzy world of entertainment's power players with a bold, insightful voice. He's not afraid to explore the darker side of human nature through stories featuring families torn apart by secrets and lies.

Nolon loves to write about big questions and moral quandaries. How far would you go to cover up an honest mistake? Would you destroy your career to protect your family? How much of your soul would you sell to get the life of your dreams? Would you cheat on your husband to keep your children safe? Would you give in to a stalker's demands to save your marriage?

David W. Wright is the co-author of edge-of-your seat thrillers including the best-selling post-apocalyptic series *Yesterday's Gone*, the paranoid sci-fi *WhiteSpace* series, and the vigilante series, *No Justice*, as well as standalone thrillers *12*, and *Crash* which was recently optioned for a movie.

David is an accomplished, though intermittent, cartoonist who lives in [LOCATION REDACTED] with his wife and son [NAMES REDACTED.]

He is not at all paranoid.

He is "the grumpy one" on the *The Story Studio Podcast* with fellow Sterling and Stone founders, Sean Platt and Johnny B. Truant.

You can email him at david@sterlingandstone.net

We swear, he almost never bites. Unless you feed him after midnight.

Also By Nolon King

Hidden Justice
Hidden Justice

Hidden Honor

Hidden Shame

Hidden Virtue

No Justice
No Justice

No Escape

No Hope

No Return

No Stopping

No Fear

Once Upon A Crime
Once Upon A Crime

Twice Upon A Lie

Three Times a Murder

Dead For Good
Dead For Good

Left For Dead

Dead Of Night

Wake The Dead

Dead For Life

Stand Alone Novels

Pretty Killer

12

Blown

Miserable Lies

The Target

Secrets We Keep

Close To Home

Heat To Obsession

A Simple Kill

Tell Me No Lies

Red Carpet Black

Fade To Black

Victim

Also By David W. Wright

Hidden Justice

Hidden Justice

Hidden Honor

Hidden Shame

Hidden Virtue

No Justice

No Justice

No Escape

No Hope

No Return

No Stopping

No Fear

Karma Police

Jumper

Karma Police

The Collectors

Deviant

The Fall

Homecoming

Yesterday's Gone

October's Gone

Yesterday's Gone Season One

Yesterday's Gone Season Two

Yesterday's Gone Season Three

Yesterday's Gone Season Four

Yesterday's Gone Season Five

Yesterday's Gone Season Six

Tomorrow's Gone

Tomorrow's Gone Season One

Tomorrow's Gone Season Two

Tomorrow's Gone Season Three

Available Darkness

Darkness Itself

Available Darkness Book One

Available Darkness Book Two

Available Darkness Book Three

WhiteSpace

WhiteSpace Season One

WhiteSpace Season Two

WhiteSpace Season Three

Stand Alone Novels

Crash

Emily's List

Threshold